Author's Commentary

It is with much prayer and extreme carefulness that I present this story to you. Today, our lives are immersed in worldly entertainment, from the innocent to the blasphemous. But rarely, if ever, does a secular entertainment industry point you to Jesus Christ as the exclusive author of our salvation. Therefore, it is my heart that the Starlore Legacy books might entertain while heralding the inerrant Word of God as true, and that there is no name given among men whereby you can be saved other than that of Jesus. As Jesus taught through parables, allegory, and metaphor, this is my attempt to likewise inspire people of all ages to search out the Holy Scriptures and follow our Lord and Savior. These books are not intended to replace, distort, or confuse God's Word. These books are also not intended to teach theology or doctrine. Therefore, please do not make the mistake of so rigidly applying this loose allegory to such and misunderstand its intent. I am grateful and humbled to be able to share my passion for serving God through literature with you. Thank you.

~Chuck Black

Praise for
The Starlore Legacy

"Wow! The Starlore Legacy series is amazing! I must say that as someone who has been making a living in the creative industries my entire career with lots of ideas and very innovative concepts for movies, projects and media, I am continuously blown away by the level of allegorical stories with incredible biblical symbolism that Chuck produces. I absolutely LOVE this Starlore series! And of course, I can already picture the movies!"

~JESS STAINBROOK, Executive Producer, *Seven Days in Utopia* featuring Academy Award winners Robert Duvall and Melissa Leo; Exclusive Advisor, *The Bible Series* by Mark Burnett and Roma Downey

"Greetings from Ireland. We have been journeying with your books for over 10 plus years. We fell in love with the *Kingdom Series,* and we've read and re-read them several times. We came across them at a local Christian bookstore as we were seeking a series to read aloud as a family. Our children were young but old enough to grasp the content and meaning of the stories and what they truly represented. We were thrilled to learn about the *Wars of the Realm* books, and we snatched up the series as quickly as we could. I still read aloud, and our youngest son, 17, who lives with us in Ireland, still enjoys our reading times. I am often nudged for "just one more chapter, Dad." When I saw that *The Starlore Legacy* series was available, again we jumped for joy. We cannot wait until the release of the 4th book. The characters are great, and your writing style always has us captivated. It's amazing how often we'll refer back to something the characters are going through and compare it to real life. On behalf of my wife and our 3 kids, we want to say thank you for answering the call to write good, godly, Christian books. You have become a part of us, and we are so grateful for how you have influenced our family over these many years. Please know that you are making an impact and that your mission is certainly a success. God's blessings on you and your precious family, and may the Lord grant you wisdom and insight as you continue to weave the tales for the *Starlore* books."

~ SCOTT CHATTERSON, Missionary, the Republic of Ireland

MERCHANT

Look for other books
by Chuck Black

The Kingdom Series
Kingdom's Dawn
Kingdom's Hope
Kingdom's Edge
Kingdom's Call
Kingdom's Quest
Kingdom's Reign

The Knights of Arrethtrae
Sir Kendrick and the Castle of Bel Lione
Sir Bentley and Holbrook Court
Sir Dalton and the Shadow Heart
Lady Carliss and the Waters of Moorue
Sir Quinlan and the Swords of Valor
Sir Rowan and the Camerian Conquest

The Starlore Legacy
Nova
Flight
Lore
Oath
Merchant
Reclamation
Creed
Journey
Crucible
Covenant
Revolution
Maelstrom

www.ChuckBlack.com

MERCHANT

EPISODE FIVE

CHUCK BLACK

Contents

CHAPTER

1

A Secret Knowledge

"Consider the cost of your freedom. Who among us is able to secure it? For he alone is able and shall buy your freedom and your future." – Micaba, Oracle of Ell Yon

B rae Thornton searched the night sky, feeling the ache in her heart stir her soul once more. It was a longing she had lived with since she was a child...a yearning to reach for the stars...to travel from world to world exploring the wonders of the galaxy. The two moons of Rayl were reflecting the yellow radiance of their sun in pink and reddish hues. Brae tucked a tussle of her chestnut-colored hair behind her ear as she walked her favorite childhood path through the country. A subtle smile formed on her lips as she filled her lungs with the sweet fragrant air of the rural farmland. The whirring of an occasional agritech bot tirelessly tending the next crop mixed with the gentle night sounds of distant creatures. The glow of Jalem, the capital city of Rayl, only slightly disrupted the crisp starry view Brae often loved to gaze upon. She turned toward home, hoping sleep would not elude her yet again.

Brae felt fortunate. The last five years at the Raylean Astrotech Institute had been grueling, but since her father's home was less than an hour's travel from the institute, she often stole away to spend a night there, especially when she needed a brief reprieve from the pressure of her studies. Having fulfilled all the requirements of the astrotech master program, she had recently been awarded the official title of "Astrotech Master." The irony of such an accomplishment was that she had never left the atmosphere of Rayl to achieve it. And now, knowing the history of her father and mother who had spent years traveling the cosmos, she still felt so bypassed, perhaps even foolish. She had made studying the stars her lifelong passion and hadn't even made orbit...not once! In three days, that would all change. The initiation of a new master into the astrotech order required an expedition to the region of space that was the focus of her master's program thesis. The purpose was to conduct additional research and gather data to either prove or disprove the hypothesis of the master's previous two years of work. The pressure to prove one's hypothesis as true was enormous, and although a master could recover from a false conclusion, it was a lengthy career detour to do so. When Brae discovered her identity as being the daughter of the legendary Navis Daeson and Raviel Starlore, it inspired her to embark on one of the most daring and controversial research projects ever attempted as a young astrotech master. Her close friend, colleague, and dwelling suitemate, Shayde, had tried many times to dissuade her simply because of the great risk of failure of the project. But Brae was stubborn, perhaps to a fault, trusting a sense of purpose in the endeavor that she couldn't explain. Now, on the eve of launching her expedition, she had come home, hoping to settle her heart in the quiet comfort of her childhood haven. And when she began to question her resolve and her motivations, the quiet confident words of her dad always realigned and strengthened her.

She looked toward home, seeing the warm glow of the kitchen light as dusk fell rapidly. Daeson would be there preparing her favorite nighttime tea, ready to spill encouragement into her life. She needed that now more than ever.

The next morning, Brae arrived early at the entrance of the Raylean Guard. She presented the document authorizing her request for a pilot for their research ship, *Stalwart*. As part of the astrotech order, she was granted a research starship to equip with instrumentation as she saw fit for her astronomical expedition. However, the astrotechs were at the whims of the Raylean Guard for supplying a pilot for such a flight. In addition to the sensors and research equipment as well as a capable shuttle, the *Stalwart* could accommodate two pilots, three additional command center crew members, and a crew of twelve astrotechs, although Brae's team would consist of just two pilots and her five team researchers.

The Raylean Guard that was to appoint a pilot for her was a vestige of the once great Raylean aerotech and miltech orders. This was a significantly reduced composite force permitted by the Morian Empire for the exclusive purpose of helping maintain order on Rayl. Under the scrutiny of the Morian subchancellor, the Raylean Guard was allowed some autonomy but with limited weapons and craft. All Raylean miltech forces were under the control of Prefect Terrok, a ruthless ruler often taking out his frustration as a Raylean puppet of the Morian Empire on his own people. Terrok was indeed a perfect puppet for the Morian Empire and its ruler, Supreme Chancellor Krish, for he was not swayed by the notions of belief in their fabled Immortal Ell Yon. In fact, Terrok had embraced the Morian culture and their love of Deitum Prime with enthusiasm, partaking in the pleasures such a lifestyle offered. As such, a loyal Raylean traditionalist found himself or herself in quite a moral and ethical quandary, especially those who had been conscripted into the Raylean Guard. Prefect Terrok had formed an elite subset of Raylean Guard cadre for his own personal protection which he called the Royal Guard, for within the masses there lurked some extreme traditionalists that despised him because of his unapologetic embracing of the Morian lifestyle. An armed faction of these traditionalists became known as Partisans.

The sentry told Brae to wait while he called in her arrival. A few minutes later a Raylean Guard pilot arrived, and the sentry snapped to attention. Brae noticed the sentry didn't seem to expect this man. The pilot offered a casual salute.

"Ensign Burns on leave, Lieutenant?" the sentry asked.

The pilot smirked. "Something like that. What do we have?"

"Pilot request for the astrotechs."

Brae caught the subtle condescending tone in the sentry's voice and tried not to let it boil her. *Haven't even made it through the gate and it's already started,* she thought.

The lieutenant snatched the order from the sentry and looked it over, then glanced toward Brae. He scrutinized her as if trying to decide if he should begin the fight with her now. Brae lifted her chin slightly and stared right back into his eyes. The pilot was typically over-confident and handsome. It seemed to be a prerequisite for their pilot program, or did being a pilot just seem to exude that? Her brief occasional exposure to these Raylean Guard pilots had always confirmed the stereotype. Further, she had never witnessed even a hint of such arrogance in her father, whom she knew could fly circles around these stick monkeys. Brae's own thoughts distracted her momentarily as she endured the smug but silent judgment of the man. She steeled her gaze again and was just about to remind him that the order was fully authorized by the regent's office when the pilot turned to the sentry.

"I'll take it from here, Dod." He looked back toward Brae with eyes a little softer than before. "The Ops Group Commander is going to have to authorize this. Follow me, miss."

The pilot wagged his head toward the door he had earlier come through, then moved that direction. Brae was slow to react as she watched the pilot open the door and walk through.

"Lieutenant Stryker doesn't wait for anyone, miss."

Brae hurried, arriving at the door just as it was closing. Her presence reversed its motion, and she slipped through. The pilot was already ten paces down the hallway. She hurried to catch up.

"That request is fully authorized by the regent's office," Brae said.

The pilot looked over at her, a smirk on his face, then shook his head. She regretted stating the obvious and hated how these arrogant pilots made her feel every time she was around them.

"Doesn't matter who authorized it. Major Kamp still won't like it and has to sign off on it."

Brae just about made a snarky reply then recanted. It would only make things worse, and she didn't care who said what as long as she got her pilot.

Three more turns, then past a flight desk surrounded by more polite but cocky pilots, and through an office area with desks too close together brought them to an office door with a bold blue identifying sign...Ops Group Commander.

Brae's escort knocked once and opened an archaic functioning door with hinges. She thought it odd, especially in a place that sent pilots to the stars. *Perhaps it has something to do with the type of man behind the door*, she thought. The pilot stuck his head in but didn't enter. Brae had taken a step to follow him but instead found herself much too close to him.

"We've got a Miss-"

The pilot stuck his head back out, his face just inches from hers. Brae's eyes opened wide as she jumped back. He stared at her, waiting.

"Ah, Astrotech Master Thornton," Brae said, trying to ignore the flush in her cheeks.

The pilot stuck his head back through the office door.

"Thornton with a pilot request from the astrotech order."

"Great!" the gruff voice of a war veteran replied. "Bring her in."

Brae thought she could hear him grumble a few choice words. This time the pilot opened the door wide and stepped aside. *Now he's a gentleman?* she thought, then realized it was a gesture only so he could make a quick exit. He handed the request back to her as she stepped past him. Once she was through the door, he stepped out. Brae watched the door slowly close.

"Not so fast, Stryker—get in here! I want you to hear this."

The pilot reached back and grabbed the door before it fully closed then stepped through. He looked at his commander with narrow eyes.

Brae took three steps toward the major and held out the orders. Major Kamp was a short, fit man with wrinkles too deep in his forehead for his age. There was nothing soft about him. He snatched the orders from her and began to read the request.

"I need a pilot for a critical research mission codenamed, Event. We're going to-"

"They're all critical, aren't they?" Kamp said, cutting her off.

Brae once again realized these guys could care less about real science. It was pointless to try explaining how important this expedition was.

Kamp looked up at her and frowned. "I don't have any extra pilots to waste on a five-day joy ride to the Omega Nebula."

Brae clenched her jaw. "It's authorized by the-"

"Regent's office," he interrupted again. "Yeah, I see that, but it doesn't say anything about authorizing me more training spots for more pilots...or more fuel for our fighters."

Brae crossed her arms and stared at the major. She wasn't going to move until she got her pilot.

Kamp eyed her over, then glanced toward the pilot named Stryker just behind and to her left.

"Lieutenant Burns will be off leave by then, sir, and it's his turn for...extra duty," the pilot offered.

Brae could only imagine what other phrase the pilot was going to use.

Kamp looked back at Brae. "What will be your proximity to the nebula?"

"15,000 miles."

Kamp's left eyebrow raised. "Your omeganite collector array is barely that close. Why?"

Brae chose her words carefully. This mission had the potential of garnering support for limiting the role of the astrotechs simply because it was what many considered "fringe science." Even within the astrotech order, Brae might be regarded too enthusiastic regarding research of a historical or legendary nature. Such was the "Event" mission.

Brae eyed the major. "Do you really want to know or are you just waiting to cut me off in my explanation?" She heard the pilot behind her stifle a short snicker.

Kamp scowled. "The *Stalwart* has enough omegeon shielding to endure that kind of exposure, but I still don't like it." He shook his head, then a wry smile ebbed across his face. He looked over at Lieutenant Stryker. He grabbed a pen, filled in a name under "DESIGNATED PILOT IN COMMAND," and signed the order. He held the document out for Brae to take.

Brae took the document and involuntarily sighed, letting her shoulders drop slightly.

"Thank you, Major. Now, how do I get in contact with the pilot to brief him on mission details?"

Brae scanned the order document. "Is Lieutenant...ah..." she turned and looked at the pilot next to her. "Stryker?"

Stryker's eyes narrowed. "Major?"

"You'll be Miss Thornton's pilot, Lieutenant. I don't want some green lieutenant piloting a research cruiser that close to the nebula." Kamp cut Stryker off before he could voice a protest. "I'll tell mechtech division to prep the *Stalwart*. Take Edge as your co...maybe this'll wipe that silly grin off his face. Dismissed."

Brae saw Stryker's reaction and decided to exit quickly. She got what she came for. She stepped through the door and began walking through the outer office area. She tucked the signed order in her mission folder and snuck a quick glance back toward Kamp's office. The door was still open, and she could see Lieutenant Stryker red-faced and protesting, but from the brief encounter she'd had with Kamp, she was pretty sure the major would have none of it.

"Oh...pardon me," Brae said as she bumped into the back of a pilot leaning over one of the desks.

"Any time, miss," the pilot said with a smile, then feigned a polite bow.

Brae focused on navigating her way out, but by the time she reached the hallway that led to the exit, Lieutenant Stryker had caught up to her.

"Hey...Thornton!"

Brae stopped midway down the hallway and turned about. Stryker walked with broad commanding steps. As tough and determined as she was, the manner of his approach was somewhat intimidating. She squared off.

"Yes, Lieutenant?"

Stryker closed the last few steps, putting his hands on his hips. He glared down at Brae.

"What is so important that we must fly that close to the Omega Nebula? Our probes often don't even make it that far."

Brae's eyes narrowed. "Mission research objectives are classified. All you need to worry about is getting us to the coordinates designated on the mission spec sheet on time and return us safely back to Rayl."

"Is that so?" Stryker said stepping closer to Brae. "Well let's get one thing straight right now. I want a full briefing with all your personnel that will be on this mission. You may be in charge of the mission, but I'm the commander of that ship, even if it is a research vessel. The safety of the crew is my responsibility, and where mission requirements interfere with their safety, I will make the call. Is that clear?"

Brae didn't like this arrogant rocket jockey's tone. *Why did Major Kamp have to choose him?*

She stepped closer and lifted her chin to show him she wasn't intimidated.

"Perfectly! But if you can't stomach a few nebula discharges to make this mission a success, *you* will be the one answering to the astrotech council during the evaluation. Is that clear?" Brae wagged her head and lifted herself up on her toes to bring her face within inches of Stryker's to emphasize her last point. She broke the fury of their locked gaze by snapping her head about and storming down the hall toward the exit. Her heart was beating fast—the anger rising up in her was alarming. Rarely did she get angry...about anything! In just seconds this arrogant, ignorant, self-centered, pajama-wearing stick jockey had rattled her. She couldn't get through the door and out of the building fast enough. Once she made the courtyard, she found a bench beneath a sprawling shade tree and sat down to collect herself. It took twenty minutes before she could think straight again. When she stood up, she took a deep breath and tried to shake off the episode, telling herself that she had gotten what she came for.

Rhett Stryker watched as the fiery dark-haired astrotech walked down the hall and out the door.

"Well, this is going to be as much fun as sand in my eye."

Rhett shook his head. He detested these intellectual high and mighty astrotechs that think everyone else is their footstool, and this Thornton woman had already proven herself to be one of the worst. He briefly considered petitioning Major Kamp once more but then realized it wouldn't bode well. *I'm just going to have to grit my teeth and get through this*, he thought. At least he could commiserate with Edge.

Rhett made his way back to the squadron ops room and found Ensign Cuttler, aka Edge.

"Hey, Edge, how would you like to co-pilot an astrotech research vessel to the Omega Nebula with me?" Rhett asked while sitting on the corner of his desk. He picked up Edge's scale model of their latest fighter, the triple-engine *Dauntless*.

"Ah...no thanks."

"That's what I said," Rhett quipped. "And it didn't do me any good either."

Edge smirked. "Oh, I see. You weren't really asking."

"Nope. Major Kamp just assigned you and yours truly to this spectacularly boring mission with a spectacularly arrogant and cold-blooded astrotech."

"He's that bad?" Edge leaned back in his chair.

"*She*, and yes, she's that bad."

Edge nodded, then smiled. "I need a change of scenery anyway. You never know...we might learn something."

Rhett shook his head. "Always the optimist." He put the *Dauntless* back on its stand. "The mission brief is tomorrow, and we launch the following day."

Edge gave a half-hearted salute. "Aye aye, cap...I'll be ready."

Rhett made his way back to his own desk. He pulled up the operational and emergency procedure manuals for the *Stalwart* on his displays and began reviewing them. They were required to be proficient on multiple spacecraft, including the astrotech's *Stalwart*, but it had been quite some time since he had last piloted the ship. After a couple of hours of study, Rhett turned his attention to the purpose of the mission. Within just a few minutes of research, he discovered that due to a recent uptick in the nebula's plasma activity, many had orchestrated flybys to catch a close-up view of one of the plasma discharges. Rhett frowned. Is that what this was...a sight-seeing mission? His disdain for the hot-headed astrotech deepened. He had more important things to do than pilot a research vessel to watch a cosmic fireworks display.

CHAPTER

2

The Still of Night

On the evening of the following day, Brae made time once more to spend a couple of hours with her dad and Rivet. The expedition weighed heavily on her mind, but she also wanted to check on Daeson. The increasing influence of the Morian Empire was continuing to shift the power and perspective of the Raylean puppet government which seemed to impact her father greatly. He grew more brooding each day and was certainly justified, for every aspect of their culture, including the tech order structures and functions, was being affected. In Brae's case, resistance to her master's research and expedition seemed to surround her on all sides. She'd had to fight for every inch of ground, from the approval of her astrotech master's research two years ago to the last detail of the mission approval process. She'd even had to fight for the assignment of that arrogant pilot.

"You look flustered, Brae," Daeson said, handing her a glass of tea. "Is everything in place for your mission tomorrow?"

Brae took the cold glass and tried to relax. She noticed that Rivet had been looking at her most of the evening.

"Yes, everything is set. I guess I'm just a bit anxious about how this is going to turn out. I've spent the last two years of my life preparing for this." She took a sip then looked over at her father. "There's a lot riding on this mission. What if it's a complete flop?"

Daeson flashed a quick smile. "You've done your research, and I know how thorough you are. Honestly, I think you've been preparing for this your whole life, not just these last two years."

Brae thought for a moment. "I suppose you're right," she said then looked toward Rivet. "But why do I get the feeling that Rivet is uneasy?"

Daeson glanced over at Rivet.

Rivet slowly turned to looked at Daeson. "I should be going with her, my liege. There could be danger."

Brae stood up and went to Rivet. As she did, Rivet refocused his eyes on her. Brae sat down next to him.

"I'm not worried about danger, Rivet. I'm just worried that my thesis isn't going to reveal anything significant, and I'll be the laughingstock of the astrotech order."

Rivet stayed silent, peering into Brae's eyes. She shivered, still not fully understanding the depth of intelligence of the bot, nor his full purpose.

"What you are about to do, Lady Brae, will shatter the powers of darkness, and there will be grave danger and much loss."

Shivers flitted up and down Brae's spine. Rivet's mechanized voice seemed to hold the spirit of the ancient oracles. Was he just philosophizing, theorizing, or foretelling? How genuinely intelligent was his artificial intelligence programming? The more she came to interact with the android, the more he made her nervous.

"Which is why I should be with her, my liege," Rivet finished, turning his head back to stare at Daeson.

"The astrotech council would never allow it without a full vetting, and we don't have time for that, but what's he talking about, Dad?"

Daeson frowned, his gaze dropping to the floor. He slowly lifted his eyes to look back at Brae.

"Wait here."

Daeson stood and exited the room. After a few minutes, he returned carrying a metallic case which he set on a nearby table. He looked over at Brae and Rivet, waiting. Brae understood and came to stand beside him. Rivet remained sitting in his chair across the room. Brae was confused. She had seen this case numerous times in the past couple of years, for within it was Daeson's Talon from long ago. He had even allowed her to practice some with it. It was a beautiful weapon, sleek in design, deadly in use. But tonight, her father seemed to hold a special reverence that surprised her.

Daeson entered a code on the case panel at which Brae could hear the mechanism unlock. He opened the case, revealing the ancient weapon lying peacefully in its place.

"Your Talon, Dad…what's this all about?"

"There's more here, Brae," he said, touching a slight recess on the inside of the case that she hadn't noticed before. A second later, she could hear another mechanism. She looked over at her father, hardly daring to wonder what he was about to show her.

Daeson lifted the false bottom of the case to reveal the unimaginable. Brae lifted her hand to cover her mouth, her eyes wide. Inside was the gleaming jeweled form of a Protector.

"Dad...a Protector!"

"Not *a* Protector...*the* Protector," Daeson said quietly.

Brae gawked at the wonder before her. This was the last piece of evidence that cancelled all remaining doubt about her father's fanciful stories of the past. Of course, there was too much to ignore and explain away for her father's rendition of the past to not be true, but the legend was so enormous and fantastical that occasionally, deep into the night, she could not fully suppress the flashes of doubt that came.

"This was given to me by the hand of Sovereign Ell Yon." There was an edge of sadness in his voice. "Since the death of your mother, I haven't had the courage to wear it...to listen and hear him."

Daeson turned, lifting a hand to Brae's cheek. He looked into her eyes, the sorrow of a thousand years and the passing of hundreds of lives framing his gaze. "I've learned to listen to Rivet's... intuition if you will. He's still a mystery to me for I don't know how much of his programming was influenced by Ell Yon. But I do know this...the galaxy is in ruins and the promises of Ell Yon are sure. At a time of his choosing, there will be a shift in the balance of power that will shake the foundation of Dracus's regime. When...where...and who...is but mere speculation. As with all the oracles foretold, we will know when it is upon us."

Daeson reset the false bottom. He touched the recess again, holding it longer this time.

"Touch here," he said.

Brae cocked her head, wondering what he was doing. Daeson gently took her finger to make the motion for her. A second later, a soft sequence of three beeps rang out. He then closed the case, picked it up, and handed it to Brae. She looked up at her father, confused and frightened. She stepped back.

"No, Dad. I can't take this!"

"The last word I heard of Ell Yon's voice was that when you were of age, I was to give this to you. Today is that day."

Brae bit her lip. She wasn't ready, not even to hold such a thing. She saw something move out of the corner of her eye. She glanced over at Rivet to see him come her way. He approached and stood in silence next to her and Daeson. Somehow, his presence helped. She slowly lifted her hand to receive the case from Daeson.

"Don't be afraid, Brae. Ell Yon will never leave you nor abandon you, no matter where your journey takes you."

Something about her father's words disturbed her. They seemed so final, like a goodbye.

"Bring the Protector with you, my lady," Rivet said, disrupting her sober thoughts.

She nodded, letting the case fall to her side. It seemed heavier than it should have...much heavier.

The pain of losing Raviel was deeper and more cutting than Daeson thought he could bear, and the passage of time did nothing to diminish the intensity of it. Caring for their baby girl was the salve that seemed to help his wound, but even that was not enough. When he had removed the Protector from his arm, he had convinced himself that it was just for a day. But a day became a week which became a year. In the weakness of his humanity, he could not help but connect his pain and loss with his service to Sovereign Ell Yon. Though his intellect knew better, the pieces of his broken heart needed to blame something for its continual state of miserable loneliness, a loneliness that only Raviel could ever satisfy. But more than that, it was fear that kept him from picking up the Protector and finding the voice of his lord once more. Would he be asked to sacrifice even more? Now that Brae was his precious treasure, a tether to the memories of his life with Raviel, would he be asked to give her up as well? It was a question he could not even risk asking, and so he walked in silence, just parallel to the path he knew Ell Yon had called him to. Wasn't that enough, not turning to the left or to the right even if he weren't centered where he was supposed to be? Knowing that their daughter would be an integral part of Ell Yon's future already threatened his resolve. In the still of the night, Daeson knew his state and was ashamed...ashamed of his cowardice. After all, he was the mighty Navi that had guided the Raylean people through the ages of darkness and of might, and yet he hid from the voice of the Sovereign.

When a year without the Protector became years, the momentum of his willful unhearing became a fearful thing in and of itself. Surely Ell Yon was disgusted with him. To appease his guilt, he had poured the passion of his past as a Navi into the life of his daughter, Brae. It was easier to play the role of a narrator in the stories of his past rather than reveal himself, for had he not she might have unwittingly exposed his guarded weakness. Daeson had given up on himself, placing the hope of his penance in the future of preparing Brae for service to Ell Yon. The irony of it all was that he had tasted the mind of Ell Yon through the Protector, and in the deepest recesses of his soul he knew that he was wrong, grossly underestimating the unfathomable depths of the Sovereign's love, mercy, and forgiveness. Yet the power of his human pain strengthened his weakness enough to deny such healing love. It was a sorrowful state, but he lived it with a purpose knowing that the human race needed rescuing more than he needed to cling to his pain for the loss of Raviel. And so, in that sorrow, he soldiered on.

Brae...Brae. His beloved daughter had the fiery spirit of Raviel but was plagued with the stubbornness of her father. Throughout their years together he tried to weed that out of her, though he also realized that there was a need for an aspect of that stubbornness for it would carry her through the challenges that were to come and were even now upon her. Although he had not donned the Protector since she was a child, there was still a keen sense of knowing that this mission she was about to embark on was the initiation of something galactic. He hardly dared consider the possibility of what it might mean. He had to repeatedly force his pain-filled heart into obedient subjection to the Sovereign, if even from his distant parallel path.

Rivet joined Daeson on the front porch as they watched the amber lights of Brae's speeder illumine a plume of dust from the old road of their country home.

"This is the beginning, my liege," Rivet said.

"I know," Daeson replied, his words threatening to expose his anguish. "Will she survive?" he asked.

Without the Protector there were things unknown, but he also knew that the answer to that question was something the Protector would never reveal. The android had a mysterious and unique connection to

Sovereign Ell Yon in a way that Daeson could never quite discern. In the years without his own connection, Rivet had become a comfort for his aching soul.

"It is unknown."

It was an unfair question, and Daeson knew it. Daeson looked over at Rivet, his companion throughout the journey of his life, and was grateful. *Would Rivet have a role in this future to come?* he wondered.

Rivet turned his head to Daeson.

"The evening is spent...rest, my liege."

CHAPTER

3

The Omega Nebula

Omegeon – an element created by the Omega Nebula that emits a subatomic particle with energy levels exceeding all other known particles. Without extreme shielding, minimal exposure to omegeon particles is deadly to all life. Miniature omegeon crystals are extremely rare and contain massive quantities of omegeon particles. Applications for omegeon beyond that of powering the Protectors are currently unknown.

Brae didn't sleep well that night. It was impossible not to think through every detail of her mission prep, not wanting to miss a single item or process. Also vying for her thoughts and attention all through the night were the cryptic words of Rivet and the stunning revelation of the Protector her father had bestowed on her. Somewhere in the dark of night, she rose from her bed and stepped out onto the balcony of her quarters in Jalem. The light pollution of the city ruined much of the glory of the starry sky, but still, with her eyes turned upward, the tug of those brilliant pinpoints of light pulled on her soul. The spectacle soothed her, and she was finally able to lie down to slumber. Unfortunately, this only made for a few fitful hours of sleep in preparation for what was sure to be a grueling, sleepless, week-long mission.

At the appointed time the next morning, Brae and her team of five astrotechs with varying degrees of experience, including her closest friend and colleague, Shayde, arrived at the Raylean Guard hangar. They began loading the *Stalwart* with the extra research equipment they would need for the mission.

The *Stalwart* was a fine research vessel, large enough to accommodate nearly all expeditions the astrotech order required. The cockpit command center was designed for two pilots with three auxiliary seats just aft of them. The passenger section was large enough for twelve people, but there were only six sleeping quarters for passengers, which is what limited Brae's team to the size it was. But in truth, Brae had a difficult time even getting four additional researchers to be part of her team since her research and hypothesis had limited support from the astrotech senior masters. The *Stalwart's* research lab and observation deck was rather spectacular, being positioned above and aft of the main fuselage. It was spacious and outfitted with high-tech equipment and sensors. The forward half of the lab had three large observation windows giving a stunning 180-degree view of the space it occupied. The vessel had a sizeable storage bay as well as a shuttle for unique mission excursions. The entire ship was designed with special shielding that provided adequate protection from radiation including the highly deadly omegeon particles.

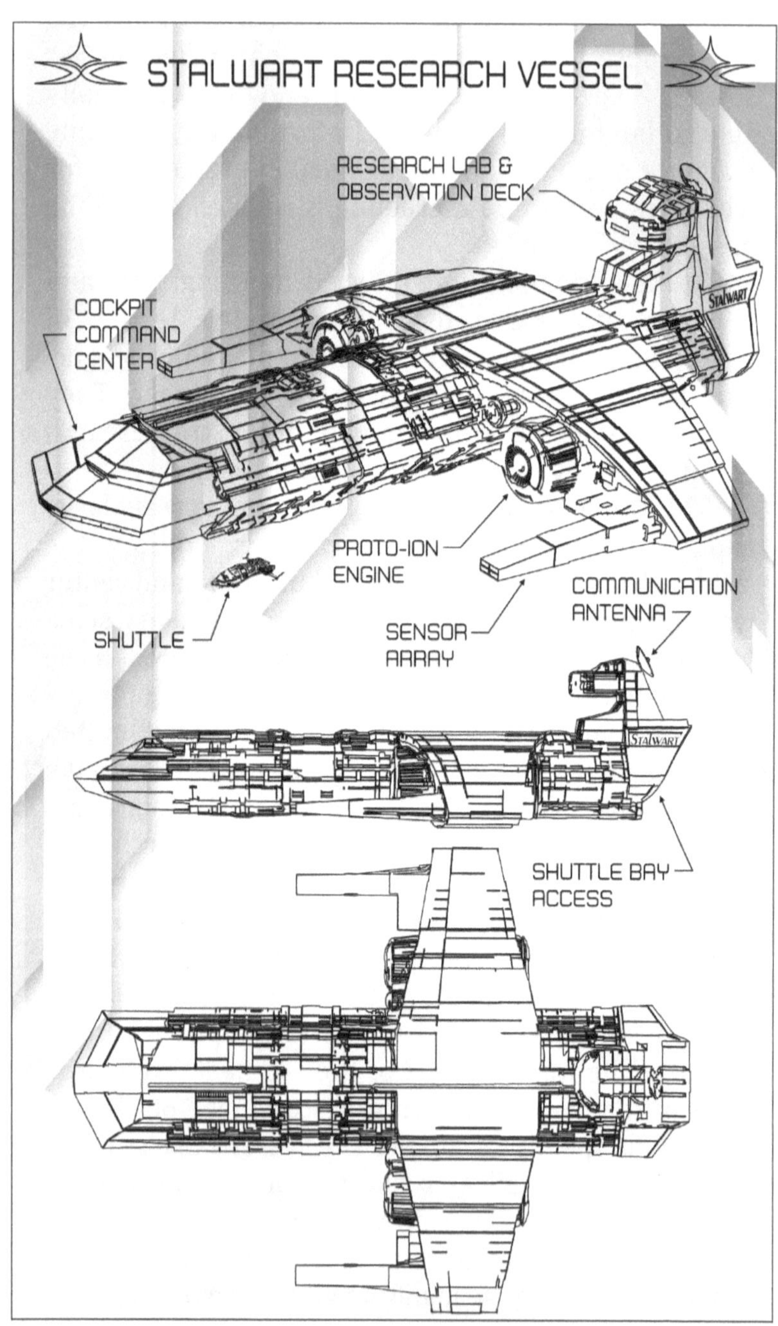

STALWART RESEARCH VESSEL
RESEARCH LAB & OBSERVATION DECK
COCKPIT COMMAND CENTER
STALWART
PROTO-ION ENGINE
SHUTTLE
SENSOR ARRAY
COMMUNICATION ANTENNA
STALWART
SHUTTLE BAY ACCESS

The *Stalwart* was powered by two large proto-ion engines and a slipstream jump drive for conduit hyperspace travel.

When Brae and her team boarded the *Stalwart*, Stryker and his co-pilot were already in the cockpit command center running their preflight checks. A ground crew of four mechtechs were busy making final preparations for the launch. Brae looked to see if there were any astrotech senior masters to send them off, but there were none. It was what she expected, yet the disappointment stung worse than she had anticipated. As launch time approached, however, the thrill of her first trek into space eclipsed any negative thoughts or feelings she had regarding her superiors. On the surface she was the professional, all-business astrotech master, but inside she was as giddy as a schoolgirl. She had anticipated this day since she was five years old. It wasn't just about traveling in space, it was about studying it...absorbing the beauty of the cosmos in all its splendor through firsthand investigation. And if her hypothesis was correct, this would be a grand initiation.

Brae was grateful for Shayde. Her friend was the only one of her team that truly understood the ramifications and the degree of her personal interest in the expedition. Ironically, if Brae had an opposite, Shayde would be it. That they were both Raylean traditionalists and astrotechs was the end of their shared commonality. Shayde loved people—Brae would rather be alone. Shayde was an optimist—Brae a realist. Shayde dressed to the nines—Brae loved casual and comfort. Shayde loved the city life—Brae would rather walk the valley and streams of the country than dine in one of Jalem's finest restaurants. But despite all their differences, the companionship they shared one with another was deep and meaningful.

Once all equipment and personnel were on board, Lieutenant Stryker and his co-pilot addressed Brae and her team. They were all sitting in their designated launch seats with Shayde sitting next to Brae at the front. As Stryker stepped forward to speak, Brae looked for any signs of predisposed animosity that might impede a successful expedition, but there were none. Stryker appeared to don the persona of a professional pilot on mission.

"Good morning. I am Lieutenant Stryker, and this is Ensign Cuttler. Master Astrotech Thornton is the mission commander of this expedition, and I am the pilot in command. For any issues or decisions regarding the execution of mission requirements, you will be directed by Miss Thornton. For any and all concerns relating to the proper and safe execution of the flight, I will be making the call. Your safety is our responsibility and our priority. If necessary, it will overrule mission requirements."

Stryker paused, briefly looking Brae's way. She knew that last bit was just for her. She couldn't help the very subtle smirk that momentarily lit upon her face. A man like him couldn't possibly understand the magnitude nor the importance of what this expedition could mean to the Raylean people.

"This expedition will position the *Stalwart* within 15,000 miles of the Omega Nebula," Stryker continued. "I don't need to tell you how potentially dangerous that can be so let's get in, get your data, and get out. Does anyone have any questions?"

Stryker waited only a couple of seconds, then nodded.

"Very well, please secure any loose items and prepare for launch."

He and the co-pilot exited the passenger area and made their way to the cockpit. Shayde reached over and squeezed Brae's hand, an ear-to-ear grin on her face. Brae's heart was racing, and her dear friend knew just what she needed. Shayde leaned close to Brae.

"I can see what you mean about that pilot...what an ogre! And an ugly one at that," she added with a wink.

Brae gave Shayde a sour look.

"You have no idea," she shot back. "I just hope he stays in the cockpit and out of our way. The less we see of him the better."

Shayde retreated, pretending to offer a serious salute. "Okay, Commander."

Brae laughed, shaking her head. "I'm serious."

When Brae heard the rumble of the massive engines, her stomach flipped. *This is it*, she thought. *This is my moment.*

Ten minutes later, the *Stalwart* roared its engines to full power and lifted off. There were port windows in the passenger area, just large enough to tease Brae with glimpses of this epic journey. She looked forward to breaking orbit when they would be able to move about the ship and get a better view, at least until they reached the slipstream conduit. But what really thrilled her was the anticipation of seeing the Omega Nebula through the lab observation deck windows once they were in their final position a few hours later.

As the *Stalwart* accelerated forward and upward, reaching into the skies of Rayl, Brae closed her eyes, thanking Sovereign Ell Yon for the chance to see her dream finally come true. A few minutes later, Brae could hardly remain strapped into her seat as the port window shifted from the sky-blue hue of the atmosphere to the speckled black beauty of space. The crisp image of the rim of Rayl was slowly changing from the gentle arc of a horizon to that of a suspended blue orb. Brae shivered with excitement. Shayde was smiling from ear to ear.

"You made it, Brae!"

"It's...glorious!" Brae responded, knowing her grin was as big and as silly as she felt.

Rhett had filed the expedition's flight plan and had received approval from the Morian Empire's Planetary Control Agency. Once they broke orbit from Rayl, any Morian intervention or oversight would be rare, especially since the *Stalwart* and their expedition was categorized exclusively as research. They would be making two slipstream jumps, the last taking them to within sub-light travel distance of the Omega Nebula. In terms of distance, the nebula was "next door" to Rayl, being just less than twelve light years away. Rhett had only ever seen the nebula from a few light years away, and even at that distance it was ominous looking. He was nearly pure-blooded Raylean but had never bought into all the fanciful tales of their people's past and the much-exaggerated part the Omega Nebula supposedly played in it. Even still, now that he was about to get close and personal with the nebula, he could not deny a measure of apprehension stirring in his soul. He wondered if it was just the potential risk they would be taking by flying so close to it or if it was something else.

The first slipstream jump was completed without incident.

"Lay in the coordinates for the Omega Nebula gateway," Rhett ordered.

"Coordinates laid in," Edge replied. "Do you want a com channel open to let the passengers know they can move about?"

"I'm not a transport pilot, Edge, and this isn't a joyride," Rhett scolded.

"Okay," Edge recanted. "I just figure we're going to be with these technoids for the next five days, and it wouldn't hurt to at least *try* to be friendly."

Rhett shook his head. "That's a great idea...you be friendly, I'll fly the ship."

Edge tapped a panel opening a ship-wide com channel.

"Attention...our first slipstream jump is complete. It will take another seventy minutes before we reach the next gateway, so you are free to move about but confine yourselves to the passenger and sleeping quarters areas. Thank you for flying Raylean Guard Transportation."

Rhett glared over at Edge. "Seriously?"

Edge shrugged and became preoccupied with some non-critical task. A little over an hour later, they approached the second gateway for their final jump. Rhett's heart quickened.

"Engage jump drive on my mark," Rhett commanded as the marker beacons designating the entrance flashed just before them.

"Three, two, one...engage."

Once more the space around them melted away as a million stars elongated into ribbons of light. For Rhett, a jump through a slipstream conduit was never dull. Every time he did it, he was astounded by the technology that allowed faster-than-light travel to occur. Many claimed it was Immortal tech. Rhett believed that it was ancient and so advanced that our scitechs could never quite figure it out, so attributing it to some mysterious alter-dimensional race of beings was the easy way out. This jump would only last a few seconds. When they exited, Rhett was not prepared for what he saw. The sheer magnitude of the nebula was enough to garner an overwhelming sense of awe, but there was much more to this nebula than its impressive size. The vibrant white and orange colors filled the *Stalwart's* cockpit canopy with random energy discharges. The boundary of the nebula was extremely distinct, like a wall of cosmic energy and material that nothing could pass through and survive.

"Wow!" he heard Edge exclaim.

Rhett immediately began checking his instruments, especially their omegeon radiation level.

"Stay focused, Edge. Let's make sure everything is functional and within spec before we do any stargazing."

Edge refocused and began tapping on his controls.

"Whoa...get a load of this, Stryk," Edge said, pointing to a center console displaying a recent scan. Dozens of spacecrafts were positioned at various distances from the nebula.

"What do you suppose they're doing here?" Edge asked.

"Same thing we are," Rhett replied. "Only at a much safer distance."

Rhett set a course that would safely bypass the observing crafts and take them in close to the nebula...much too close for his comfort. He took a deep breath.

"Here we go."

He engaged the *Stalwart's* engines and began piloting the course he had plotted. It took over an hour to close in on the coordinates designated on the mission spec log. Rhett sent Edge back to the passengers to check on them. A few minutes later he returned.

"Hey, Stryk," Edge called as he entered the cockpit command center. "One of the astrotechs has asked for us to let Thornton into the cockpit to get a close-up view of the nebula. She said Thornton would never ask for herself."

"Ha! I don't think so," Rhett blurted. "She'll have a view from the observation deck soon enough."

Rhett made a final course correction which brought the full fury of the nebula in view. It caused both pilots to stop and gaze. A moment later Rhett looked over at Edge.

"Fine," Rhett said, "bring her forward...but only for a few minutes. Let the others know they can have access to the lab as soon as we fix our position."

Edge disappeared and Thornton arrived a couple of minutes later. Rhett motioned to the co-pilot seat...it would give her the best view.

"This is it," Rhett said as he decelerated the *Stalwart* to a stop. "What orientation is best for your sensors?"

When there was no response, he glanced over at Thornton. White flashes of plasma light softly reflected off her rose cheeks. Her eyes sparkled in wonderment as the energy from this massive living nebula danced in blue, white, and orange arcs in front of them. Rhett had seen the phenomena growing with each passing moment of their approach as he piloted the *Stalwart*, but evidently not quite as Thornton had seen it, with complete adoration and amazement. It was breathtaking...frightening actually. It made him feel small and insignificant. So much uncontrollable energy.

"Brae! Our spectral analysis is—" Shayde burst into the cockpit, immediately yielding to that which demanded awe and respect from all who beheld it.

"My whole life I wondered what it would be like," Thornton said, her voice soft like Rhett hadn't heard or ever expected from the geeky astrotech. "It's beyond what I imagined."

She slowly turned her glowing face toward Rhett, the wonderment lingering as if enchanted by some magical place. He was momentarily surprised by the astrotech. He had never thought of this intellectually obstinate scientist as anything but annoying, but this place changed her, at least temporarily.

"Orientation?" he asked again, being careful to stay focused. Failing to do so almost always meant problems for a pilot. And he had a feeling that this could be just as dangerous as any combat mission.

"Oh...sixty degrees off the starboard with the front plane of the Nebula boundary," Thornton said then snapped her head toward Shayde, her terse but cool annoying attitude fully resumed. "Are the spectrograph, magnetometer, imager, and collector array calibrated and functional?" Thornton asked.

"Uh huh," Shayde said, still mesmerized by the nebula.

"Well, let's start our analysis and see if we can pinpoint magnitude and location of the Event."

"Excuse me...event?" Rhett asked. He clenched his jaw, trying not to jump to conclusions.

"Yeah...the Omega Event," Shayde replied. "The whole reason for the mission."

Rhett glanced to the nebula and then back to Thornton. "I thought that was just a name you gave this expedition. But you're saying there's actually going to be an event? As in some sort of discharge event?"

Thornton nodded...Rhett frowned. "Just how large of a discharge are we talking?" he asked.

"Well, Lieutenant Stryker, if we knew that, we wouldn't have had to fly twelve light years to find out."

She flashed him a condescending smile then stood and exited the cockpit. Oh, how he despised these smug intellectual tech know-it-alls. "Tell Ensign Edge to get his hide back up here," he commanded over his shoulder, but it didn't feel like the last word. He doubted he would ever have the last word with Thornton.

A few seconds later Edge slid into the co-pilot seat, a wider than usual grin on his face. Rhett shook his head...he didn't want to know.

"I like her," Edge volunteered.

"I don't," Rhett countered.

"That's why I like her," Edge laughed out loud.

"How would you like to EVA to clean space fungus off the hull?"

Edge kept smiling and occupied himself with his instrumentation.

"I'm surprised by you, Stryk. Beneath all that sci-tech geekiness, she's a looker."

"I hadn't noticed," Rhett replied. "This is no joyride, Edge. We're already too close to this nebula. If there is a discharge like they're expecting, we're going to need to punch it to the slipstream gateway pronto. Double-check those course calculations and have alternate ones ready for whatever direction we are oriented. There's no telling what heading will be the safest exit."

"Will do, Cap," Edge replied, his mission tone now evident.

Once the *Stalwart* was positioned and oriented, Rhett began unstrapping himself. "I'm going to find out just how stupid dangerous this discharge is supposed to be."

"Give her a kiss for me," Edge teased.

Rhett slapped the back of his head.

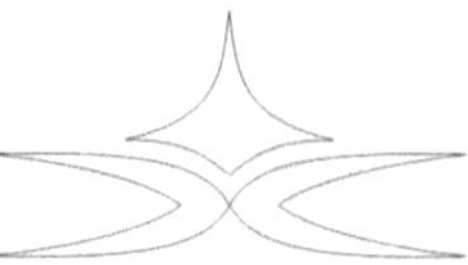

CHAPTER

4

High Stakes

In the realm of the Ruah, deep inside the Omega Nebula, Kalem, the First Admiral of Ell Yon's Aurora Galactic Fleet stood on the observation deck of his star cruiser flagship, the *Advent*. This was his home. Though this *Advent* was not the original ship from when he had been given command of Ell Yon's fleet many centuries ago, he had kept the name for each of the previous five star cruisers he had commanded. Doing so forced a continual reminder of the day that Admiral C'fir Dracus had turned against Ell Yon and the Commander to form the Torian rebellion...the Scourge. Thousands of years had passed, and the accumulating destruction following that fateful day seemed to have no end. Kalem, like all Immortal Malakians still true to Sovereign Ell Yon, had good days and difficult days. In the last few centuries, it seemed there were far more difficult days than good ones. Dracus's tactics and resourcefulness testified to the brilliance of Ell Yon's nemesis. Except for that one sliver of humanity called the Rayleans, it seemed as if Dracus owned the will and hearts of nearly all of mankind. And it was humanity that was now the exclusive focus of both the Malakians and the Torians, for it was in the realm of humanity that this galactic battle would be won or lost.

From his lofty space perch, Kalem watched the hundreds of beautiful ribbons of vessels stream across the broad window of the observation deck, exiting and entering the breathtaking blue orb of their world, Tsiyyon. In the realm of the Ruah, Tsiyyon was positioned within the fiery walls of the Omega Nebula and therefore there had never been a mortal that had ever seen the planet and the system to which it belonged. This was the abode of Sovereign Ell Yon and the Commander, and the home of all Malakian Immortals.

Kalem sensed another powerful figure step up next to him.

"Is your fleet positioned as I've commanded?" Kalem asked.

"They are, pattern foxtrot with all battle stations on alert," came the reply.

"Very well," Kalem said.

Though both men seemed taken by the view, their silence was simply a prelude to a conversation supremely significant.

"It's unusual that both of our fleets have been called home to Tsiyyon at the same time," Kalem's companion offered.

Kalem nodded.

"I sense your heart is heavy. I hardly dare ask why we're here, along with all of the other fleet admirals, so I'm told."

Kalem nodded again.

"Galec, you and I have witnessed the unbelievable and the unthinkable." He turned his head slightly Galec's direction without fully looking at his fellow admiral. "But what we are about to witness this day is beyond anything you can imagine."

Galec waited patiently.

"Come with me, my friend," Kalem said, turning away from the stunning visual before them.

A few minutes later, they entered the *Advent's* docking bay where a hundred men and women snapped to attention. They walked to a large executive class transport where the ship's crew welcomed them and prepared for launch. Once seated, Galec looked toward Kalem.

"You've always accused me of being slow to speak and rather cryptic in my replies to you. Are you trying to get even with me, Kalem?" Galec asked, no smile evident on his face.

Kalem looked at Galec for the first time.

"No, Galec. I just don't think I can explain it without you seeing with your own eyes."

Galec frowned. Kalem knew Galec didn't like being surprised, but there was no better way to communicate what was about to happen.

Within a few minutes they were skimming the atmosphere of Tsiyyon to reach the far side of the planet, then began traveling on a course toward the largest of the three moons. The surprise on Galec's face was evident. In the distance, the peripheral boundary of the Omega Nebula was clearly evident. Flashing waves of plasma energy rippled across the massive expanse of space before them.

"The nebula is more active than usual," Galec commented.

"Yes," Kalem returned.

On the far side of the moon, Galec's eyes opened wide. A structure not dissimilar to that of a slipstream conduit gateway came into view.

"I don't understand," Galec said. "We haven't been using slipstream conduits for centuries. Why this, and why now?"

"This conduit is unique. Besides offering temporal protection for light speed travel, it will protect us from the boundary of the nebula," Kalem answered.

"But we don't need protection if we are just passing through it," Kalem countered.

Kalem looked at Galec, his eyes alone conveying his message.

A few seconds later, the crew engaged a slipstream drive engine as they entered the gateway. When they exited, their vessel had come to a full stop at a space station tangent to and touching the nebula boundary. There was a powerful energy shield protecting the station and their ship from being incinerated by the powerful bursts of energy. Kalem looked toward Galec, seeing astonishment in his face. He would have smiled were it not for their solemn mission.

"Rather intimidating, wouldn't you say?"

Galec huffed. "You might say."

The pilot of the transport radioed for clearance to dock and soon they were entering the bay of the large station.

"Why wasn't I informed of the existence of this station?" Galec asked, his countenance grim.

"Don't be insulted. I was told just last week," Kalem said. "There are things of which only Ell Yon and the Commander know, and this won't be the last."

Galec pursed his lips, nodding. "These are the things that concern me most."

Kalem put a hand on Galec's shoulder. "Your discernment is keen, my friend."

After transiting various corridors and platforms, they entered a massive geodesic room that seemed to have no ceiling at all. Occasionally a discharge from the boundary of the nebula, which was a stone's throw away, would arc and impact the place where a ceiling would be. It was then that one could see the transparent dome shield protecting and pushing back against the energy discharge. It was frightening and beautiful all at the same time.

Standing before them were the ten other fleet admirals. They snapped to attention to welcome Kalem and Galec. Kalem returned a salute then all turned their attention to the two figures standing on a platform that was positioned directly in contact with the Omega Nebula boundary wall. They both turned and in unison, all twelve of the fleet admirals dropped to one knee. Sovereign Ell Yon stepped forward to speak as the Commander remained behind and motioned with his hand. The fleet admirals stood waiting to hear the words of their Sovereign.

"Admirals of the Aurora Galactic Fleet, the war with C'fir and the Torians has been long and costly. You have done well in your duties, honoring us by your faithful service and commitment. The infusion of Dracus's Deitum Prime into the realm of humanity has altered the essence of life itself. As you know, we have been working on an antidote to permanently destroy the genetic altering agent, and we have succeeded."

The subdued exclamations that rose throughout the cadre of fleet admirals indicated their excitement. Galec looked to Kalem, noticing that he alone did not seem encouraged. Kalem caught Galec's gaze, his eyes darkening to dismay. Sovereign Ell Yon paused to allow the low rumble to subside.

"In truth, we've known the formula for the antidote since the day Deitum Prime was first revealed."

This initiated significant surprise from the admirals, yet none dared ask the most obvious question…why did they wait until now?

"The timeline for the implementation of the Solution is for me alone to establish. Just know that nothing you have fought for…nothing you have sacrificed for is in vain. We fight for the precious souls of humanity in every quadrant of the galaxy, and our fight is far from over. What is about to happen will initiate the cleansing of the galaxy, but it is only the beginning, and your commitment to see this through must not fail. Do you understand?"

"We understand, Sovereign Ell Yon," Kalem called out for all of the fleet admirals, his salute confirming his oath. An instant later, all the other eleven admirals joined in a unifying salute.

Ell Yon received the affirmation with solemn respect. He nodded and the admirals dropped their salutes, eager to hear the implementation of the Solution. The Commander stepped forward to stand beside his father. The admirals waited patiently as, for the first time in their immortal lives, they watched the Sovereign seem to struggle to speak his next words. To the last admiral, it terrified them all.

"There is one and only one antidote to the vile Deitum Prime of Dracus. It is locked in the genetic code of the royalty of the Ruah and flows in the veins of my son."

Though silent, the admirals were visibly confused by the Sovereign's words.

"To transfer the antidote to humanity, the Commander must enter their domain, taking on the fully human form of a man."

At this, the admirals could not keep their tongues.

"Sovereign…Commander…surely an interphasal translator could accomplish this," Admiral Lucien implored.

"We've investigated every other option," the Commander said. "This is the only way."

"But you will be exposed and vulnerable to the Torians and their attacks," another admiral stated.

"As a human, you would become…mortal!" Galec finished.

This last statement stunned them all. The Sovereign and the Commander stood in silence, waiting for the admirals to recover themselves. Kalem reached for Galec, placing a steady hand on his shoulder. When Galec looked to his commanding admiral, it was evident that more was to come.

"Settle your heart, my friend," Kalem whispered. "The others will need you."

Galec took a breath, steeling his countenance for whatever else may come. When they were ready, the Commander looked to his father and waited for his subtle nod, then stepped forward.

"Though the antidote is locked within my genetic code, there is only one catalyst that will unlock it so that it may be propagated to the rest of humanity."

The Commander's countenance set firm and resolute.

"I must die there."

Before the admirals could voice further protests, the Commander lifted his arm to subdue them.

"Do not be dismayed, servants of Sovereign Ell Yon. This is a day that hope is born to humanity…and a day of celebration. You will discharge this message. C'fir Dracus knows what you now know and will do everything in his power to stop us. Never before have your missions to humanity been more dire…more weighty. Fulfill them with every fiber in your being and be courageous for those you lead. Do we have your oath as such?"

Every admiral immediately bent to one knee.

"We are one under the Sovereign...we so swear," came the unified decree.

A solemn hush ensued as the moment lingered.

"Rise up, admirals," Sovereign Ell Yon commanded. "And witness a new era in the realm of humanity."

Father and son turned and embraced. The Commander then walked to the edge of the platform where a doorway to a chamber embedded into the boundary of the nebula opened. Within the chamber brilliant flashes of light were arcing around its periphery. Just inches away on the nebula boundary wall, energy swells were building to a cacophony of frightening power.

"Come, Kalem," the Commander called.

Kalem quickly stepped up onto the platform and came to the Commander. The Commander lifted the Protector from his arm and handed it to his first admiral.

"I bid you to keep this for me. You will know when it is time."

Kalem received the Protector, bowing as he did so. The Commander then entered the chamber, turning to face his father. Sovereign Ell Yon slowly lifted his own Protector, opening his hand. Fierce arcs of blue power danced across the jeweled ribbons, at times leaping off the Protector entirely and joining with the expanding bursts of nebula charges. The Sovereign hesitated. Kalem saw pain in his eyes as he had never seen before, a tear trailing down his noble cheek. For a few brief seconds, father and son exchanged a gaze of pain, power, and purpose that no other being could ever know. The Commander tilted his head forward ever so slightly, and Sovereign Ell Yon unleashed the Protector. The consuming energy permeated every atom of the Commander's body. Kalem watched with great trepidation as the power of the Protector dismantled the fabric of the Commander's being, thrusting him into and through the crushing power of the nebula in a final burst of explosive energy. Kalem and his admirals had to shield their eyes from the white-hot light, enduring the initiation of the Solution for humanity. In an instant, it all stopped, silence filling the void of sound. With his arm still outstretched, Sovereign Ell Yon remained a statue of power and pain, a visage seared into Kalem's memory forever. The only movement he saw was the single tear trickling down the face of his lord. Kalem struggled—how does one console his lord? Hardly more than a whisper, Kalem heard the Sovereign's command.

"Dracus is on the move," Ell Yon said, lowering his arm. "Dispatch your fleets."

Kalem snapped a salute, then turned to join his admirals just as he heard multiple hails from their communicators.

"Admirals, return to your fleets and prepare for battle!"

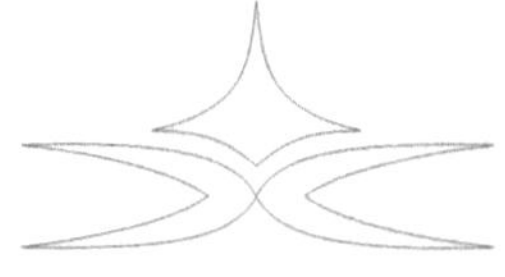

5

The Event

Brae was becoming discouraged. After five days, the nebula had not given up any secrets. She was tired and frustrated, allowing herself only two hours of sleep every third shift, and it was starting to take its toll on her. She retreated to her cubicle to catch a few minutes of sleep before the next shift started. Before she laid down, she reached for the case that she had felt compelled to bring with her. She pressed her finger onto the reader, instantly hearing the unlock mechanism activate. Slowly she opened the case. There was enough room in the upper portion of the case to hold Daeson's Talon and a remote hover probe she had wanted to take. She activated the mechanism to unlock the lower hidden compartment, slowly lifting the upper compartment to reveal the gleaming sleek form of Immortal technology—the lost Protector. She stared at it with a renewed sense of awe and wonder. A hundred images of the stories her father had told her flashed across her mind. Was all of it really true? She had to remind herself of the evidence of the truth of her father's words, Rivet being not the least of such. But perhaps the greatest evidence of all was resting in the case before her. How else could her father, a simple geo-mapper pilot, have acquired such a priceless antiquity?

She still hadn't mustered the courage to try wearing it. It frightened her. If this truly was the Protector that Ell Yon had first given to mankind...to Daeson Starlore many centuries ago, then who was she to dare such a thing? With an extreme sense of awe and fear, she ran her fingers across the jeweled ribbons encircling the smooth silvered vambrace. Midway down the length of it, Brae felt the slightest of tremors. She paused, and then it reached for her. Micro arcs of blue energy intercepted her synaptic gaps and carried her into the Ruah. Blinded by pure white light, she couldn't see where the Protector had taken her. Energy seemed to completely abandon her body as she fell to her knees.

"Daughter of Sovereign Ell Yon, be prepared to see glory and be prepared to see loss."

The voice was powerful and mysterious. As fast as it had come upon her, it vanished away. The next thing Brae felt was Shayde pulling on her arm.

"You're pushing too hard, Brae. You didn't even make it to your bunk before you fell asleep."

Brae yawned, realizing that she had fallen asleep on the floor. Slowly she remembered her encounter with the Protector. She glanced toward the case on her bed, wondering if Shayde had seen it, but the case cover was closed.

"Wow...I guess you're right. What's up? Has anything happened?"

Shayde frowned. "No, and our fearless lieutenant wants to talk to you."

Brae smirked. "I can only imagine," she said with a huff. Glancing in the mirror, she straightened her clothing while wiping some sleep from her eyes. "Let's go see what Mr. Charming wants, shall we?"

As Brae entered the sensor lab, Stryker was looking at one of the sensor displays. He turned and looked at her, lifting an eyebrow.

"We've all had a lot of fun, but it's time to take her home. This mission is complete," Lieutenant Stryker said.

"No, Stryker," Brae protested. "If we leave now, we will miss the Event. This mission is not over."

Her weary voice betrayed her. Stryker frowned, looking very unconvinced.

"Are there any indications that we're any closer than when we first arrived?" he asked.

Brae wanted to lie, but her silence gave all the testimony Stryker needed.

"Sorry, Thornton." Stryker glanced at his arm band, reading the date and time. "According to your mission briefing and the time designated and authorized, the mission is complete. Shut it all down and secure the lab. We'll be jumping to slipstream in twenty minutes." He turned to leave.

"Lieutenant Stryker," Brae called out. He turned. "One more day...Ple—"

"Stryk, you better get back here," Edge's voice boomed over the ship intercom.

"Brae, you need to see this!" Shayde called out from the spectrograph console.

Stryker's eyebrow raised, then both he and Brae spun about and darted away from each other. The ship shook as the first wave of plasma discharge hit the hull.

"What's happening?" Brae asked, steadying herself as she made her way to Shayde.

"I'm getting Purlee numbers that are off the chart. Plasma discharges are starting to spike all across this region of the nebula."

"This is it," Brae exclaimed. The thrill rising inside her was difficult to contain. "I want full bandwidth recording on all spectrums. Verlin, make sure our data drives stay online and the backup power supplies are functional." Brae began giving orders to every member of the research team, making sure not a single sensor was overlooked, or a data point was missed.

"Thornton, how long do we need to maintain this distance for your analysis?" Stryker's voice boomed over the com. She was instantly annoyed, having to break her concentration on the event of a lifetime to answer. "As long as it lasts!" she responded.

Lieutenant Stryker's lack of acknowledgement indicated a reciprocated annoyance. After an hour of what appeared to be an increasing level of nebula energy outbursts, Stryker appeared in the research lab. He went to the large front observation window and stared at the cosmic monster looming just a few thousand miles away. Brae took a few seconds break from analyzing the endless stream of data pouring into their memory banks and came to stand beside him.

"Glorious, isn't it?"

Stryker stayed silent for a moment. "I was thinking ominous." He glanced over at Brae.

"If the intensity of these plasma events increases, I'm going to have to pull us back."

Brae glared over at him. "You can't. This is just a prelude to the Omega Event I've been anticipating for years."

"The *Stalwart* can only handle so much. I told you that the safety of this ship supersedes any astrotech discovery. I'll not sacrifice the safety of this crew for that. Are we clear?"

Brae was about to respond but was interrupted.

"I'm getting a massive energy buildup at 23.2, 31.8 degrees." Shayde called out. "Nothing recorded so far is even close."

"That's it," Stryker said turning to leave. "I'm pulling us back."

"Too late!" Shayde exclaimed.

Brae and Stryker turned to see the Omega Nebula appear to swell in one region of space then explode a shockwave of plasma energy outward right toward their ship. The speed and magnitude of the discharge was frightening.

"Brace for impact!" Stryker yelled, grabbing a vertical handle just to the right of the observation window.

Brae reached for the handle to her left, but the plasma wave hit the ship, and she missed her grip. She felt a strong hand grab her right arm which kept her from falling as the ship shuddered against the forces blasting throughout its structure. For a few seconds, Brae wondered if the ship was going to tear apart under the stress. She stole a glance toward Stryker, wondering if he thought the same. His eyes were looking upward at the steel girders then at the edges of the observation window, not realizing that he was still holding tight to Brae's arm. Slowly the groaning and quaking of the ship subsided. He let loose of Brae's arm, his face stern with concern. Without a word, he left and returned to the cockpit.

After checking on her research team and validating the data they had collected, she made her way to the cockpit.

"How's the ship holding up?" she asked.

Stryker looked perturbed.

"It's holding...barely," Edge answered. "Whatever that was, it nearly took us out. Most systems are still functioning but if another one comes—"

"I'm taking us out of here," Stryker finished. "Whether you've collected your precious data or not." He shot Brae a fierce look, then punched in a heading.

Brae stayed silent, deciding she wouldn't win another round with him.

"Hang on, Stryk," Edge said. "Take a look at this."

Edge pointed to the center glass instrument panel. A pulsing blue dot displayed with a number beside it.

"What is it?" Brae asked.

"Get me a tighter resolution scan," Stryker ordered.

A moment later, the display expanded to show a small craft apparently adrift and even closer to the nebula than the collector arrays in front of them.

"Looks like a small merchant ship of some sort." Edge was unusually sober. "And scanners show one life on board."

Lieutenant Stryker looked over at Edge. "Impossible! Check it again."

Edge reached for a panel on his side of the cockpit and deftly slid his fingers multiple times across its control icons.

"It's weak, Stryk, but it's there. Somehow there's one life on board."

Stryker touched his com menu then clicked the transmit button.

"Unidentified craft, this is the *Stalwart* with the Raylean Aerotech Forces broadcasting on all emergency channels. Please state your condition."

Silence.

"Unidentified merchant craft, this is the *Stalwart*. Do you need assistance?"

Silence.

"Where did it even come from?" Edge mumbled to himself.

Stryker's face grew taut with frustration. He looked over at Edge's scanner display. "I'm not risking this ship and the eight souls on board for one life. We're already closer than we should be to ensure our omegeon shield integrity isn't compromised."

Brae couldn't take her eyes off the image displaying the craft that was drifting dangerously close to the nebula barrier. Something indescribable was pulling at her soul, much the same as when she looked up at the stars as a little girl. The ache inside her cried out, yearning to be soothed. What was this?

"We have to go there and help," she said quietly, speaking the words without trying.

"Did you hear what I just said?" Stryker replied.

Brae broke her gaze from the image of the merchant ship and looked at Stryker.

"Clearly, they're in trouble. We need to help," Brae countered.

"If that nebula discharges again and we're closer than this, we won't survive. The risk is too great."

Edge seemed mesmerized by the life-sign scanner. "I've heard strange stories of abandoned ships like this. This gives me the creeps."

Brae ignored him. "This research ship has a shuttle with omegeon shielding."

Stryker pursed his lips, eyes narrowing to slits.

"I can pilot it," Brae said. "Give me one hour." She then turned and exited the cockpit, unable to quell the overwhelming compulsion drawing her to this obscure ship next to a nebula that could reach out and dismantle her in a moment.

Rhett couldn't deny a sense of obligation to help a spacecraft in distress. It was a generally accepted space-farer's code. Rhett looked over at Edge, frustrated by the situation and that girl.

"Go, Stryk. I'll keep the ship safe until you return."

Rhett shook his head. "That nebula acts up again you withdraw 10,000 miles...got it?"

Edge nodded. "Aye, Cap."

Rhett unstrapped and hurried back to the research lab where Thornton was just finishing giving additional instructions to her research team. He crossed his arms and waited in the doorway until she came his way.

"Step aside, Lieutenant. I'm doing this."

"And you understand that I have all the authority to stop you," he rebutted.

Thornton glared at him. "Please," she said with great difficulty.

Rhett stepped aside. "This way to the shuttle bay," he said, making room for her to walk by.

On the way, they passed by the passenger sleeping quarters where Thornton ducked inside and rejoined Rhett carrying a small instrument case. When they arrived at the shuttle bay door, he entered a sequence on the entry pad and the door disappeared into the wall on the left. Inside, he stopped at a series of lockers. Opening one, he grabbed an EVA suit.

"Put this on first—no telling what condition that ship is in." He held the suit out to her then reached for his own.

"You're coming with? Don't trust me?" she asked, taking the suit.

"Nope," he replied. "You go out there and get yourself killed, and it's on me."

"So, you're pretty much just worried about your career," Thornton said as they donned the EVA suits over their clothing.

Rhett struggled to find a comeback. This woman had the innate ability to irk him beyond any other person he had ever met. He checked Thornton's suit then nodded. He turned back to a third locker, entered a code, then retrieved a class one plasma blaster and holster. After checking the blaster's charge, he strapped the weapon securely around his waist. As they turned to approach the shuttle Rhett suddenly remembered something significant.

"This isn't the *Stalwart's* shuttle," he said stepping up to the side entrance of the sleek looking craft.

"What?" Thornton exclaimed. "What do you mean?"

"The *Stalwart's* regularly assigned shuttle is undergoing maintenance and wouldn't be ready by launch date," Rhett explained. "Ops substituted this one, the *Guardian*."

"What about omegeon shielding?" Thornton asked.

"It has it...probably better." Rhett grinned. "And she's well equipped, much better than the original. It even has a couple of mini-plasma guns."

"Well, we won't be needing those," Thornton said as Rhett entered the access code to open the shuttle door. A second later, the door split open horizontally in the middle, the top portion lifting up, and the bottom portion lowering down to form a four-step ladder.

"Maybe not, but I love flying anything with a gun," he said, leading the way into the shuttle.

Thornton huffed. "I'll bet you do."

Rhett just shook his head. *What a killjoy*, he thought.

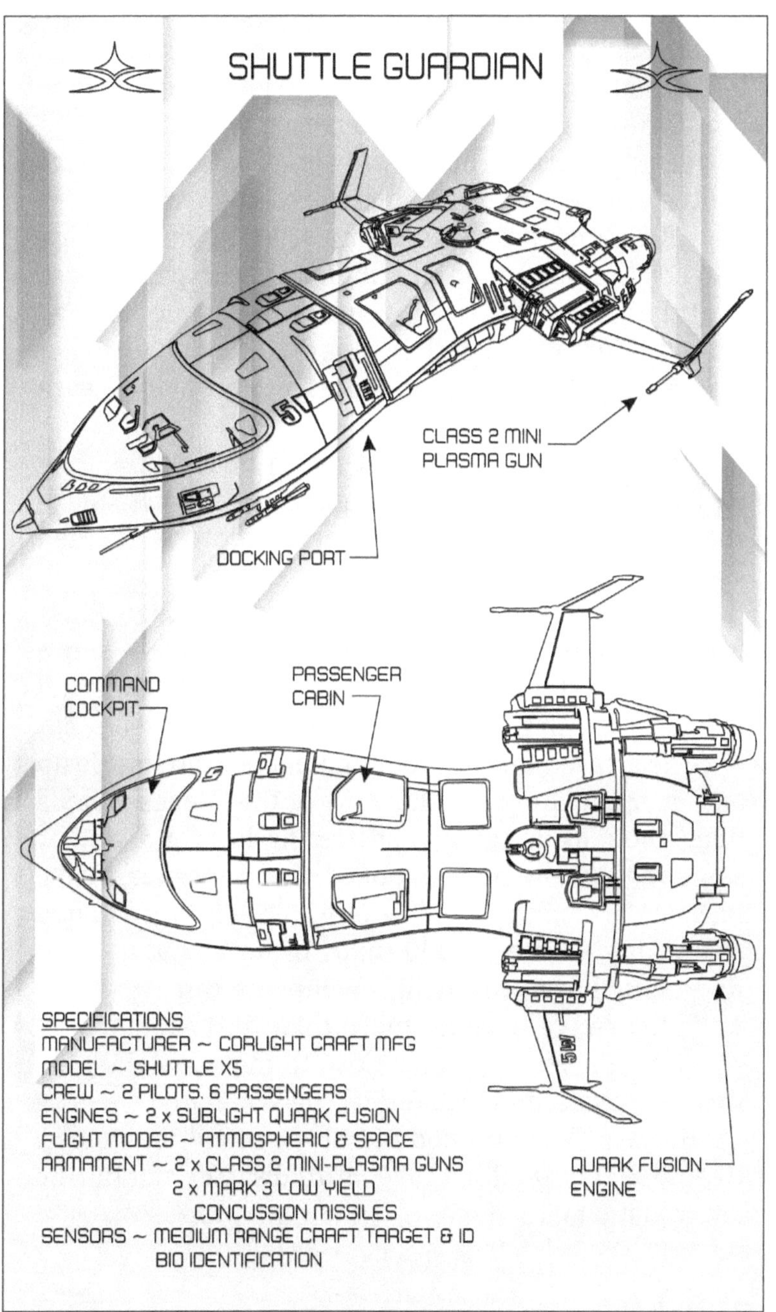
SHUTTLE GUARDIAN
CLASS 2 MINI PLASMA GUN
DOCKING PORT
COMMAND COCKPIT
PASSENGER CABIN
QUARK FUSION ENGINE
SPECIFICATIONS
MANUFACTURER ~ CORLIGHT CRAFT MFG
MODEL ~ SHUTTLE X5
CREW ~ 2 PILOTS, 6 PASSENGERS
ENGINES ~ 2 x SUBLIGHT QUARK FUSION
FLIGHT MODES ~ ATMOSPHERIC & SPACE
ARMAMENT ~ 2 x CLASS 2 MINI-PLASMA GUNS
2 x MARK 3 LOW YIELD
CONCUSSION MISSILES
SENSORS ~ MEDIUM RANGE CRAFT TARGET & ID
BIO IDENTIFICATION

The *Guardian* was a sleek maneuverable craft able to carry six passengers and two pilots. It was powered by two sub-light quark fusion engines, an innovative new thrust technology that was recently finding use on smaller spacecraft. This hybrid vessel was more than a shuttle and less than a fighter. The only tech that the *Guardian* didn't have was a jump drive engine allowing it to use the slipstream conduits for hyperspace travel. Rhett had flown the craft once a couple of months ago and was duly impressed. Having it to rely on for what may be a potentially perilous excursion helped ease some of his apprehension.

He pointed to the co-pilot seat for Thornton, then closed the side door and did a quick inspection to make sure everything inside was locked down. He then strapped in next to his annoying co-pilot.

Confirming their imminent launch with Edge, Rhett issued a shuttle bay open command to their ship's command system. As the large aft door of the *Stalwart* opened, their first view of space was unimpressive, but once he cleared the bay door and piloted the shuttle up and over the *Stalwart*, the view of the Omega Nebula filled their front canopy, shattering his courage. For some reason, the nebula looked even more terrifying. Plasma discharges and energy swells threatened everything within 20,000 miles of its boundary, and Rhett felt like he was flying a wimpy tin can.

"I figure we have no more than thirty minutes of shielding once we get that close to the nebula. We do this clean, safe, and fast. Got it?" he said flatly.

He saw Thornton nod out of the corner of his eye. He hoped this wouldn't turn into a disaster. If it did, he knew just who to blame.

5

The

Merchant

"He shall bear the weight of authority for the galaxy and will be highly esteemed. He shall be called Reclaimer, Commander, Merchant, and Ruler of Peace." ~ Eziam, Oracle of Ell Yon

Brae couldn't deny the feelings of apprehension rising inside her, but she wasn't about to let Stryker know it.

"You actually know how to pilot a ship?" Stryker asked.

"Small ships like this shuttle...yes."

"Who taught you?"

"My father is a geo-mapper on Rayl," Brae replied, not daring to reveal more than that.

Stryker's left eyebrow raised. "Hmm."

"What?" Brae asked.

Stryker tapped a course correction on his display. "Respect. Some of those geo-mappers fly in some pretty dicey terrain."

If he only knew, she thought. Here in the cockpit of the shuttle, the nebula seemed even more vivid and frightening, emanating massive bursts of plasma energy. She activated the life-scanner on her display and focused it on the coordinates Edge had relayed to them.

"I'm getting the same readings as Edge...one life-sign, but it's weak."

Stryker hesitated. "For the record...I don't like this."

He pushed the throttles of the shuttle forward, and Brae felt her body being pulled into the padding of her chair. Within a few minutes they were approaching the omegeon collector array where nearly fifty collectors were silently gathering micro doses of the powerful but deadly particles.

"Look at those collectors," Brae exclaimed.

Stryker shook his head. "Looks like some of them are fried from the burst."

Brae swallowed hard. She hated to admit it, but Stryker's concern about the force of another discharge was probably dead on. Their small shuttle wouldn't stand a chance.

"Keep an eye on the internal omegeon radiation level," Stryker said, sliding the graphic from his screen to Brae's. "If it rises above 35 pico-megs, we're aborting."

"If what you said is true and this shuttle has the same or better shielding than the original shuttle, it shouldn't be a problem," Brae returned.

As they passed by the collector array, Brae felt her stomach churn. Now the only thing between them and the colossal cosmic display of raw unfettered power was a tiny merchant ship. She felt so small and vulnerable. The merchant ship was just a spec in the center portion of their canopy. Brae pointed.

"Yep...I see it," Stryker said.

After ten more minutes of nearly full power, Stryker began decelerating.

"Remarkable…I don't see any significant damage," Brae said after completing a high-resolution optic scan of the craft.

"How can you tell?" Stryker asked. "It's a rickety old ship. No wonder the life-sign is weak."

Once they were within two hundred feet, Stryker slowed and performed a 360-degree fly-around before positioning the shuttle on the topside of the ship, preparing to connect with its docking port. Brae immediately began unstrapping.

"Thornton, we need to do this quickly, but it doesn't mean we rush procedures. That's the quickest way to end up dead. Wait for me."

Brae smirked, then remembered a similar warning from Rivet that had saved her life. She knew this about herself, but it perturbed her that Stryker seemed to know it too.

"I'm just going to prep a probe to enter the ship first." Brae continued unstrapping and stood. "There's no telling if that ship has adequate omegeon shielding. Maybe that's why the life-sign is so weak."

Stryker was concentrating on the final positioning maneuvers for docking.

"Check."

Brae went to the crew section of the shuttle and found her instrument case. She opened it so that Stryker couldn't see its entire contents. She removed the hover probe, calibrated it for omegeon detection and activated it. She heard the docking mechanism latch just below her feet. Moments later, Stryker joined her.

"We're locked in. Is the probe set?"

Brae nodded. She glanced once more toward the cockpit canopy. It was completely filled with a raging nebula just an arm's length away. She double-checked that her helmet was locked as Stryker punched in the code on the hatch access panel to open it. Multiple panels slid from the center outward like an iris opening on a camera. Brae heard a brief "whoosh" as air rushed to fill the void between their ships. Stryker reached for the region of the access panel of the merchant ship that read, "EMERGENCY ACCESS ONLY." He looked up at Brae. She read the concern in his eyes.

"*Stalwart*, this is shuttle *Guardian*. We've docked and are preparing to enter the ship. Confirm your status."

"*Guardian* this is *Stalwart*. All systems green here, Cap. FYI...besides the other observation craft we passed to position ourselves, I'm getting some long-range hits on Raylean Guard ships. Are you aware of a mission in this region of space?"

"Negative, *Stalwart*. At least we'll have support if something goes wrong."

"Copy, *Guardian*."

Stryker's jaw tensed. He then pulled on the emergency access lever, and the merchant ship's hatch opened. It took a couple of seconds for the air pressures to equalize. At first glance, nothing appeared out of order through the hatch. Stryker looked back up at Brae and nodded. She dropped the probe through the hatch, and it immediately whirred to life. She tapped on the controls on her arm, guiding the probe deeper into the ship.

"Well?" Stryker asked.

"I must position it far enough away from the hatch to get a valid reading. Procedures...right?"

Stryker's eyes narrowed, but he waited. When Brae was satisfied, she accessed the probe's sensor display.

"Atmosphere, normal. Omegeon radiation at...33 pico-megs."

Stryker shook his head. "That's too close, but we're here. Let's get in and get out." He then checked his weapon before stepping through the hatch and into the merchant ship. Brae followed.

As soon as Brae entered the merchant ship, chills flitted up and down her spine. She prepared herself for the worst, but the ship looked completely abandoned. The silence was eerie.

"I don't get it," Stryker's voice boomed through Brae's headset which made her jump. "Where's the crew? What happened here?"

"I don't know," Brae replied, "but the probe indicates that the life-sign we were reading is this direction." She pointed toward a long dark corridor. She maneuvered the probe to lead the way. Two beams of light emanated from the probe, partially illuminating the dark corridor.

Stryker clicked on his helmet light. "Let's go."

They passed numerous doors until they came to the last one in the corridor. The probe waited patiently at the door.

"This is a cargo hold," Stryker said. "You sure about this?"

Brae had the hover probe scan once more.

"Whoever...or whatever it is, is in there." She swallowed hard. Her heart was beating fast. Something profound was happening, and she had no idea why or how to explain it. She was not a fearful person, that trait ran in her blood. So to admit that fear was threatening to undo her steady demeanor was extremely unusual.

"Something is really off about this," Stryker radioed.

Great, even Stryker feels it, Brae thought. *Was this a really bad idea?*

He reached for the panel that would open the door. She just about reached to pull his hand back.

Don't be afraid...you are chosen.

The deep whisper formed inside her head and pushed outward toward her ears, but the words were not her own. She turned around, looking for the author of them.

"What's wrong?" Stryker asked.

"I...I don't know," Brae said. "Something..."

"Something what?" Stryker pressed.

Brae tried to shake it off. "Nothing...let's go."

Stryker frowned, drew his weapon, then pushed the panel, and the cargo door slid away. The probe entered first, and they cautiously followed. The hold wasn't all that large since the merchant ship was a Class F craft, but even still, there was no mistaking what the origin of the life-sign was. In the center of the hold was a small life suspension pod, its blue and amber ribbon lights softly illuminating the empty space around it. Such pods were rare today. Only a few large ships had them as "space life rafts" used to preserve the lives of crews of ships whose life support systems had failed. They were designed to put the occupant in a state of suspension until help could arrive.

"What the...why is this here?" Stryker asked.

Brae stepped up beside him. Slowly they approached. The upper half of the pod was curved glass, offering a clear view of the occupant. Brae's first glimpse stunned her.

"It's a child!" she exclaimed.

Stryker seemed too shocked to say anything. He just stared through the glass cover in silence. Brae gazed at the peaceful, still face of the child. The boy looked less than a year old. He was thin, almost sickly looking. Why was he here? Who would abandon a child in the depths of space? How long had he been here? A week...a year...a century?

Stryker holstered his blaster then turned his attention to the pod's indicator and control panel. "His vitals are weak but sustainable."

Brae looked over at him. "What do we do?"

For the first time since she met him, the cocky pilot seemed at a loss for words. He turned his gaze once more to the face of the lad.

"*Guardian*, this is *Stalwart*. We just picked up a mayday call from one of the observation craft."

Stryker looked over at Brae, serious concern in his eyes.

"Are the other Raylean Guard ships close enough to render aid? They're way more equipped for it than our research vessel," Stryker radioed.

"Unsure, shuttle. I'll keep you advised. Just hurry it up and get back here."

Although Brae didn't know Edge well, she could tell the tension in his voice clearly affected Stryker.

Stryker looked back at the pod.

"The pod's too large to fit through the hatch, and with the radiation level near peak, we don't have time to EVA it to the shuttle considering what Edge just relayed." He tapped his arm control to check the environmental conditions of the cargo hold. "Oxygen, carbon dioxide, carbon monoxide, ammonia, and methane levels are all within tolerance. The temperature is 48 degrees...cold but bearable. Help me figure out how revive the child and open this thing," Stryker ordered. "We only have minutes."

Brae turned her attention to the control panel. "I don't know anything about these pods," she murmured. "Only that the sequence to suspend and revive is elaborate."

"We don't have time for elaborate," Stryker returned.

Both of them focused on trying to decipher the revive sequence. After a couple of minutes of false tries, Brae's last attempt initiated a graphic indicating a green "Time to Revive" bar and a percent that slowly began incrementing toward 100. The pod pulsed to life with an array of sounds and gas ports flooding the chamber with a concoction evidently designed to revive the child. In the middle of their efforts, an urgent radio call burst through their headsets.

"Mayday, mayday! *Guardian*, this is *Stalwart*. We are under attack!" Edge's urgent words were interlaced with the sound of multiple concussions in the background.

Brae looked to Stryker, shock on his face.

"*Stalwart*, what's your status? Who's attacking?"

Two seconds of silence seemed an eternity.

"*Guardian*… Ray…Guar…destroyers!"

The broken transmission hinted at the unthinkable.

"Get out of there, Edge!" Stryker yelled. No response.

"*Stalwart*…come in, *Stalwart*!"

Stryker looked at Brae with fierce eyes. "We have to leave now!"

Brae glanced down at the pod control panel—55 percent. She spread her hands across the glass cover, just inches from the face of the child. Without knowing why, Brae could not...would not leave the boy.

"The child," she pleaded.

"Our crew!" Stryker exclaimed, grabbing her arm to pull her away.

Brae jerked her arm out of his grip.

Sixty-two percent.

Stryker glared back at her, eyes red with rage, teeth clenched.

"I'm launching the shuttle as soon as the engines are online. If you're not on board, I'm leaving without you."

He turned and exited the cargo hold. As the door swished closed behind him, Brae suddenly felt alone and abandoned. The headset clamored with multiple attempts by Stryker to contact the *Stalwart*, but there was no reply.

Eighty-four percent.

The bar graphic was painfully slow.

"Thornton, get back to the shuttle now...that's an order!" Stryker's voice boomed through her headset.

"On my way," she lied.

Ninety-three percent.

Brae began looking for an override but couldn't find one. The floor beneath her shuddered. Had Stryker left her? Thirty seconds later, the pod reached 100 percent. The top half of the pod split, spilling its gaseous concoction into the cargo hold. Brae didn't wait for it to fully open before lifting the child out while grabbing the thermal blanket he had been lying on. She quickly wrapped the boy, cradled him in her arms and ran. The peril that was crushing in around her was almost too much. Desperately she slammed the cargo door release with her elbow then stepped through and into the long corridor. She tapped in a command for the probe to "Return To Ship."

"Thornton!"

"I'm almost there, Stryker. I'm coming!" she said, running as fast as she dared. The probe led the way, dimly lighting the eerie corridor.

All of a sudden, the ship jolted to the left, nearly toppling Brae and her precious payload. She stumbled up against the wall of the corridor, using her body to protect the child. She looked down at the face of the small boy and couldn't tell if he was even breathing. His face was still and white. She resumed her desperate sprint back to the shuttle.

"The *Stalwart* is under attack and a destroyer is coming our way. We need to leave now!"

Just then, a powerful energy blast tore through the hull of the merchant ship. Brae tumbled to the ground taking all of the impact on her shoulder and back as she cradled and protected the unconscious child in her arms. The walls of the vessel groaned as the steel hull of the corridor behind her began to buckle. She gained a knee, turning to look toward the frightful sound. All at once a section of the corridor just 50 feet away ripped open. The rush of the ship's air pulled her and the child toward certain ice-cold death.

"Thornton, do you copy?" Stryker's voice clamored in her head as she held tightly to the child with one arm while desperately reaching for a handhold with the other, but the smooth walls and floor offered nothing.

This is it, she thought. *This is the end of me...of us.* She stole a glance at the child as they slid down the smooth surface of the floor toward the gaping hole in the hull. In that fraction of a moment, the child opened his eyes, and time seemed to stand still. The chaos of the moment melted away as she glimpsed eternity in the brilliant eyes of the boy. It took her breath away, dissolving even the fear of impending death. But it only lasted a split second as the crushing sound of collapsing steel and escaping air violently imploded on her senses once more. Brae closed her eyes, knowing there was nothing left but to embrace her end. Then it all stopped. Was such a death so quick there was no pain to feel? She opened her eyes. Just a few feet away from her, standing at the edge of the shredded hull of the corridor was a giant of a man interceding between Brae and the child and certain doom. His thick arms were stretched forward toward the breach with vambraces on each arm emanating beams of energy that seemed to offer a protective shield, momentarily sealing the breach in the hull. The man wore a flexible metallic looking suit unlike anything Brae had ever seen. He turned his head to look over his shoulder at Brae.

"Get the child to safety!" he commanded.

Brae instantly recovered her feet and resumed her run back up the corridor. At its exit, she stole a glance back toward her mysterious savior. At that moment, the rest of the hull began to collapse, and the man was gone in an instant. She hit the air lock button to her left and the corridor door slammed shut, isolating the hull breach from the rest of the vessel.

"Thornton, the engines are online. I'm leaving now!"

"I'm at the hatch. Help me get the child through!"

Brae positioned herself to push the lad up through the hatch just as Stryker's face appeared. He hoisted the child up and through the hatch opening, then reached for Brae. He jerked her up and into the shuttle in a second, then handed the child back to her. He closed the hatch, his face unreadable...stolid. Without a word, he lunged back to the cockpit and slid into the captain's seat. Before Brae could make her own seat, another explosion ratcheted the shuttle and slammed her up against the bulkhead once more. This time, the boy's eyes opened briefly as he gasped for air. She felt the shuttle careen off to the side as she scrambled to make the co-pilot seat, still cradling the child as she went.

Stryker's hands flew across the controls then landed on the throttle, shoving them forward. The shuttle jolted from the instant thrust command.

"Raylean Guard vessel, we are a Raylean astrotech exploration craft. Cease your attack!" Stryker radioed.

Just then, the merchant ship they had just abandoned exploded in a horrific display of fire and twisted metal, segments of the ship careening in every direction. One smaller section of the destroyed ship slammed into the back of the shuttle, nearly obliterating them.

"Why are they doing this?" Brae exclaimed looking over at Stryker.

"Raylean Guard forces, cease fire! We are a Raylean astrotech exploration craft!" Stryker repeated.

Stryker rolled the shuttle one hundred eighty degrees and pulled back on the stick, maneuvering between debris onto a course back toward the collector array. It was then that they were able to get a full view of their impending doom. A Raylean Aerotech Force Drakken class destroyer was in pursuit.

"That's the *Gravitas*!" Stryker exclaimed. "This is insane!"

"What of the *Stalwart*?" Brae asked, strapping herself into the seat while trying to secure the unconscious child as well.

"*Stalwart*, do you copy…Edge, are you there?" Stryker radioed.

A second later, an image of terror filled the screen. Smoke and fire surrounded a badly bleeding Edge—his countenance looking as if he had already submitted to his impending death. The image flickered in and out.

"Hang on, Edge! I'm coming to you."

"Negative, *Guardian*. Don't...know...why. Shields gone...hull breach. Goodbye Cap—."

One brief image of white-hot plasma flames engulfing Edge and the entire innards of the *Stalwart* flashed...then she was gone. Brae looked up and saw a brilliant flash of a distant explosion.

"No!" Brae screamed, covering her mouth in disbelief. She couldn't stop imagining Shayde and the rest of her research team screaming in the horror of consuming plasma fire quickly followed by the ice-cold vacuum of space.

"Those blasted devils!" Stryker grimaced. Another plasma round passed just beneath them.

"*Stalwart* shuttle to *Gravitas*. Cease fire! We are a Raylean research vessel! You are firing on a friendly spacecraft—CEASE FIRE!"

His radio call was answered with a double class 2 plasma cannon burst that nearly ended them. Stryker was able to narrowly jink up and left to avoid sure destruction. They made the collector array, weaving in between each collector to shield them from further attack. Brae was still too stunned by seeing the *Stalwart* destroyed to think clearly. It simply was unfathomable. The *Guardian* canopy filled with the image of a collector as Stryker swerved, narrowly missing one of its extended panels.

"Surely they won't destroy the collectors." Brae said just as a massive plasma cannon burst tore through four collectors. One of the collectors collided with the shuttle's starboard engine nacelle initiating alarms throughout the cockpit. The impact sent them tumbling end over end. Stryker worked fervently to regain control and shut down the right engine.

"We've lost the starboard engine...we're not going to survive this," he muttered. "We can't outrun them, and we've nowhere to hide."

The *Gravitas* was closing in fast—the speed of a damaged research shuttle was no match for such a war machine. Brae knew all too well that a direct hit of a destroyer's plasma cannon would incinerate them in an instant. Stryker was doing his best to keep the *Gravitas* at a distance, and the collector array was helping, but time was their enemy. In the chaos of their flight and of dealing with the loss of the *Stalwart* and her team, she had nearly forgotten the child that was still cradled in her lap. A cool touch fell on her cheek. She looked down and beheld the face of the child...a child that was gazing up at her with eyes that caused her to tremble. Though the child was pale and weak, his gaze undid her. In that moment she knew. The balance of the galaxy fell on this single moment of escape. They had to live...*he* had to live! Why...why did she have to bear such a lofty responsibility as this? Once again, the frightful chaos of their plight seemed to disappear into a moment of extreme reflection. And all from the glance of a lowly child. As his hand fell from her face, something out the port window caught her eye. Brae turned her head to the left. A single glimmer of light shimmied off some distant vessel.

"Stryker—look!" she pointed.

Stryker turned and squinted. "What is it?"

"I'm not sure, but it's our only hope."

"I don't think so. I'm getting nothing on my sensors," Stryker argued. "It could be just a chunk of ice meteor."

Another plasma round exploded into a collector just in front of them. Stryker had to juke hard right, then swerve extremely close to another collector as he turned one hundred eighty degrees back toward the destroyer.

"What are you doing?" Brae exclaimed as the distance between the two vessels closed quickly.

"I'm going to use what remains of the array to cover us as we reverse our direction. If we don't get hit, it should buy us just enough time before the *Gravitas* can turn around and pursue."

It was frightening to see the destroyer quickly loom large in their canopy. Stryker zigzagged in and out of the remaining collectors with the finesse of a Terridon. One more plasma burst nearly wiped them out, but they survived, passing just beneath the underbelly of the *Gravitas.*

"Where is it?" Stryker asked. "I still have nothing on my sensors."

Brae searched the space all around them but could not find it. She glanced down at the lad, but he had fallen unconscious again.

"Ell Yon...where?" she whispered.

A single glint of light just off the starboard caught her eye.

"There!" Brae said.

Stryker rolled right, pulling hard on the stick. The vessel, if that's what it was, was as black as the space surrounding it.

"It must have some sort of electromagnetic cloaking tech. I see it, but there's still nothing on my sensors."

The *Gravitas* had turned and was now joined by two other destroyers.

"This is bad," Stryker said.

"More cannon fire coming at us," Brae said pointing to their warning system.

"We're out of options, Thornton."

All at once the shuttle lurched, its structure straining against some unknown force.

"Shuttle craft, shut down your engines," came a command over their radio channel.

"They've got us in a grappling field," Stryker said. "Well, one way or another, it's over," Stryker said turning his head toward Brae while simultaneously pulling the throttles back to idle. He frowned, grief and anger lacing his face. The look of disdain on his face alarmed her.

What? He's blaming me for this? Brae wondered. She instantly became furious.

"Incoming," Stryker said calmly, leaning his head back against his headrest. He lifted his chin as if to face death with dignity. Then the space around them exploded in a wash of plasma energy that would surely end them. But it did not. The shuttle shuddered from the force, but a fraction of a second later the plasma dissipated around them and into the black ship that had grappled them. Brae, Stryker, and the child then began to experience extreme acceleration, sinking deep into the cushions of their seats. The child's increased gravitational weight on Brae's chest momentarily caused her to lose her breath. The shuttle's inertial dampeners were helping but could not overcome the acceleration from the towing ship. Twenty seconds later, the g-forces subsided, and Brae could breathe again. She checked to see if the child was okay. He was unconscious and barely breathing. She was concerned. In less than a minute, the Raylean destroyers were out of sight and out of range, and they were on course for the nearest slipstream gateway.

Chapter

7

Legends from Afar

Rhett was too angry to speak, too distraught to think. All he knew was that the worst of all tragedies had befallen him. Death would have been better. As captain of his ship, he had abandoned his crew, and they had died because of it. Their tragic fate fell directly on his shoulders. Remorse dripped from him like black tar.

"Edge!" he whispered so softly Thornton hadn't heard it. Saying his name seemed to solidify the horror of a tragedy that he should have stopped. Why had he allowed this arrogant astrotech to influence his better judgement? He knew it was the wrong decision...had felt it in his gut. His father had told him that a decade of specialized flight training could not replace a pilot's instinct. *Trust your pilot instinct!* The words shouted at him from the depths of his soul. Why had he listened to her...why had he let her influence him? These emotions were so consuming that he didn't know what to do with them. He didn't trust himself in this condition. He tried to stuff them away so he could think...respond.

Both he and Thornton sat in silence, processing what had just happened.

"Have you ever seen a ship like this?" Thornton asked, breaking the silence.

"Never," Rhett grunted. "For all we know, our fate might be worse than if we'd died back there."

"Thanks," Thornton snapped sarcastically. "I'm concerned about the child. He's barely breathing. We need to get him medical attention."

Rhett slowly turned his head her way, teeth clenched. "Trying to save him is the reason our entire crew is dead!"

Thornton's eyes narrowed. "Listen, Stryker. We both lost people and—"

"I should have never listened to you! Had I been with them I would have—"

"Died, Stryker! You would have died!"

Rhett slammed his fists into the consul in front of him. "You don't know that!" he screamed. He glowered back at her. Her stubborn countenance shifted to one of fear. Thornton cradled the child as if to protect him. Her reaction jolted Rhett out of this irrational emotional state. This was not the behavior of a professional...of a veteran combat pilot. He took a deep breath.

"I'm...sorry," he muttered.

Thornton lifted her chin, eyes of fire replacing the fearful look that had briefly lingered. She said nothing, and it felt like further condemning judgment. Oh, how he disliked this woman.

"Why did they attack us?" Rhett whispered. "Why destroy the *Stalwart*? It doesn't even have any weapons."

Thornton looked over at Rhett then to the child in her arms. "I think it was because of him."

"What?" Rhett said incredulously.

The shuttle suddenly lurched forward. Rhett checked a few instruments.

"They're pulling us in."

A large docking door opened in the aft section of the ship. Rhett felt like they were being swallowed by some dark unknown monster.

Once the shuttle came to rest in the dock and the doors were shut, they waited for the bay to fill with atmosphere. Whoever this was, their technology was impressive. Every aspect of the ship was designed with a sleek yet functional purpose.

A large luminescent panel in front of their craft shifted from amber to pale green.

"Ready to meet our captors?" Rhett asked.

Thornton said nothing in response. She was already unstrapped and moving to vacate her seat. The concern was evident in her face. Rhett tried to give her a hand with the boy, but she refused, cradling him closer to herself. At the shuttle door, Rhett pressed the release latch, and the door parted horizontally to reveal the innards of this alien ship. Puffs of vapor momentarily clouded their vision, then cleared. Standing before them were a man and a woman, faces stern yet somehow expectant. They were clearly leaders of distinction by their stature and attire. Four armed and ready guards were beside them, two to the left and two to the right, bearing weapons Rhett had never seen before. A few seconds passed without a word or an action by anyone in the bay.

"We need help for the child," Thornton said. "Do you have medical personnel and equipment on board?"

The man motioned for them to step forward. "Come."

Rhett and Thornton stepped out of the shuttle and toward the man and the woman. The two looked earnestly at the child, their faces illuminating with wonder and adoration.

"I am Regent Nistra," the man offered with a slight bow.

"I am Regent Vee Taal," the woman said, offering the same greeting. "We are a research craft with limited medical capabilities, but what we have is yours. Please follow us," she urged, then they both turned and exited the dock.

The two regents escorted them to a small but comfortable medtech bay. It was evident that she had not understated their medical capabilities.

"This is our medical assistant. He will do what he can to help the child. We must receive another vessel but will return shortly."

For the next thirty minutes, the medical assistant attempted to ascertain what was wrong with the child but could not diagnose the problem. He finally placed the boy under a warming blanket.

"I'm sorry, without knowing what is ailing the child, I dare not administer any medicine." The medical assistant shook his head. "I'm afraid I've done all I can do. He needs to see a medtech master." The man then turned and exited, leaving Rhett and Thornton alone with the child.

Thornton stroked the boy's cheek then felt his forehead. She bit her lower lip, something Rhett hadn't seen the astrotech ever do.

"Perhaps he was in the suspension pod too long," Rhett offered. "He's right...we need to get him to a proper medtech facility."

"What if he doesn't make it that long?" Thornton asked.

Rhett was completely out of his element. All he knew how to do well was pilot spacecraft. He fumbled for something to offer but nothing came.

"I have an idea. Stay with him," Thornton said then ran out of the medtech bay.

"Wait—" he began, but she was gone. He turned back to the child, walked over, and looked down at him, seeing his face truly for the first time. He studied the child's features closely. There was nothing remarkable about him. He thought about the plight of the boy. What had happened to have led to him being alone in the cold dark region of space next to a dangerous power-surging nebula? Strange. The child was so still. He reached down and touched the lad's arm. It was cool to the touch. Shivers flitted up and down Rhett's spine. He pondered how the life of a child could so alter the course of his own.

After a few minutes Thornton returned carrying her instrument case that had held the probe. She set it on a table next to the bed the child was lying on.

"What are you going to do with that?" he asked as she deactivated the lock mechanism.

When she opened it, Rhett was surprised to see an elegant but archaic weapon where the probe should have been. He was about to comment, but then she opened a hidden compartment to reveal something that rattled him. Rhett's mouth opened wide.

"Where did you get that, Thornton?"

Thornton carefully lifted a Protector out of the case.

"My father."

"I don't understand...your father is a Keeper?"

"No," she replied looking over at Rhett. "Not exactly."

"What does that mean? Did you steal this?" Rhett exclaimed, his thoughts racing to conclusions. When she didn't reply, he could hardly contain himself. "No wonder they were attacking us! You brought this on us!"

"Calm down, Stryker, I didn't steal it and neither did my father."

"Then explain," he said, crossing his arms.

Thornton looked conflicted, hesitant to answer. Rhett just stared at her...waiting. Surely this Protector was the reason for the bizarre actions of the Raylean Guard. The Protectors were not allowed off world, and here in front of him was a master astrotech holding one.

"This Protector has been in my family for centuries," Thornton said, then offered nothing else as if that would satisfy him.

"I don't believe you. Every Protector is guarded and kept in accordance with extremely strict Raylean Guard protocol and has been for a thousand years. The fact that I am looking at one right here...right now...tells me something nefarious is happening."

"Not this one," Thornton rebutted. "This is the fabled lost Protector. My father only just recently told me of its existence. I was as shocked as you are."

Rhett wasn't convinced, not even slightly. "How is this possible? Who's your father that he would have access to such a thing?"

"I can explain later," Thornton said turning her attention back to the child. "Right now, we need to help him, and I think this might be the way."

Rhett glanced over at the little boy. His skin was gray and gaunt. "How?"

She looked up at Rhett. "I honestly don't know." She gently laid the Protector next to the child, but nothing happened.

"Seriously…that's your plan?" Rhett chided.

Thornton glared up at him with a scouring look. "Have you ever worn a Protector?"

Rhett's eyes opened wide. "Me? Are you kidding? I don't even believe in this stuff. I just know that there are a lot of powerful people that would do just about anything to get this Protector back where it belongs."

"You are absolutely no help at all." Thornton declared, shaking her head. She lifted the Protector and held it in her open palms, as if it might explode at any moment. Just then, the device monitoring the child's vital signs began to alarm.

"He's not doing well," Rhett said, trying to ease his sardonic tone.

Thornton's face became taut with angst. She grabbed the Protector with her left hand and placed it just above her right forearm.

"You're not going to…," Rhett began, but before he could finish, Thornton pushed the Protector down onto her forearm. He watched amazed as the solid mass of the Protector seemed to melt around her skin, encapsulating her forearm. He'd seen a Keeper do this once before and was stunned then as well.

Thornton's eyes opened wide, and Rhett was taken aback at what he saw. The very color of her eyes seemed to brighten to a frightening hue. It was impossible to tell if she was experiencing thrill or terror. She fell to one knee, and Rhett reached for her.

"Thornton…you okay?" he asked, steadying her so she wouldn't faceplant.

Her head bowed low as she tried to get on top of whatever it was that had taken her. She grabbed his arm and tried to stand. When she lifted her head, something was different about her. She glanced briefly at Rhett and seemed to look clear through him. Then her gaze fell on the child. Stepping closer, she leaned over to stroke his pale cheek. She didn't smile, but there was a knowing written on her face that caused Rhett to stare in wonder. She lifted her right hand over the child, touching her thumb and forefinger briefly together and then opening them wide. An amber beam of light emanated outward toward the child. Rhett knew that many Rayleans would often visit a Keeper of the Protectors to be scanned for Deitum Prime, but he had never partaken in such an archaic ritual. Thornton manipulated the beam to scan the child's entire body. When complete, the percentage of Deitum Prime was flashing brightly in the suspended display. Thornton looked up at Rhett with a glow in her face that hinted at the knowledge of a deep mystery. She turned her hand so that Rhett could see it...zero percent.

"What does that mean?" Rhett asked, but before Thornton could answer, the vitals of the child dipped even lower.

Turning the Protector back to the child, Thornton opened her hand wide. The amber beam instantly disappeared as blue arcing streams of energy began travelling along the jeweled ribbons of the Protector. Three seconds later, Thornton's hand erupted in a brilliant shower of radiant energy, bathing the child in its luminescent glow. Thornton seemed saturated by the event, her eyes closing to endure it. For the next thirty seconds, it seemed as though life itself was being poured into the child from the Protector. All at once, the blue beam of energy stopped, and the Protector fell silent. Thornton collapsed and would have hit the floor hard had Rhett not grabbed her at the last moment.

"Hey...are you okay? Wake up!" He picked her up and carried her to another medtech bed next to the child. After gently laying her down, Rhett felt for a pulse.

"Thornton!"

No response. He looked down at the Protector on her arm. He cautiously reached for it and pulled it off her arm. It yielded, and he was once again amazed at the tech that seemed to defy physics.

"Wake up, Thornton...as much as I don't like you, I'm not doing this alone...wake up!" he said tapping her cheek with his hand.

Thornton moaned, opening her eyes. She blinked a few times.

"There you are...what just happened?" Rhett asked.

Thornton tried to sit up, but Rhett had to help her.

"The child...is he all right?"

Rhett glanced over at the instrument displaying the vitals of the young boy. Every vital was now perfect.

"Hmm...yes, whatever you did seems to have worked. His vitals are normal. You okay?" Rhett asked.

Thornton took a deep breath. She reached for her arm and rubbed where the Protector had been.

"Don't worry, it's right here," Rhett said handing the Protector back to her. "What was that all about?"

"Hand me the case," she commanded, carefully swinging her legs over the bed to stand.

Rhett frowned. He retrieved the case and gave it to her. *I think I liked her better when she was unconscious,* he thought.

Thornton opened the case, but before placing the Protector inside, she lifted the small plasma pistol out. She fastened it about her waist, oddly transforming this star-gazing astrotech into something else.

"You actually know how to use that thing?" Rhett asked.

Thornton wasted no time in placing the Protector back in the case and locking it.

"No. I just like how it brings out the color in my eyes." Tucking the case away, she went to the child. "His name is Jeshu."

Rhett looked dubious. "And how do you know that?"

"I—" she began but just then Regents Nistra and Vee Taal returned.

"I'm sorry we don't have the ability to properly treat the child. How is he doing?" Nistra asked.

"He's doing much better," Thornton answered. "Vitals are now normal." The child's cheeks had turned a healthy pink color. She picked him up, leaning his delicate head on her chest and shoulder.

Just then another man entered the medtech bay and was greeted by Nistra and Vee Taal.

"There are no other survivors," the man said. "Every ship in the region was attacked and destroyed. Hundreds of lives were lost."

Rhett looked at Thornton. Her eyes conveyed the same gut-wrenching sorrow that he felt. He shook his head in dismay...somebody would pay dearly for this.

The new arrival looked over the shoulders of Nistra and Vee Taal. "Is he the one?" he asked softly, his face transforming from one of anguish to one of hope.

"Yes...we believe so," Vee Taal said, stepping aside.

The man approached Thornton and the child slowly, then Rhett saw him perform the most remarkable thing...he knelt to one knee and bowed his head. Nistra and Vee Taal followed suit. Rhett stared in confusion. After a moment of unexplainable reverence, the three regents stood.

"We strongly advise that you do not return to Rayl," Nistra said.

"And that you don't attempt to contact anyone there...*anyone*," Vee Taal added.

"There's too much at stake. Prefect Terrok will stop at nothing to kill the boy," the third regent said, turning to gaze at the child once more.

Rhett was frustrated, as if everyone in the room knew something significant except him.

"I don't understand. What is so special about the child?"

Nistra broke his gaze from the boy. He looked at Thornton, then to Rhett. "You truly don't know?" he asked. Rhett slowly shook his head.

"Our ancient oracles foretold of a coming sovereign...one who would rise up and conquer all evil in the galaxy. We each have dedicated our lives to searching the stars for the fulfillment of the legend. We are convinced that the Omega Nebula was the herald of such a mighty sovereign. When our study of the nebula revealed an impending unique and unexplained energy swell, we knew the time was at hand. We've traveled from the edges of the galaxy to witness the advent of such a thing."

"The Event," Rhett heard Thornton whisper.

Nistra turned back, looking earnestly at the child. "One day, this child will rule the galaxy."

Rhett struggled to hide his cynicism. He glanced toward Thornton to see if she was as shocked by their misplaced reverence as he was. Her countenance revealed nothing...as stolid as a stone wall. Perhaps she was too stunned to react. Then Rhett realized that if the adoration these three regents held for what they thought was a future galactic ruler would advantage them, he was willing to use it. One thing they had right—for reasons incomprehensible, the Raylean Guard, his own aerotech force, had tried to kill them and had succeeded in killing Edge and the rest of the research team. He stymied any irreverent response and instead humbled himself.

"Honorable regents, we are indebted to you for saving us from the attack of those destroyers. I can only imagine that this puts you at great risk as well."

Vee Tal searched Rhett's eyes. "Perhaps, but we have resources and have plotted a safe way home. It's you that needs to be concerned and wary. We can repair your shuttle and even equip it with a slipstream jump drive so that you can navigate through the gateways."

"You must do whatever it takes to protect the child," Vee Taal added.

Rhett's eyes widened. *Protect the child? For how long?* he thought. The weighty task was only now beginning to settle on his mind. At the very least he had to find a caregiver...someone who could truly tend to and raise the abandoned child.

"We will also refuel your shuttle and provide food and monetary assistance."

"That is most gracious of you."

Rhett noticed that Thornton was silent throughout the remainder of the conversation with the regents. When the regents left to give them an opportunity to discuss their plans, Rhett turned to Thornton.

"You didn't say much through all of that," he said crossing his arms.

Thornton continued to hold the child tightly to her chest.

"And you didn't seem surprised by his absurd statement about the child ruling the galaxy one day," he added.

"I know something they don't," she replied, looking at the peaceful face of the little boy.

"What's that?"

Thornton turned and looked at Rhett. "He already does."

Rhett would have laughed if the conclusion he'd come to wasn't so serious.

"You have lost your mind...and so have they!" he said pointing toward the doorway.

Rhett began walking to one end of the medtech bay and back, talking more to himself than Thornton. He'd given up on anything reasonable coming from her. "I'm surrounded by insanity. How did this happen to me? None of this makes sense," he muttered, running his hand through his hair. "I have to get back to my squadron."

Thornton laid the sleeping child down and looked over at Rhett.

"Didn't you hear those regents? It's not safe!" she said sternly but with a hushed voice.

He came to the opposite side of the bed the child was lying on and looked straight into Thornton's eyes. He glanced toward the door and lowered his voice too.

"And we know nothing about these three...whoever they are. What I do know is that Major Kamp and Colonel Whitmore would never authorize an unwarranted attack on their own craft, let alone unarmed civilian vessels."

Rhett's eyes narrowed. "My crew is dead—I have to get to the bottom of this, and it starts with contacting my squadron operations officer, Major Kamp."

Thornton glared back at Rhett, that fiery look in her eyes once again.

"It all makes perfect sense if you'd quit being so bullheaded and listen for once."

Rhett stood straight and crossed his arms, anger threatening to rule him again.

"Fine...try me." He looked down at Thornton through slitted eyes.

Thornton fumbled for a start to her explanation, then huffed. "You already think I'm mad. Just consider this...what if the regents are right? You'll be putting the child at risk just by revealing that you're alive. You have an obligation—"

"My obligation is to fulfill my duty as an officer in the Raylean Aerotech Force."

Thornton frowned. "The same force that just tried to kill us all? Maybe it's time you rethink your obligations!"

"I know exactly where my obligations lie," he rebutted with rising volume. "And it's not with some—," just then, the boy beneath them stirred. Rhett paused, looking down at the child. For one fraction of a moment, something in his soul stirred. He looked back up at Thornton, her face full of anger and concern. He had heard about the bond between a mother and her child. Though not his mother, was Thornton somehow feeling a bond to this mysterious child already? In their intense exchange, he realized his face was just inches from hers. He took a breath, softened, and backed away. Thornton seemed confused by his response.

"I'll take you and the child someplace safe," he said in quiet voice. "Then I'm going back to Rayl to investigate."

He walked toward the door then turned back to Thornton.

"You good with that?"

Thornton thought for a moment then shrugged. It was the best he would get from her, so he took it and exited the medtech bay.

Brae watched Stryker exit the room then immediately turned her attention back to the child.

She swallowed hard, trying to get her mind around what was happening. As frustrated as she was with Stryker, his ego, and his scheme to abandon her, she couldn't really blame him—even she was struggling with the reality of what this all meant and who the child was. It had taken her two years to accept the bizarre story of her family's past, and now this! It frightened her...no, terrified her. Her encounter with the Protector was in and of itself nearly too much to absorb, but what had been revealed to her by Sovereign Ell Yon regarding the child was beyond profound and something she could only ponder privately in her heart. No one, especially Stryker, would understand...not now...perhaps not ever. One thing was certain—from this moment forward, the course of her life would change forever.

She reached down to stroke the soft cheek of the child. "Jeshu," she whispered.

How could she possibly serve as the watchguard of one so vital to the future of the entire galaxy? She imagined the weight of such a future falling on the vulnerable and innocent child. Compassion and a spirit of protection welled up within her.

"I'm not strong, little one, but I will be for you. I'm not fearless, little one, but I will be for you." Brae gently smiled, tears brimming her eyes.

The child stirred, opening his eyes to look up into hers. He reached up and touched her face, a quiet smile lighting on his lips and in his eyes. She reached for his tiny hand and pushed it against her cheek, then kissed his fingers.

"We'll do this together."

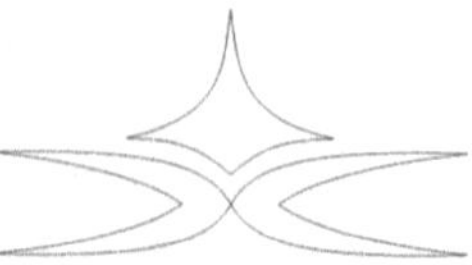

CHAPTER

8

A Conspiracy of Betrayal

After three days with the regents, it was time to part ways. As promised, the regents had completely repaired their shuttle and modified it with a jump drive engine that would allow them to utilize the slipstream conduits. They also outfitted them with food, supplies, and a significant number of Morian credits, the most widely accepted currency in this region of the galaxy. Additionally, they reconfigured the shuttle transponder to transmit a unique identifier that would not associate them with the destroyed research vessel, the *Stalwart*. Once they had launched, the regent vessel disappeared through a conduit, never to be seen again.

"Our best play is to take you and the child to Jypton," Rhett said as he laid in a course for the next slipstream gateway that would take them there. "Even though they too are ruled by the Morian Empire, there's enough isolation from Rayl to afford anonymity for you, and it's close enough for me to travel back to Rayl without much difficulty."

Thornton just nodded. Sitting next to him in the co-pilot seat, she began tuning in the shuttle sensors. Her quiet submission to his plan made him uncomfortable.

"The regents gave us enough Morian credits to set you up and purchase all necessities for well over a year...maybe two."

Thornton just nodded again. Rhett turned away, frustrated that he couldn't dismiss the rising feeling of guilt. Was he abandoning them? Thornton's silence just made it worse, and he knew that she knew it.

He accelerated and entered the gateway. The space around them melted into streaks of kaleidoscopic light. Thirty seconds later, the space around them reformed into the splendor of a hundred billion stars of the Aurora Galaxy. The beautiful planet of Jypton filled a large portion of their front view. Once they entered its atmosphere, there was no turning back. He looked over at Thornton.

"Look, we need answers, and I'm going to find them for us. I'm not abandoning you...I promise."

Thornton's countenance was indeterminate. She looked over at him, eyes holding the confidence he'd come to expect from her, but there was something else too.

"We'll be fine. You need not concern yourself with us."

Rhett turned away, clenching his teeth. Even when he was trying to be nice, she had the ability to frustrate and humiliate him. He focused on his atmospheric entry and on coordinating with the appropriate Jyptonian authorities for gaining flight path approval. He selected a spaceport in a moderately sized city that would afford the necessary supplies and not bring attention to them. It took the remainder of the day, but Rhett had successfully arranged appropriate dwelling quarters near a food market and purchased a small hovercraft in case Thornton needed to travel. That evening Rhett and Thornton managed to get through their last few hours together with only a few minor skirmishes. The three of them ate well, and both Rhett and Thornton were astonished at how much the child devoured.

The next morning, Rhett prepared to leave. At the doorway, Thornton held the child in her arms. The boy already looked very healthy and unusually alert. Thornton wore a look of confidence, but Rhett couldn't help but think she was feeling afraid and abandoned.

"Thornton, I'll be back...soon...I promise," he said trying to encourage her.

Silence.

"I've just got to figure this out so we know what our next move is," he followed.

Thornton stared at him for a moment.

"And if something happens to you? If they catch you like the regents said might happen? Then what happens to us?"

Rhett hadn't seriously considered that outcome.

"Nothing's going to happen to me...I'll be back."

Thornton slowly shook her head in disgust. The little boy she was holding reached out his right hand to Rhett. Rhett reached and took his hand.

"Hey little guy...don't worry, I'll be back."

"It won't matter what you discover about the Raylean Guard, Rhett Stryker. What matters is that you discover whose hand it is that you're holding right now and what your responsibility is to him."

Rhett froze as he felt the soft pudgy fingers of the child. What if there was even a shred of truth in the words of the regents?

"Rhett Stryker," the little boy said with imperfect but clear pronunciation. Both Rhett and Thornton looked at the child in amazement. The child pulled back his hand, instead becoming preoccupied with the light fixture hanging above them. Thornton looked up at Rhett, then turned and closed the door. Rhett held up his hand to stop it then closed his fingers to a fist and grimaced. He considered abandoning his personal mission altogether, but then realized that he would have no peace until he knew what had happened. He had to know for Edge's sake...for the entire crew. He stood staring at the blank door then spun on his heels and made his way back to the spaceport and the shuttle waiting there. Before long, he'd passed through multiple slipstream conduits and entered the Kayn System. Now he was within standard communication range. He tapped in the frequency of his ops squadron scheduling receiver. His thumb hovered over the transmit button as a dozen conversations and a hundred thoughts raced through his mind. *What if—*

He changed the frequency to a generic planet-to-off-world com station.

"Rayl global com station Baker Baker Zulu, this is Raylean transport shuttle *Aviel*. I need a patch through to a private communicator."

"This is global com station Baker Baker Zulu. Relay your communicator identifier code."

Rhett tapped in the communicator code and in just a few seconds, Major Kamp came into view on the screen. The man's face instantly lit up in a visage of shock. Rhett saw his hand move quickly and then the com screen went blank. A few seconds later, a text only message appeared.

"No communication allowed...disappear!"

Rhett's brow furrowed. He responded.

"Must talk. Where to meet?"

Long seconds ticked by. Finally, an encrypted response came.

"Two days, Bethsdal...corner of Summerset and Ankosh...1800."

"Two days!" Rhett said out loud.

Major Kamp rarely showed emotion, so that three-second shot of his reaction to the com call was enough to make Rhett more than uneasy. It sobered him greatly.

Over the next two days while Rhett waited for the meeting with Kamp, he did everything he could to investigate the events that had happened at the Nebula. Much to his surprise, there wasn't a shred of information being broadcast about the attacks on the spacecraft there...nothing! He considered reaching out to a couple of his fellow pilots in the squadron but decided that Major Kamp was still his best bet.

Better minimize my exposure to just one contact, he thought.

Well ahead of the arranged meeting time, Rhett navigated to the city of Bethsdal. He found the corner of Summerset and Ankosh and waited. Exactly at 1800, a sleek ground speeder pulled up to the corner. The wing-style door opened, and Major Kamp motioned for Rhett to get in. Kamp held a finger to his lips as he accelerated the craft to cruising speed. Rhett reluctantly obliged. A few minutes later, Kamp pulled the speeder off the road and into a parking position near a large three-acre flower garden near the center of the city. He exited the craft and Rhett followed him.

When they had walked a fair distance into the garden and there was no one near them, Rhett stopped.

"Enough, Major. What in the galaxy is going on?" Rhett demanded.

Major Kamp turned about to look at him. He shook his head. "I thought you were dead. I was told you all died in a mishap...some sort of nebula plasma discharge."

"And you believed them?" Rhett asked.

"At first, yes, but when I tried to orchestrate a recovery mission, I was shut down immediately." Kamp looked over at Rhett, eyes narrow. "The more I investigated the more walls I ran into until—"

"Until what?" Rhett prompted.

"I received a private communique from Prefect Terrok's exec threatening me and my family if I continued to investigate. Then the guy told me that if you show up, I was to report it directly to him. It wasn't too hard to deduce that you weren't dead but that they wanted you dead."

Rhett eyed Kamp closely. He had never known Kamp to exhibit fear of any kind, not even in battle. But there was something close to it in his eyes right now.

"What happened up there, Stryker? This was supposed to be a research mission...what did you do?"

Rhett was stunned by the question.

"Do? I didn't *do* anything! We were rendering aid to a small merchant ship when our own Raylean Guard ships attacked us. It was the *Gravitas,* Major! I radioed over and over that we were unarmed and a Raylean research vessel, but they would not relent." Rhett paused, teeth clenched remembering seeing Edge in his final moments. "They killed Edge and the entire research team for no reason!"

Major Kamp turned away, rubbing his forehead. He cursed. "How did you escape?" he asked without turning back.

"I was in the shuttle when it happened. We narrowly escaped, but they were after us."

Kamp snapped back around. "We?"

Rhett hesitated, wishing he hadn't divulged that Thornton was still alive. If Prefect Terrok was involved, this was a conspiracy that went to the highest levels... perhaps even the Morian Empire itself.

Kamp shook his head, holding up his hand. "Never mind...I don't want to know." He looked Rhett square in the eyes. "I don't think they got what they were after, whatever that is, but if they think you might still be alive, you'd better disappear, Stryker, and never come back. I have a buddy serving over in Terrok's Royal Guard," Kamp's expression turned dour. "He's disappeared, and his family too."

Rhett raised a fist to his lips, thinking...trying to make sense of it.

"Why, Major...why would they do this to their own people?"

Major Kamp looked back at Rhett. "You tell me... you were there."

The image of the little boy holding out his hand to Rhett flashed across his mind.

"I need to go."

Major Kamp seemed to understand. He put a hand on Rhett's shoulder. "Watch your back, Stryker."

Rhett nodded. "You too, Major."

On his journey back to the shuttle, Rhett had a lot to process. Thornton's research mission had catapulted him onto a completely different and unwanted trajectory. As unpleasant as the facts were, at least he now had something upon which to act.

Whether or not the child they had rescued was as prophetically grand as certain people thought, his existence had initiated peculiar and fatal actions by the highest levels of the Raylean government. Regardless of what Rhett believed about the boy, those dire actions would force his next move. The feeling of betrayal by the Prefect and by his own Raylean Guard was difficult for Rhett to accept. The more he dwelt on it, the angrier he became. Torn between his patriotic heart to serve in the Raylean Guard and the truth of this horrific attack on innocent people, he was forced to sever his allegiance in order to move forward. Thornton had accused him of being stubborn. He had to admit she was right, but now he would be stubborn about their survival. He tried to imagine what his life would be like for the next few months...perhaps years. He shook his head.

"Why did it have to be Thornton?" he muttered.

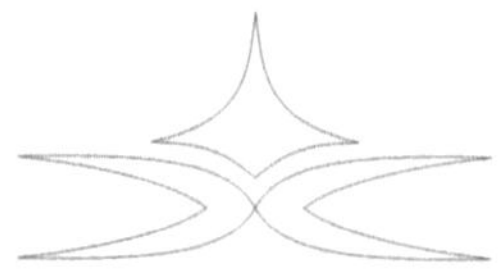

CHAPTER

9

Wisdom and Stature

While still on Rayl, Rhett didn't dare return to his home in Jalem, but he needed the credits and supplies he had stashed there. He thought about contacting his two brothers and his parents, knowing they would anguish over his disappearance, but it was too risky to reach out to them. The solution he landed on was to hire a cleaning service to enter his dwelling, but on the way there, he intercepted one of the young gals and paid her a substantial amount to acquire and hide the items he was looking for. One such item was a key to a lock box located outside of the city that contained a stash of handheld weapons not registered with the Morian Empire. Many of his fellow pilots had done the same thing, and he was sure there were many more than he knew of.

And then there was Quilla. His relationship with her had grown each week, and he really liked her. He only considered contacting her for a moment, quickly realizing that if discovered, she would be put in harm's way. That would have to wait...would she wait?

It took another five days to complete his clandestine activities, but on the eighth day after leaving Thornton and the child, he was on his way back to Jypton with a fully equipped shuttle and a plan to remain under the Raylean Prefect's radar for as long as it took. His greatest concern now was how he was going to coexist with the one woman in the galaxy that seemed to despise him. And truth be told, he could hardly tolerate her in return. He took a deep breath, fully embracing the fact that in order to be safe, his life was likely about to get very boring and frustrating.

It had been over a week since Stryker had left Brae and the child. Images of Shayde and her research team haunted her as she relived those frightful moments over and over. When the tears of mourning came, the child would lean his sweet head on her shoulder and wrap an arm around her neck. The empathy he demonstrated at such a tender age was uncanny. She thought often of her father and considered multiple ways she might try to contact him, but logic and reason always won out. She was sick thinking that he might come to believe she was dead. Twice, while the child slept, she opened her case and gazed at the Protector. As she slid her fingers across the jeweled surface, the stories her father had told her filled her mind, and she imagined this powerful vessel of Ell Yon being used in such profound ways to save and deliver her people. How would the Sovereign use it now? It was odd, being exiled to the very planet that had started their journey as a people so long ago. Understanding her father's distinctly significant role, which began on Jypton many centuries earlier, provided a personal connection here that surprised her.

Throughout the week she had tried to find out some information about the catastrophic events at the nebula from the broadcasting agencies on Jypton, but there was absolutely nothing to discover. This unnerved her even more, for Stryker's sake. Knowing who the child was and knowing the propensity for evil that Prefect Terrok had, there would be a price on their heads. As she thought about Stryker, she found herself becoming angry with him all over again. He was such a stubborn pilot, putting the child at risk for the sake of his own curiosity. Each day he didn't return, she became more anxious, but she also become more amazed by the boy. His appetite was beyond normal, and his development was simply extraordinary.

On the evening of the eighth day, there was a knock at the door. Brae's heart began to race. She went to the door and viewed the entry monitor. She pressed the door release lever and there stood Stryker, tall and grumpy.

"Thank Ell Yon it's you!" she said a little too cheerfully. She almost felt like hugging him but knew that it was simply out of relief than for any other reason.

"Of course it's me...I told you I'd come back."

Brae smirked...*nope...definitely no hug.*

"Look, Thornton," Stryker began, taking a deep breath, "before we start at each other again, I just want to say—"

"Rhett Stryker!" called a small voice from around the corner. A second later a small boy came walking into view.

"What the?" Stryker exclaimed. He looked at Thornton with eyes wide.

The little boy came to Stryker with arms upstretched. Stryker picked him up and held him, gawking in wonder at the boy. He shook his head.

"What….what is happening, Thornton?"

Brae slowly shook her head. "I don't know. Every morning I wake up it's like he's a week older than the day before. His development is off the charts. He started walking three days ago and now—"

"I'm hungry," the little boy said clearly.

Stryker's eyes widened further. "You know this isn't normal, right?"

"Tell me about it," Brae said. "Where did Rhett go?" Brae asked, stroking the child's back.

The boy turned to look Stryker straight in the eye.

"He took the shuttle to Rayl. I'm hungry."

Stryker's mouth dropped open. He set the boy back on the ground, looking at Brae.

"Seriously…what's happening here?"

Brae grabbed Stryker's arm, pulling him into their dwelling as she closed the door behind them.

"I can hardly keep enough food here for him," Brae said. "His metabolism is four times normal, I'm sure of it, but so is his cognitive development. He's learning as fast as I can teach him. This child, Stryker, is remarkable to say the least."

Stryker just continued to gawk at the child, speechless.

"What do we do with him?"

Brae bit her lip and folded her arms across her stomach. "Feed him, protect him, and teach him. That's all we can do."

Stryker ran his hand through his hair. "Wow!"

Both Brae and Stryker just stared at the boy as he masterfully completed a puzzle on Brae's glass tablet designed for children twice his age. He looked up at them and smiled then began another.

"I never thought I'd say this, but I'm glad you're back. It's a bit unnerving being responsible for Jeshu alone."

"So, you missed me," Stryker quipped.

"Ha! Like I miss having a canker sore."

"Yeah, thought so," Stryker returned.

"I missed you," Jeshu said, glancing up to look their way.

"I missed you too...Jeshu," Stryker replied awkwardly. They watched as Jeshu became preoccupied with the glass tablet once more. Stryker leaned over to talk softly to Brae. "This is really creeping me out...going to take some time to process." He thought for a moment. "Do you get the feeling that before long he'll be teaching us?"

Brae nodded. "All the time," she whispered back. Brae realized she was too close to Stryker for her comfort zone. She backed away. "By the way, the dwelling across the hall is open. We should rent that for you."

Stryker nodded, looking relieved. "We can probably afford that for a few months, but I'll need to figure out a way to earn credits if this turns into a long ordeal."

Brae felt her tension ease hearing him say that.

"What...you're not going to bug out on us again?"

Stryker looked at her, shaking his head. "You know, you'd be so much easier to get along with if you weren't—"

"Weren't what?" Brae prompted.

"If you weren't...you!"

Brae shook her head, turned, and squared off with him.

"I don't know what it is about you, but every time I'm with you more than five minutes I want to scream."

"Well, I used to be calm and collected until I met you," Stryker replied.

Brae took a deep breath, closed her eyes, and shook out her hands.

"Look, neither of us wanted this, and we certainly don't like each other, but that doesn't matter because it is what it is. Can we at least try to coexist without such back and forth caustic verbiage all the time?"

Stryker looked like he was trying to control his emotions too. He nodded.

"Agreed."

"Promise?" Brae asked.

"Yes, do you?" Stryker asked, a bit of a smirk on his face.

Brae nodded and stuck out her hand.

"I see...we're shaking on this?" Stryker asked.

Everything about this guy irritated her, even trying to agree not to be irritated. She just left her hand in the space between them without saying anything. Finally, he reached out and took her hand. She gave it one solid shake then let loose, at which time Jeshu began to clap, as if learning something new for the first time.

Stryker squinted. "Is that a coincidence?"

"Who knows," Brae said, walking over to the boy and scooping him up. "Let's get you some food while Rhett moves in next door."

"Hmm, that's the first time you've called me by my first name."

"For his sake," Brae quickly added. "It'd be weird having him call you, 'Stryker.' Besides, I'll bet you don't even remember my first name."

Brae flashed a quick glance his way. He squinched up his face, looking like he was about to voice a comeback but instead closed his mouth, spun about, and exited the dwelling.

In an attempt to be true to their agreement, Brae did her best to abide with Rhett. She could tell that he was also making an effort to do the same. As a result, they were successful for short periods of time without much bickering. Over the next few months, Jeshu continued to astound both of them. They were thoroughly tasked with teaching and providing new material for him to learn. The questions the lad asked were profound, causing them to have to study and prepare themselves for a child with an insatiable desire for knowledge.

For Brae, watching Jeshu grow, develop, and learn was like watching a miracle take place in slow motion. At times, she trembled when watching him, knowing deep down she was a witness to the fulfillment of eons of ancient oracles. She ached to be able to share this with her father, for Daeson Starlore had sacrificed greatly for this day. If only Rhett could share in her enthusiasm, but instead, as the days wore on, the man seemed to withdraw further from her and the child. Every attempt she made to draw him in, including what she would consider grand efforts of kindness, seemed only to distance him further. To his credit, although he was becoming more and more emotionally detached, he never faltered in fulfilling his role as provider and mentor for Jeshu. After a time, Brae came to accept this. *After all*, she thought, *it's certainly not as if we're bonded.*

Rhett discovered he was exactly what he'd thought he was when it came to raising a child…lousy. Granted, this was no ordinary child, but then again, he was witnessing all stages of childhood development in a vastly accelerated fashion. Regardless of Jeshu's apparent age, Rhett found it extremely challenging to be the man he thought he should be for the boy. This bizarre circumstance brought an endless stream of doubts and questions that apparently had no answers. Perhaps the most unnerving aspect of this entire ordeal was the fact that whenever Rhett taught Jeshu something, it was only a matter of time before the boy not only mastered it but exceeded his own ability in the task. It left Rhett feeling entirely inadequate. This, coupled with the fact that Brae was an impossible woman to abide with, began to gnaw at his soul. Anticipating the end of it was difficult to quell, for his sense of obligation to both Brae and Jeshu would not release him.

It quickly became evident that Jeshu's rapid growth would be difficult to explain to those near them. Isolating themselves only worked for a short time, and then they were forced to move residences every so often so as not to draw attention. There was also a sense that Jeshu needed some interaction with other children his apparent age which added to their challenges.

Months later when Jeshu looked to be about nine years old, Rhett realized that whatever strange future was in store for the boy, he would need to know how to defend himself.

"Jeshu, I see you've been playing with other boys from time to time."

"Yes, we have fun together," Jeshu said, glancing over his shoulder to smile at Brae who was working on her glass tablet. She nodded, smiling back at him.

"Have you ever had to fight one of them?" Rhett asked.

Jeshu looked confused. "Why would I ever do that?"

"Well, sometimes others want to fight you even if you don't," Rhett replied. "Sometimes there are bullies, and we have to stand up for ourselves...or for others."

Jeshu's confusion disappeared in an instant. "Yes, I've seen that. But what they want isn't worth fighting over."

Rhett put a hand on Jeshu's shoulder. "One day, it will be."

Jeshu became solemn and silent as he considered Rhett's words. "Yes, it will be." He looked up into Rhett's eyes. "But not for the reasons you think, and my fight will never be with our people, no matter what they do. Will you teach me how to fight?"

As often happened, Rhett was taken aback at the boy's response. He noticed that Brae was now completely tuned into what was happening.

"Yes, I'll teach you how to fight," Rhett said. "As an aerotech pilot I was trained in hand-to-hand combat and with small weapons fire. I'll teach you everything I know."

The subtlest of smiles lit upon Jeshu's face as he considered Rhett's offer. He turned to look at Brae. "And will you teach me all you know about fighting, Brae?"

Rhett laughed. "Thorn...Brae is an astrotech master, Jeshu, not a fighter."

Brae put down her glass tablet and came to them.

"Try me, Stryker," Brae said placing her hands on her hips.

Rhett stood and squared off with her. "Come on, Thornton...don't be ridiculous."

"Step back, Jeshu," Brae said, taking on a fight stance.

Rhett huffed. "Fine."

In one quick move he grabbed her arm, using it as a lever to spin her about to secure a behind-the-back armlock. Before he could apply crippling vertical pressure to her arm, she reached behind her back with her free arm and grabbed her wrist to prevent Rhett moving it upward. She then stomped on his foot with her heel. He recoiled just enough so she could push her locked arm downward, then smash the elbow of her free arm into his face. When he doubled over from the blow, she executed one quick twist to reverse the lock on him while checking his free arm so he couldn't recover. A second later she released him. He stood straight, rubbing his bruised cheek, and his pride. Brae looked pleased with herself.

"So, you know that move...I didn't expect you to actually elbow me in the face."

Brae's smile faded.

"Sorry...doesn't really work without it though."

She went to the kitchen and returned with an icepack. He begrudgingly took it and sat down.

"Let me guess...your mysterious father."

Brae nodded.

"Seems like he's the one I should take lessons from," Jeshu said with a smile.

"Ha, ha," Rhett mocked.

Jeshu put a hand on Rhett's shoulder. "I'm excited to learn all you have to teach."

Rhett looked up at Brae. "I guess you'll have two teachers. I have a feeling you'll be a quick study though.

It's also time to start adding some physical training to your schedule."

Brae came beside Jeshu, offering a peace smile to Rhett then turned her attention to Jeshu. "I agree. Are you ready for that?" she asked.

Jeshu lifted his chin. "I am."

As Rhett had predicted, Jeshu's ability to learn and employ their training was unparalleled. Intermixed with the hand-to-hand training, Rhett and Brae also taught him how to handle class one and class two plasma weapons. But when Brae revealed the full functionality of Daeson's Talon to Jeshu, his eyes lit up. Rhett became an observer only since this was an archaic weapon with which he had no experience. He watched Brae expertly handle the Talon and was impressed. There was more to her than he had ever given her credit for. Unfortunately, it did little to increase his tolerance for her annoying personality.

Often in the evenings, before he left for his own dwelling, Rhett would hear Brae regaling Jeshu with stories of their Raylean history, beginning with the embellished rendition of their escape from the mighty Jyptonians. Occasionally he would stay later than usual just to hear her stories, cleaning a plasma rifle as an excuse to linger. It was one of the few times Rhett didn't mind being in Brae's presence or hearing her voice. Something about her fantastical stories resonated in him. She told them with such passion, and though he convinced himself that much of what she said was fanciful legend, he knew that she believed every word, and he was oddly jealous.

I could never have childish faith like that, he thought.

Rhett would watch Jeshu's face light up with each telling. There were moments when the boy's eyes flickered with a gleam that caused Rhett to shiver.

Without understanding why, Rhett found himself wanting to run away, afraid that one day he might actually realize what the boy was all about.

Brae and Rhett mentored young Jeshu on Jypton for a year and a half, exhausting themselves in the pursuit of providing intellectual as well as physical training. It seemed to Brae that although the boy's development was accelerated, it was not linear. When Jeshu looked to be about twelve years old, she began to have thoughts regarding the possibility of journeying back to Rayl.

"Where is he?" Rhett asked after entering Brae's dwelling.

"On an errand for supplies," Brae answered. Before he could sit down, she approached him. "I think we should consider returning to Rayl."

Rhett paused before speaking. Brae knew it was his way of tempering his responses to her to reduce the chance of the conversation becoming hostile. She waited. Although she still found him irksome, the man was still with her and Jeshu, honoring his word. She could at least respect that.

"The memory of Prefect Terrok is long," Rhett reminded. "I'm not sure it's wise to consider this just yet."

"I don't get it," Brae said. "A year and a half ago, you were the one that risked everything to go back to Rayl. Now you get cold feet?"

"That was before I learned that the tyrant was executing anybody, and their families, who asked questions about our Omega Event."

Brae fell silent as she thought about her father. Had Terrok targeted him simply because the Event mission was hers? Every day that passed without knowing his fate weighed heavily on her heart.

"Then how long do we wait, Stryker?" she shot back. "When is enough enough?"

"I don't know, Thornton. I just don't think—"

"It's okay," came a young but calm voice from the entrance. Brae and Rhett instantly stopped to see Jeshu enter and set a couple of bags of supplies on the floor. More than once, the lad had interrupted an escalating conversation between the two of them in order to restore peace.

"It's time, and you need not worry on my behalf," Jeshu said with a quick smile. "We can go."

Brae came to him and put her hands on his shoulders.

"Are you sure?" she asked. He lifted a hand to her arm.

"Yes, it's time to reconnect with our people...for me to learn our ways and to see the Sovereign Sanctums," Jeshu said to reassure her. He glanced toward Rhett. "If we stay away from Jalem, it'll be safe."

Rhett came to stand beside Brae.

"Very well, I'll begin preparing."

Ten days later, Brae, Rhett, and Jeshu were in their shuttle leaving the atmosphere of Jypton. Jeshu was glued to the starboard window as they exited the blue orb of the planet, his excitement evident by a broad grin.

"It's easy to forget he's still just a boy," Brae said smiling as she looked at the lad.

Rhett looked over his shoulder. "Yes, I agree."

"You agree?" Brae said, "and you admit it?"

Rhett shook his head then refocused on his flying.

"Will you teach me to fly, Rhett?" Jeshu asked, temporarily breaking his gaze from the spectacular view to gaze at all of the instrumentation of the cockpit.

"Of course, Jeshu, one day," Rhett replied.

"My father's a good pilot too," Brae said.

Jeshu offered a gentle smile. "I know. He flew many great missions for our people."

Rhett glanced toward Brae, confusion on his face. She ignored him.

"Perhaps he could give you a few flying lessons as well," Brae added.

The smile on Jeshu's face diminished. "Perhaps."

"Jeshu?"

"Yes, Brae?"

"How much do you know…I mean about all things?"

The lad became quiet…thoughtful.

"I must learn all things, but as I do, it's as if I'm being given keys to unlock much more. Before you were, I was, but I must work to know this. Remembering is like cleaning a window. With each stroke of knowledge and wisdom I gain, I see and remember more."

All along, Brae knew from where Jeshu had come, but hearing him speak it as a boy was surreal and difficult to absorb. She glanced over at Rhett. He looked as if he wanted to speak his mind but was struggling with his words.

"Do you know why you're here?" Rhett asked.

The lad became solemn. He turned to look out the starboard window again.

"Yes," came his soft reply.

Brae looked at Rhett and he at her. Neither dared ask more. Brae felt for the case at her feet.

"That thing still makes me nervous," Rhett said, noticing her attention to it.

"I know it's for him one day…I just don't know what I'm supposed to do with it."

"Keep it out of sight, that's what you do with it," Rhett chided.

Brae silently agreed, though she didn't give him the satisfaction of admitting it.

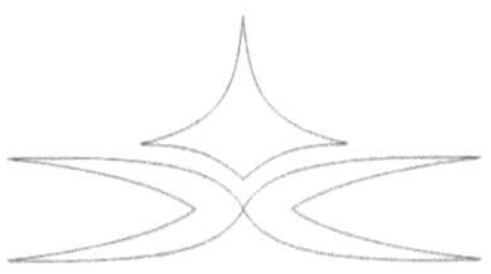

CHAPTER

10

Son of the Sovereign

Morian Empire – A powerful galactic force that has successfully conquered 27 systems and 32 planets. The Morian Empire's home world is Moria, the wealthiest planet in the alpha quadrant of the Aurora Galaxy. The empire is ruled by First Leader Chancellor Krish and his congress of 24 delegates. The Morian Empire began conquering other worlds 112 years ago, subduing the Kayn System and the planet of Rayl 69 years ago.

Immediately upon entering the Kayn System, Brae and Rhett could tell that things were different from when they had left nearly two years ago. Morian security ships showed up everywhere on their scanner.

"That evil Empire is slowly tightening the noose around our necks," Brae muttered.

"Better keep that kind of talk to yourself, Thornton," Rhett rebuked. "If one of the pilots in our squadron were to say something like that, she could pretty much kiss her career goodbye."

"What good is a career if you spend your days pandering to a regime that is sapping your resources and killing your people?" Brae shot back.

"It's not the Morians we need to be concerned about," Jeshu interjected while staring out one of the starboard windows. "Beware of the Keepers and the Builders—they are the real threat to our freedom."

Brae slowly turned to look at Jeshu, stunned by his statement. She glanced toward Rhett, seeing the same confused look on his face. Although Brae had learned from Daeson to be skeptical of the sincerity of some of the Keepers, she had never considered them a threat to freedom. After all, the Builders and the Keepers were long-time established orders to collect omegeon and orchestrate the reproduction of and keep guard over the Protectors. These were the most esteemed positions of authority among all Rayleans...in every city.

"How do you mean, Jeshu?" Brae asked.

Jeshu broke his gaze from the starboard view. "You've worn the Protector, Brae. Don't you know why?"

Brae swallowed hard. That one touch with Ell Yon through the Protector had indeed changed her. Such great love...such fierce justice. Jeshu returned to his stargazing, and Brae was once again bewildered at the unusual and dramatic things that Jeshu said, even now at the apparent age of 12.

As they approached Rayl, a large Morian security cruiser hailed them.

"Shuttle craft, identify yourself," came the terse command.

"Two fighters are coming fast," Brae said, pointing at the scanner on her front glass.

"This is shuttle *Aviel* returning from Jypton," Rhett radioed. "We have three souls on board and are on course for the city of Zareth." He glanced Brae's way, flashing a look that said, "I hope that worked."

Before a response came, the two Morian fighters had bracketed their shuttle, sending the distinct message that they were the authority here.

"This is not looking good," Rhett said glancing from one side of the shuttle to the other to keep an eye on the fighters.

"Shuttle *Aviel*, execute a full stop and prepare to be grappled for docking and inspection. Confirm compliance," the voice demanded.

Brae scowled, eager to voice her disgust, but Rhett held out his hand to shush her.

"Shuttle *Aviel* will comply," Rhett radioed back. He turned to look at Brae as he initiated reverse thrusters to slow the shuttle to a stop.

"You had better chill, or we won't make it to orbit!"

Brae realized he was right. One wrong word with a Morian inspector, and it could mean the end of them. The Morians were reasonable until you hinted at resistance, then they might just kill you. Brae felt for the case holding the Protector.

"What if they find the Protector?" she exclaimed.

Rhett looked concerned. "That's not all we have to worry about. My blaster from the *Stalwart* is registered," he said tapping the weapon on his hip, "but I have a case of unregistered weapons at the bottom of our supplies. If they find those, it's over."

"Great, Stryker...unregistered weapons?"

He glared back at her. "I'm pretty sure the Talon in that case of yours isn't registered either, Thornton."

Brae gulped.

Before long, the *Aviel*, formerly the *Guardian*, had been grappled and brought into a large docking bay on the Morian security cruiser. Brae, Rhett, and Jeshu were forced out of the shuttle and made to stand by for inspection. Brae placed an arm over Jeshu's shoulders and pulled him close to her as the stolid fierce Morian security team boarded the shuttle. Rhett's blaster was the first to be taken and validated. Soon after, they began emptying all of their belongings onto the floor of the docking bay, taking time to inspect every single item. The closer they got to Rhett's weapon case the more anxious they both became. But when they discovered Brae's case holding the Talon and the Protector, the lead inspector zeroed in on it. He held it out before Rhett.

"Open it," he ordered.

"I don't have the code," Rhett said.

The eyes of the man turned fierce.

"I do," Brae said stepping forward while handing Jeshu off to Rhett.

The inspector's eyes narrowed, flashing a final scolding look at Rhett then turning to Brae.

"Do it," he commanded.

"It's a family treasure passed on for generat—"

"Silence! Just open it!" the inspector demanded.

Brae's heart began to pound. She treasured the Talon, but what if they discovered the Protector too? There was no telling what the consequences might be. With trembling fingers, she entered the code to deactivate the lock. When the inspector heard the click, he quickly spun the case around and lifted the cover. The man's eyes opened wide. He turned and placed the case on a nearby table then signaled for another inspector. After a brief conversation, the second inspector quickly disappeared. The inspector lifted the Talon out of the case, examining every detail. Retrieving a device from his belt, he scanned the Talon. A moment later he had his results.

"This weapon isn't registered with the Morian Empire Customs Agency. Where did you get it, and to whom does it belong?"

Brae's earlier anger with the Morian Empire was fully replaced by apprehension and fear. Stories of minor infractions leading to imprisonment and even death were common. The heavy boot of the empire kept all their planets in subjugation. There was no tolerance for anything less than full and willing compliance. Calamity was collapsing in on them from two sides. They had already discovered her Talon, and it was just a matter of minutes before they would be face down with blasters against their heads once they discovered the case full of unregistered weapons that surely exceeded any power level limits imposed by the Morian Empire.

"It belongs to me, sir," Brae replied. "It's a gift from my father who received it from the Jyptonian Aerotech Force for service rendered many years ago."

The inspector didn't look convinced. Just as he was about to rule judgment, a Morian chief security officer arrived.

"What do we have, Agent Bork?"

The man snapped to attention, presenting the Talon to the man. "It's an unregistered weapon, sir."

The chief took it from his subordinate and handled it comfortably.

"Ah...a Talon. And a relic at that," the man said, activating the button to transform it from blaster to short blade. The action stunned the other inspector.

"I haven't seen one of these in a long time," the chief said, handling it as if he knew exactly how to use it. He stopped his inspection and glanced past Brae to Rhett. Brae's anxiety peaked when she saw the man's gaze lower to Jeshu. He walked past her to stand before Rhett, then bent over slightly so he was eye to eye with Jeshu, the extended short blade Talon still in his hand. She could hear the soft buzz of the Talon's stasis field fully activated. Brae could hardly control the trembling that was spreading throughout her body as the chief inspector leaned into Jeshu. He gazed into the boy's eyes for a moment then lifted the Talon up between them. He smiled, but his façade of kindness didn't fool Brae—the man was smart and dangerous.

"Do you know how to use this, my boy?" he asked sweetly.

Jeshu smiled back. "A little, but I hope to get much better."

The chief hesitated then nodded. He deactivated the Talon blade, and Brae took her first breath in minutes. The chief straightened and patted Jeshu's shoulder.

"Let them have it, Bork," the chief said handing it back to the man.

"But it's unregistered, sir. I was going to confiscate—"

"It's a relic, and class one weapons like these aren't illegal...not yet," the chief interrupted. "Besides," the chief continued, walking toward the table where the case was still sitting. "If you were any good at your job, you'd know that they have something much more important to show us."

Brae stole a glance toward the shuttle where the other inspectors were just now getting to Rhett's case, but unfortunately, that wasn't what the chief was referring to. By now two other inspectors had come to see what their chief was doing. Brae noticed that the chief's gaze was locked on her case, still lying on the table. He looked up at Brae, and her heart nearly failed her.

No...not the Protector!

"Which one opened the case?" he asked.

Agent Bork pointed to Brae. The chief looked at her with sharp eyes and a sickening smile. He pointed at her then curled his finger to motion for her to come to him. Brae swallowed hard and slowly walked his way. The chief grabbed her shoulder and spun her around so she was facing the case and also Rhett and Jeshu. The man was now behind her. He placed a firm hand on her shoulder and spoke with his lips just inches from her ear.

"Open the case."

It took everything in her not to shrink away from his sinister voice as shivers flitted up and down her spine. Was the Protector something she should die for? She glanced at Rhett, never having seen such great concern in his eyes. Her gaze dropped to Jeshu. The lad's eyes held no fear. He offered her the slightest nod. The man's grip tightened, then moved closer to her neck.

"Now!" he demanded.

Brae placed her finger over the bio scanning recess and the case's lower compartment opened. Her heart broke in two for she felt as though she had just betrayed every Raylean, her father, Sovereign Ell Yon, and especially Jeshu.

"Ah...see Agent Bork, you must dismiss the obvious to find the real treasures."

The chief used his grip on Brae's shoulder to move her aside. Back at the shuttle, the inspectors had retrieved Rhett's case and were placing it on a table, investigating how to open it. There was nowhere to run...nowhere to hide. All they could do was face their impending doom in silent subjection.

The chief lifted the case's lower compartment to reveal the Protector. The smile that was on his face slowly diminished until his countenance became indeterminate. Without touching the Protector, he turned to look at Brae.

"Why do you have this?" he asked forcefully.

Brae stumbled for words, a bit stunned by his response. He lifted the case and held it before her.

"Where did this come from, and why is it off world?"

Agent Bork and his comrades seemed as stunned by the chief's reaction as Brae.

"My father was a Keeper many years ago. This Protector was bestowed on him for safe keeping. He has since passed that responsibility onto me."

The chief looked very concerned.

"Agent Bork, shut down the inspection," the chief ordered as he closed the lid on the Protector.

Agent Bork whistled to the men at the shuttle just as they were about to open Rhett's case. He made a cutting motion across his neck, and they stopped.

The chief looked at Brae, his face laced with anger and concern.

"Are you trying to start a war?" he asked. "I don't care where you go or what you do with this as long as you get it off my ship immediately. Is that clear?"

Brae nodded, taking the case that the chief was handing to her.

"Give her back the Talon and get their belongings back on that shuttle now!" he ordered to every inspector that had come to watch the ordeal.

"Sir, I don't understand. Why aren't we prosecuting them?"

"Idiot! In exchange for their cooperation as a subjugated planet, Chancellor Krish has agreed to leave the Raylean's superstitious relics untouched." The chief pointed to Brae's case. "This is one of those relics. Do you want to explain to the Captain why his ship violated an edict issued by the First Leader himself?"

Agent Bork's face turned white. "No sir!"

"Strike this inspection from the logs. This ship was never here. Is that clear?" the chief asked.

"Yes, sir!" Agent Bork said, snapping a salute.

The chief took one more look at Brae, frowned, then spun about and exited the bay. Within the next fifteen minutes, all of their belongings had been loaded back on board the shuttle, and Rhett was firing up their engines. Once clear of the bay doors, Brae reached over and grabbed Rhett's arm, taking three or four deep breaths.

"That was horrible!" she exclaimed.

Rhett took a deep breath too. "No kidding...I thought we were dead."

Brae couldn't stop a nervous chuckle and soon Rhett and Jeshu had joined in, laughing and thanking Ell Yon for their narrow escape. A few minutes later, Rhett was piloting the *Aviel* to enter Rayl's atmosphere and navigating to their destination.

Rhett and Brae chose a region of the planet of Rayl on the same continent as the capital city of Jalem, but over 1800 miles away in the city of Zareth, positioned in the arid northwest region. The monetary gifts from the three regents had stretched much further than they expected, and Rhett was able to supplement their needs with an occasional contract flying job. Because of this, they were able to rent a dwelling near the outskirts of the city with extra land and a detached guest home for Rhett. The location allowed them to enhance their training of the lad, and they did so with renewed zeal, for as Jeshu transitioned from boy to young man, his thirst for knowledge and skill continued to increase greatly.

Jeshu's ability to assimilate whatever they threw at him was uncanny. Every day that went by, Brae and Rhett were astonished by him. Brae couldn't help but wonder about the connection between Jeshu and her parents, Daeson and Raviel, but Jeshu didn't seem ready or able to elaborate on it just yet. Brae had considered and even tried at numerous times to share more of her own unique journey with Rhett, but it always seemed to be preempted by his lingering cynicism, or whatever it was that motivated him to keep his distance. Although they shared a common goal for the sake of Jeshu, they simply could not find common ground on which to relate to each other. After having spent so much time together, the cycle they had settled into seemed set in stone. For some unknown reason, Ell Yon had forced the two of them to each play the role of mentor for Jeshu. She had to daily submit to that call and keep her ill-feelings toward Rhett in check, hoping that one day she would be free to separate herself from their entangled lives. Although it took an extreme amount of self-discipline, both Brae and Rhett continued to stay isolated from their former lives and people for Jeshu's sake.

After a few weeks of getting settled, Jeshu began to insist on visiting the city's Sovereign Sanctum.

"We run the risk of the authorities connecting us to the Omega Event," Rhett warned.

"That's a risk we have to take," Brae replied. "He's eager to study the ancient oracles and the history of our people. There are things at the sanctum that he can't learn anywhere else, at least not in the way he wants to learn them. Full access to many of the historical archives can only happen there."

Rhett didn't look convinced. "It's not that simple. To gain entry to a Sovereign Sanctum…any sanctum, he has to be registered in the Raylean database. How do you plan on doing that?"

Brae huffed. "We register him."

Rhett rolled his eyes. "He has to be at least 20 percent Raylean as verified by a genetic scan, we have to prove place and date of birth, and he needs a family name." He wagged his head at Brae. "What's his family name?"

Brae glared back at Rhett. She was too tired to fight with him again. "Why don't we just ask him?"

Right then, Jeshu walked into the room, grabbed a piece of fruit off the table then fell onto a couch in the living room.

"Ask me what?"

Brae raised an eyebrow, motioning for Rhett to proceed. Rhett went to Jeshu and sat down next to him.

"Well, you've been eager to visit a sanctum, but we need to register you with the Raylean database first, and they're going to need some information about you," Rhett explained.

"What kind of information?" Jeshu asked then took a bite of the fruit.

"First, they'll do a genetic scan to see if you're at least 20 percent Raylean."

"That won't be a problem," Jeshu said.

Rhett shrugged and nodded. "Okay. They're going to need proof of place and date of birth, and I'm afraid that *will* be a problem."

Jeshu thought for a moment, then he looked up at Rhett. "How about we just tell them the truth?"

Rhett's eyes widened, looking to Brae for some help.

"What do you mean?" Brae asked.

Jeshu looked her direction.

"That you found me on an abandoned merchant ship in space, and you don't have a record of my place or date of birth."

Brae and Rhett looked at each other then burst into laughter. Rhett shook his head.

"You know...that might work as well as anything. Especially for a sanctum as remote from Jalem as we are. I'm pretty sure they don't think much of Zareth anyway so an orphan being registered here won't even be noticed."

Jeshu offered a polite smile to show his approval.

"Well then, that just leaves the question as to your family name," Rhett continued. Brae came closer, joining them on a chair opposite Jeshu.

"Do you know what your family name is?" she asked.

Jeshu's brow furrowed as if he were trying to remember. "I guess not, but can't we just pick one?"

"Hmm." Rhett stroked his chin. "What are you thinking?"

"How about Starlore?" Jeshu offered, glancing toward Brae.

Brae nearly fell out of her chair. Rhett still had no clue as to her real identity, and she certainly hadn't told Jeshu.

"Starlore...as in the ancient Navi Starlore of the legends...the one that freed our people from Jypton?" Rhett asked.

Jeshu nodded. "I've been thinking a lot about the stories Brae has been telling me. I like that name. I think I'd like to be a part of the Starlore legacy," he said with a confident nod.

Brae was still too shocked to speak. She just stared at the lad, wondering how much he really knew about her. With every revealing secret she learned about Jeshu, she became more and more intimidated by his life...his knowledge...his mission.

"I can't think of a reason why that wouldn't work. It's unique and rare, but surely there are others that carry that name as well," Rhett said. "We'll go tomorrow."

Jeshu's face lit up with an ear-to-ear grin. He jumped off the couch. Rhett and Brae stood with him. Jeshu reached for Rhett, giving him a hug.

"Thank you!" Jeshu then turned, coming to give Brae a hug. As he did so he whispered into her ear, "It's a good name."

Suddenly everything fell into place. For the first time since the revelation of who she was, she clearly saw the lives of Daeson, Raviel, and now hers whose purpose was to prepare Rayl for Jeshu's arrival. It was a humbling thought. Brae's eyes brimmed with tears, and Rhett cocked his head to one side. When Jeshu released his hug, he bounded out of the room gleefully. Brae wiped her eyes, embarrassed any time Rhett saw weakness like this in her. When he just kept staring at her, she finally dealt with him.

"You wouldn't understand so just bug off."

He frowned. "That's your excuse for anything you don't want to explain, and I don't buy it, but whatever," he said throwing his hands in the air. Rhett walked to the door, frustration evident with every step he took.

Brae actually felt a twinge of sympathy for the man.

"Hey, Rhett," she called.

At the door, he stopped to look at her.

"I don't think Jeshu is a part of the Starlore legacy... he *is* the Starlore legacy."

The frustration evident on Rhett's face dissolved away. He thought for a moment, then returned a quick nod and exited the dwelling.

Zareth's Sovereign Sanctum was small, but Jeshu didn't care one iota. When they arrived, Rhett and Brae registered Jeshu just as they had planned, and it worked perfectly, his genetic scan returning a "100 percent Raylean" status. Rhett seemed surprised but relieved because the registering agent didn't seem the least bit concerned with any of the other details, including the family name of "Starlore."

Once Jeshu was fully registered and allowed access to the sanctum, Rhett occupied himself with supply errands to avoid remaining at the sanctum, a place that made him uncomfortable. Brae noticed a glow in Jeshu's eyes once they entered the sanctum. As they sat listening to a Keeper regale a small crowd with a story from their Raylean past, Jeshu hung on every word, often looking to Brae to deny or confirm parts of the oration that didn't seem right. When it was over, Jeshu raised his hand.

"Yes, young man," the Keeper said.

"The Protector that you have, why do you wear it?"

The Keeper lifted his arm, pulling back his sleeve to reveal the gleaming Immortal wonder. He smiled a condescending smile.

"It is the duty and the right of each Keeper to wear the Protector, revealing to all who are willing, their level of Deitum Prime so as to help them better abstain from the dark substance."

Jeshu seemed lost in thought. "May I see it?" he finally asked.

"Certainly," the Keeper offered. "Anyone with Raylean blood is welcome to come and see."

Jeshu and several others went forward to get a glimpse of the Protector. Brae stayed close behind, wary of what might happen. The Keeper pulled his sleeve up further and bent down so the young ones could see better.

"Does it hurt to wear?" one of the children asked.

"No, not if you're pure from Deitum Prime. Only one who is worthy can bear it," the Keeper gloated.

Some of the children reached out to run their fingers along the silver and jeweled lines of the Protector.

"In stories of old, the Protector did much more," Jeshu said, reaching for the Protector. "Why is it silent today?"

The Keeper eyed Jeshu closely. Just as the lad's fingers came close, a single arc of blue energy leapt from one of the jewel ribbons to touch his finger. Those around gasped, but the Keeper had completely missed it.

"You are young and naïve to ask such a question, boy," the Keeper said. "Only those who wear the Protector understand such things. Sovereign Ell Yon speaks only to those who are worthy enough to wear a Protector."

Jeshu pulled back his hand. "What does the Sovereign speak to you?" Jeshu asked, tilting his head.

Brae could see the muscles in the man's jaw tighten.

"Who would like to have the Protector scan them for Deitum Prime? It's the privilege of every Raylean to allow the Protector to do so."

One little girl stepped forward. The Keeper looked relieved, focusing his attention on her. He placed his thumb and forefinger together, then separated them to reveal a beautiful amber beam of light. With a steady pass from head to toe, the Keeper used the Protector to scan the girl. When he was done, he showed the girl and her father the number, being careful not to let others see.

Jeshu stepped forward, but Brae reached for him, pulling him back. "Not yet, Jeshu," she whispered. The Keeper looked disappointed, clearly hoping to reveal the reason for the boy's obstinate behavior. Jeshu looked up at Brae, a fiery gleam in his eye. It startled her...actually it frightened her. On their way back to their home, Jeshu was unusually quiet. The Sovereign Sanctum of Zareth had affected the lad in a powerful way—it changed him. Brae knew that this would be the first of many visits to this and other Sovereign Sanctums.

Eight months later when Jeshu was the apparent age of 16, Rhett came to Brae one evening. They sat on the porch looking out over the country, a faint outline of distant mountains on the misty horizon. Jeshu was in his room studying the last shreds of the ancient oracle writings. Brae could tell something weighty was on Rhett's mind. Usually, their heavy conversations didn't end well. She gave herself a peptalk about watching her tongue and being slow to speak, reminding herself that they usually could find some sort of compromise if their emotions didn't derail them too much. She waited.

Rhett looked over at her.

"I don't have anything left to teach him," he said bluntly. "Truth is, I haven't had anything to really teach him for the past two months."

Brae wondered if this was Rhett getting ready to exit. The thought both pleased and discouraged her. They had managed to settle into a routine that seemed to work, but the underlying tension between them was wearying.

"There's one more thing he needs." Brae took a sip of her tea. She hadn't offered any to Rhett since he despised the taste.

Rhett seemed disappointed. "What's that?"

"He needs to learn how to be a pilot," she said turning his way to get his reaction.

Rhett's eyes lifted. He looked over at her.

"Why don't you teach him? Supposedly you know what you're doing," he said without as much sting as she might expect.

Brae nodded. "Yep...I could do it." She heard Rhett snort. "But you can do it better."

At that, Rhett froze. He pursed his lips together, his eyes narrowing to slits.

"I get it...you're trying to keep me from punching out."

Brae allowed a brief smile. "Yep."

Rhett took a deep breath, then sighed. "Well, for some strange reason it worked. Fine, I'll teach him. All we have is the shuttle, but it's a good one and should give us enough maneuverability to train him on the basics and even a few fighter maneuvers."

"Do you mind if I ride along?" Brae asked politely, not wanting to jeopardize what she'd gained with Rhett on Jeshu's behalf.

Rhett eyed her closely. He held up a finger. "On one condition...you don't say a word."

Brae knew that would be almost impossible. She made a motion as if pretending to zip her lips shut. Rhett just shook his head.

"Yeah...like I believe that," he said.

The next day, pilot training for Jeshu began, and he took to it like an orb fish to the sea. Within minutes, Rhett knew the lad had the hands for it. Rhett was an experienced instructor, knowing just when and what to throw at a new student pilot, but what Jeshu exhibited in piloting aptitude was simply unprecedented. As with all of his other training, it was a matter of just a few months before Jeshu had perfectly mastered and exceeded the capabilities of the shuttle. There were moments when he seemed to tap into skills and training that Rhett knew nothing of. During those times, Rhett just watched as he had learned to do this past year, learning from the young man in quiet amazement.

To his surprise, Brae said very little during the instructional time. But once his pilot training with Jeshu was nearly complete and she got what she wanted, any vestiges of kindness or compromise from her disappeared. Rhett continued to abide with her as best he could for Jeshu's sake, but now that he was coming into his own, Rhett couldn't help but seriously consider parting ways.

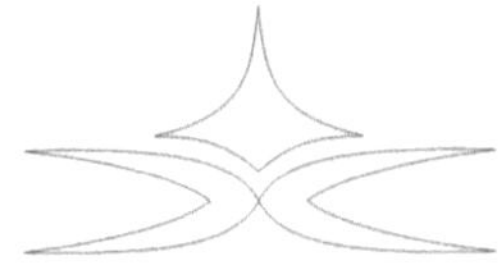

CHAPTER

11

The Beginning of an End

Raylean Guard — A remnant military force of the original Raylean aerotech and miltech orders allowed and monitored by the Morian Empire for the purpose of keeping the Raylean people in order. The Protector Keepers and Builders are granted authority over the Raylean Guard by Prefect Terrok.

Royal Guard — A small select force condoned by the Morian Empire to provide protection and security for the Raylean Prefect, Amidus Terrok, and his palace grounds.

Jeshu was now a young man of an apparent age of 18. Brae was daily dealing with a multitude of quandaries. Where would this end? What would be her role in the days to come? After all, she had taught Jeshu everything she knew, including her master-level courses as an astrotech. In the last few months, all she could do was to feed him resources in all of the other tech fields and hope it was enough.

Brae noticed that as of late, Rhett had become more distant from her and Jeshu than usual. One evening after Jeshu went to bed, Rhett lingered. Brae was exhausted and in no mood for another tense conversation with him, but when he wouldn't leave, she was forced to deal with it.

"Okay, Stryker, what's on your mind. I know you're not hanging around because you like me."

"True but wow, Thornton, you'll never be accused of equivocation," he said, flopping himself down on one of the lounging chairs in the main living area. He looked especially agitated this evening, and Brae wasn't in the best of moods either. He shot a derisive look her way.

"What?" she said from the kitchen.

"Where do I start?" he asked rhetorically. "I really want some straight answers on a few things, and don't tell me I wouldn't understand...I don't want to hear that anymore."

Brae sighed. "Answers to what?"

"Well, for example, you've never explained what Jeshu meant months ago when he said, 'Your father flew many missions for our people.'"

Brae put the last couple of dishes away and sat down opposite Rhett.

"That's not a question, it's an observation."

Rhett sneered, already frustrated. "You're impossible...never mind," he said, moving to stand up.

"Okay...I get it," Brae said, taking a deep breath to relax.

Rhett stopped then sunk back into his chair.

"I thought you said your dad was a geo-mapper pilot. How does that work?"

Brae thought for a moment, considering telling him the whole story. Would he even believe her, or would it be more ammunition for the unending cynicism he loved to cling to? She decided to start with something easy.

"My dad *is* a geo-mapper, or at least was when we left, but he actually served as an aerotech fighter pilot for many years."

Rhett squinched his face. "I guess that makes sense why he would know some hand-to-hand, but if that's true, then why haven't I heard of him? He can't be that old, and the aerotech order is pretty tight."

"I think his missions were pretty classified," Brae countered, hoping that might satisfy him.

"I had top-tier classification authority...never saw a pilot named, 'Thornton.'" Rhett crossed his arms as a skeptical interrogator might do. Brae felt her annoyance rising.

She glared back at Rhett. "Let me ask you something...do you even believe in Ell Yon and the Immortals? Surely you must admit that Jeshu is beyond normal...sent by Ell Yon from the Ruah."

Rhett's expression didn't change. He stared back at Brae in silence. If he didn't at least admit this, she wasn't going to waste her time trying to explain her father's whole 1500-year time-traveling-save-the-Rayleans thing.

"Clearly Jeshu is special," Rhett admitted. "His metabolism alone is a biological phenomenon. And obviously he's extremely gifted...brilliant beyond anything I've ever seen. But it doesn't mean it all can't be explained by natural causes. Geniuses are born every day in the galaxy, and there are freaky metabolic anomalies that medtechs have recorded in years past."

He paused, looking to Brae for some reaction. She offered none.

"As crazy as these last couple of years have been, I haven't seen anything yet that defies normal space and physics," he continued. "Have you...honestly?"

Brae thought of the massive warrior who appeared out of nowhere, saving her and the child aboard the derelict merchant ship. It was the one and only instance she could think of, and she had to often convince herself it wasn't some hallucination she'd had. She hadn't dared tell Rhett because she knew he wouldn't believe her. He was so frustrating she could hardly stand it. Her lips curled to a slight smirk.

"If I had, would you believe me if I told you?"

Rhett's eyes narrowed. "I guess that depends on how crazy it was."

Brae shook her head. "See...that's what I'm talking about. You'd only believe me if *you* thought it was believable. That's why I can't trust you, Stryker. It's why I'll never trust you, not with anything serious."

"All I'm saying is that people believe what they want to believe. I'm a guy who believes his eyes...facts and science. There's a lot of crazy people out there wanting to believe in stuff that's just a bunch of hogwash. You, an astrotech master of all people ought to know this. I'll bet your own order doesn't buy half of what you believe, do they?"

Rhett's comment struck a sore nerve in Brae. Her annoyance with him transformed to near fury. She jumped up.

"You are absolutely the most impertinent, annoying human I have ever encountered! I can't take this anymore."

Rhett stood up to face her. "Hey…this was never my idea. I've wanted out of this from the beginning. I can't believe I ever let you get me into this."

"Blaming me again? Will that ever stop? You're such a child!"

Rhett's nostrils flared. "I just asked you a simple question about your father. Why do you always have to get so haughty and insulting?"

"Me…me?" Brae laughed. "Do you hear yourself? And for your information, my father is ten times the pilot you will ever be!"

"I doubt your father ever saw the inside of a real cockpit let alone an aerotech fighter!"

Brae's rage was unstoppable. They had both now crossed the line and there was no coming back. Her mind raced with a dozen ways to strike back.

"Why don't we go see him?" came a calm voice from the stairwell.

Brae and Rhett both froze. They looked over to see Jeshu sitting halfway up the staircase. He stood, making the last few steps to the landing. Brae suddenly felt foolish and embarrassed. She stole a quick glance toward Rhett and saw the same in his face.

"I'm sorry, Jeshu. Did we wake you?" Brae asked.

Jeshu smiled. "No—I wasn't asleep yet, but I think you may have woken the neighbor half a mile down the road."

Brae lowered her gaze, trying to flush the rush of anger that lingered from her exchange with Rhett.

"Go see whom?" Rhett asked.

Jeshu walked to Brae and put a hand on her shoulder.

"Your father, Brae. It's time."

Brae lifted her eyes to see the warmth of Jeshu's gaze. Already, she could feel it…the love of something larger than the galaxy itself. She felt so small in his presence. *Does Rhett feel it?* she wondered. *Could* Rhett feel it?

"Really?" she asked.

"Yes."

Jeshu was now taller than Rhett. He lifted his other hand, placing it on Rhett's shoulder. Brae could tell this made her contrary associate uncomfortable. He sighed.

"Will it always be like this for you?" Rhett asked. "Your growth being so accelerated?"

"No, my time has nearly come, and your roles will soon end," Jeshu answered.

Brae furrowed her brow. "What do you mean?" she asked.

"You've done well with me," Jeshu continued. "I chose both of you for this purpose, and now I must step into that which my father has called me to."

"No," Brae petitioned. "Surely not yet. You're still so young."

"It's time, Brae," was all he said.

In the last few weeks, the continual growth of Jeshu's stature and authority had been undeniable. There had been brief moments when Brae had looked at Jeshu and seen frightening power. His eyes had changed from boy to beyond man in a matter of weeks. Deep down she had known he was close. She had also realized that Jeshu's final transition was probably more difficult for Rhett to handle than for her.

Jeshu glanced from Brae to Rhett. "I do hope you two will part ways as friends."

One of Rhett's eyebrows lifted signaling once again his stubbornness. But then again, she couldn't see that ever happening either. Jeshu's hands squeezed their shoulders. "Let's prepare and leave in a week's time...agreed?"

Both Brae and Rhett nodded.

One week later, Brae could hardly contain her excitement as the outline of her father's farm came into view. It had been nearly three years since she'd last seen Daeson. Had he thought her dead this whole time? She felt Jeshu's hand on her arm. He said nothing, but the warmth of his touch helped to steady her.

Before the transport speeder had fully settled to the ground, Brae was exiting the half open door.

"Let me at least get it on the ground, Brae," Rhett exclaimed, trying to hurry the craft's shutdown.

"Oops," Brae said, returning briefly to grab the silver case from next to her seat.

Brae ran to the front of the house, onto the porch, and up to the door.

"Dad!" she shouted.

She punched the access code, and the door unlocked. A good sign, she thought. Inside she scanned the surroundings. Most everything still looked familiar. She set the case on the entry table.

"Dad!" she shouted again.

Then from the entry of the kitchen, Daeson appeared, his face taut with cautious anticipation.

"Brae?" he exclaimed.

Once his gaze fell on her, tears filled his eyes, and the two of them ran to embrace each other. Brae buried her face in Daeson's neck and wept.

"I didn't know if anything had happened to you," she said, not wanting to let go of him.

"Nor I you, precious daughter."

When her heart was satisfied, she let go and looked up at him. His eyes showed the edge of age, perhaps a little more than they should have for just three years.

"I've missed you so," she said. "You wouldn't believe what has happened, and why I couldn't come to you."

Daeson smiled, "I can only imagine. I can't wait to hear all about it."

The door behind them darkened as a figure appeared.

"Dad, this is Rhett Stryker, the pilot of the research vessel I chartered for the mission. Rhett, this is my father—" It was then that Brae realized Rhett only knew them as "Thorntons." "Elias Thornton," she finished.

Daeson didn't miss a beat. He reached for Rhett, and the two men exchanged handshakes as Brae looked behind Rhett.

"Where is he?" Brae asked.

"He walked into the field," Rhett answered. "Don't ask me why."

"Where is who?" Daeson asked.

Brae strained to look out the door, then turned back to her father. Grabbing his hand, she pulled him to come with her.

"Come...you'll see."

After a short search, they found Jeshu in a field kneeling next to a stream. When they approached, his back was turned to them.

"Jeshu," Brae called. "I'd like you to meet my father."

The young man stood and turned to face them. Daeson became still, staring at Jeshu for a moment. Both Brae and Rhett stood as still as statues, watching something significant yet unknown transpire before them.

"Hello, Elias," Jeshu said with a gleam in his eye, somehow knowing to carry the ruse for Rhett's sake. He walked to stand before Daeson.

Slowly Daeson's countenance melded into a canvas of ancient joys and sorrows, the look of remembrance filling his eyes. He fell to one knee, never breaking eye contact with the warm glow of Jeshu's gaze.

"My lord…is it really you? Are you the one we wait for?"

"I am," Jeshu said, and the ground beneath them seemed to tremble.

Tears brimmed Daeson's eyes as Jeshu placed a gentle hand on his shoulder. Brae looked on in wonder, witnessing the intimate scene unfold. A young man, ancient of age, blessing an older man, whose life was but a vapor.

Jeshu kneeled to be face to face with Daeson. He lifted his hand, opening it to reveal the delicate flower of the Wild Crimson Rose.

"Perform the Reclamation Ceremony for me," Jeshu said, offering the flower to Daeson.

Daeson shook his head. "I am not worthy to do so, my lord."

"Do so to fulfill the oracles of the Sovereign."

Daeson nodded, slowly lifting the flower from Jeshu's hand. Peeling the petals off one at a time, he layered them. Jeshu opened his hand as Daeson twisted the petals until a single red drop fell into the open palm. Daeson dipped his finger into the red fluid, then swiped across Jeshu's brow and down each cheek.

"As a symbol of the passing of the Death Mist and of our future reclamation," Daeson said, his voice nearly cracking on the last word.

Jeshu leaned his head forward toward Daeson. With his hands on Jeshu's shoulders, Daeson gently kissed his forehead. Brae dared not move or speak, knowing that what she'd just witnessed was the initiation of a mission that would shake the fabric of the entire galaxy.

Jeshu stood, lifting Daeson with him. "A little longer, old friend."

Daeson nodded. Just then, footsteps were heard, and a metal form appeared from behind a nearby tree.

"Rivet!" Brae exclaimed.

On his approach, Rivet quickly scanned Brae and Rhett but made straight for Jeshu, stopping beside Daeson. He was carrying the case Brae had left on the entry table. The android lowered his head as Brae had never seen him do.

"Commander," Rivet said.

Jeshu lifted his hand and touched the top of the bot's head. When he pulled back his hand, Rivet raised his head and lifted the case for Jeshu to see. Brae's heart began to race. All of the stories Daeson had told her about the Protector flashed across her mind. If Jeshu truly was the son of Ell Yon, what would this mean? She glanced toward her dad and could see a reverent fear in his eyes as well. Jeshu placed his hand on the top of the case and the locking mechanism released without a code being entered. He then looked to Daeson.

"Christen me for my father's work," Jeshu said.

Rivet turned slightly, offering the Protector to Daeson. Brae could see the alarm in her father's eyes. He hadn't worn the Protector since her mother had died. Would he...could he don the Protector now? Daeson looked up at Jeshu, a plea in his gaze.

"It's okay, Elias, don't be afraid. You are highly favored in the Ruah," Jeshu said with a confident nod.

Daeson slowly lifted the Protector from its case, holding it as one might a treasure of infinite worth. With his left hand firmly holding the Protector, he positioned it above his right arm. Both Brae and Rhett took a step toward him, knowing what donning the Protector had done to her. Daeson hesitated, took a deep breath, then pressed the Protector downward and onto his arm. Although Brae and Rhett were ready, they were not needed. Daeson merely closed his eyes and waited a few seconds. When the synaptic interface was complete, Daeson's eyes opened, and Brae stared on in wonder. She was seeing her father for the first time in her life as he was meant to be. The transformation was remarkable—from gentle father to noble leader...from humble servant to fierce warrior...from Elias Thornton to Navi Daeson Starlore, ancient hero of the Raylean people.

Jeshu smiled as he beheld the revived visage of his gallant servant of old. The Son of Ell Yon knelt down before Daeson, spreading his arms wide. With Jeshu's face turned upward, Daeson lifted a closed hand inches from his face. The moment stretched as Brae and Rhett looked on in awe. Daeson opened his hand and immediately a brilliant, blinding, blue light spilled onto the noble brow of Jeshu, bathing him in the glorious flame of the Sovereign. The brightness, along with an emanating bass rumble, amplified with each passing second until Brae had to shield her eyes from its brilliance. She lifted her arm to cover her eyes but couldn't help from trying to see what was about to happen. She and Rhett stepped back as the ground began to quake, a nearly subsonic sound generating from the Protector. The moment reached its crescendo then instantly fell silent and still. The silence lingered until finally Jeshu opened his eyes and stood. There was a new strength in him that Brae had only seen glimpses of in weeks past. Like her father, Jeshu too had transformed into something more than he had been a moment ago. Slowly the intensity of what they had witnessed faded. Jeshu looked to Rivet and nodded then pulled Daeson aside to speak briefly to him privately. Rivet closed the empty case he was still holding and turned towards Brae. He walked to her, politely tilting his head.

"It is good to see you again, my lady."

Brae reached for Rivet's hand. "It's so good to see you too, Rivet. Did you miss me?"

"I did. It's been quite boring here without you."

Jeshu and Daeson now joined them. Rivet looked over at Rhett, inspecting him. After a moment of silence, he turned back to Brae.

"Are you bonded to this man?" he asked flatly.

"No! For goodness sakes, no!" Brae exclaimed.

"Good," Rivet replied.

Everyone laughed. Everyone except Rhett.

"I see...you've even programmed your android to insult me," Rhett grumbled.

Daeson went to Rhett. "Don't worry," he said putting a hand on his shoulder. "Rivet isn't your typical android. It'll take a while before he starts to like you."

"Hmm, well I'm not sure I'll be around long enough for that to happen," Rhett replied.

After a short time of polite conversation, Rhett made known his intentions to leave. Much to Brae's chagrin, Daeson implored him to stay, but Rhett would not be convinced. A few minutes later, Brae found herself standing with Jeshu and Rhett alongside the transport speeder they had rented to bring them from the spaceport. Brae felt awkward saying goodbye to Rhett, considering everything they had been through, and yet she couldn't deny that she was eager to see him go.

SPEEDER

SPECIFICATIONS
MANUFACTURER ~ PUREFLIGHT CORP.
ENGINE ~ BETATRON-XL TURBINE
SPEED ~ 365 MILES PER HOUR
RANGE ~ 780 MILES
FLIGHT MODES ~ SURFACE TO 5000 FT
NAVIGATION ~ INERTIAL AND GLOBAL
SATCOR POSITIONING
CREW ~ 1 PILOT, 3 PASSENGERS
FEATURES ~ COCKPIT ENVIRONMENTAL
CONTROL W/NIGHT VISION
THERMAL AND CANOPY
HUD DISPLAY

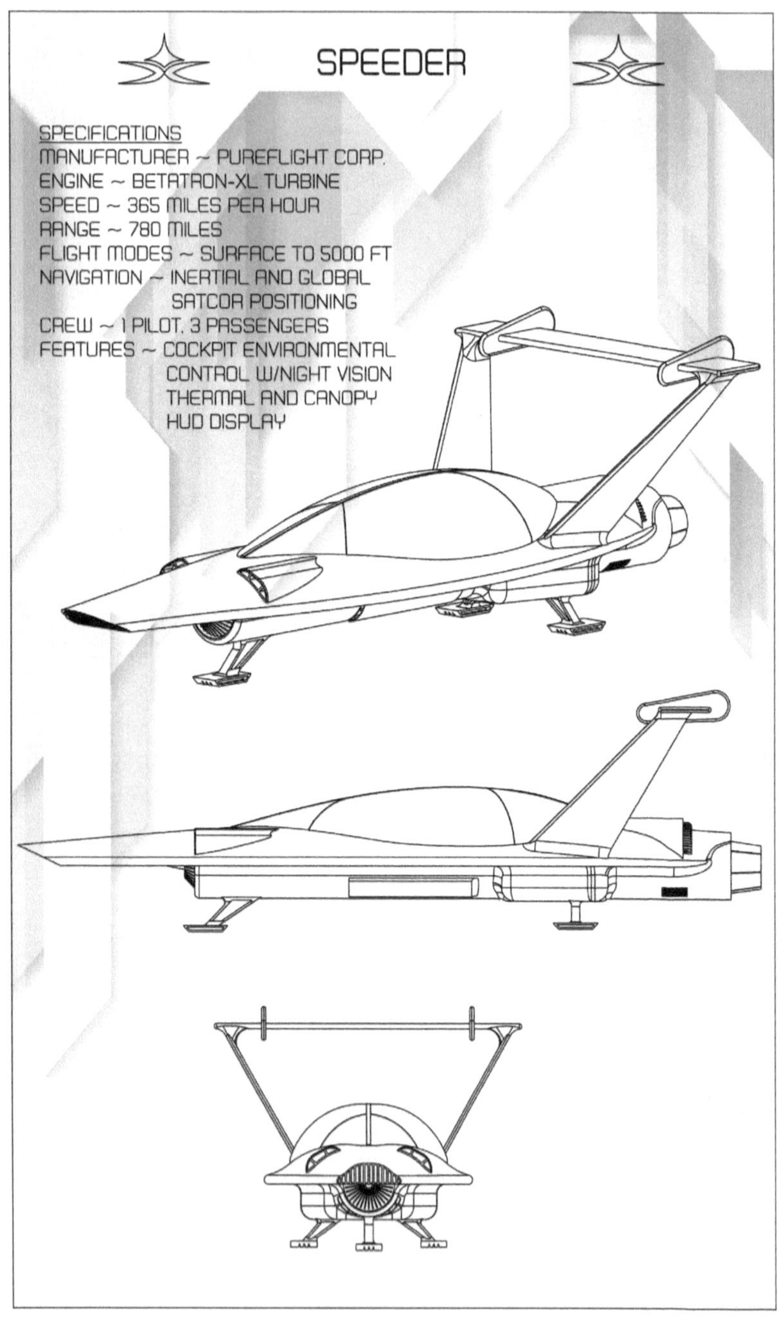

"I'll send another transport out for you," Rhett said.

"No need," Jeshu replied. "We'll not need it."

Though Rhett looked confused, he didn't argue. Brae sensed he was just as eager to be on his way, and the fewer words spoken the better.

"Be careful in Jalem," Jeshu warned. "Although the immediate threat has greatly diminished, there's still great opportunity to find trouble."

Rhett nodded, then Jeshu reached out and embraced him.

"Thank you for your sacrifice," Brae heard him say quietly.

Rhett half-heartedly returned the embrace, smiling sheepishly. Jeshu then stepped away, leaving Brae to face him alone.

Rhett offered her a crooked smile. Brae shrugged her shoulders and flashed a quick smile in return.

"Still leaving after seeing what just happened?" she asked. It was meant as a jab at him, but then rebuked herself because it might have sounded as if she was wishing he'd stay.

"I saw a bright light," Rhett replied.

Brae huffed. "Your lack of belief is stunning."

"And your blind belief is just as stunning," Rhett countered.

"After all this time with him, you still don't see it?" Brae asked. Then a moment of realization dawned on her. "I get it...you're afraid!"

Rhett glared at her. "You never let up do you, Thornton? You think you're so smart and know people so well." He shook his head while opening the gull door to the speeder.

A dozen responses were on the tip of Brae's tongue, but what was the point? She realized that the harder she tried to convince him, the further away he would go. She crossed her arms, choosing not to say a thing. *Let's just get this over with*, she thought.

Rhett paused before getting in the craft. He looked over at her. Brae braced for another insult.

"Look, Thornton, I know we never really got along much...or ever, but I appreciate what you did for him."

Brae tried a genuine smile, but it just wouldn't come.

"Thanks for what you did too, Stryker," she said. "I hope you find what you're looking for."

He nodded then seated himself into the speeder.

"Hey," Brae said grabbing the door to keep it from closing. "Where *are* you going?"

Rhett looked like he was trying to decide if he dared say anything. "I'm going to find my parents and my brothers...and someone else," he added hesitantly.

Brae was momentarily shocked. "Wait...you have a girl?"

Rhett eyed her closely. "Had a girl. Find that hard to believe, do you?"

"Well...I...ah..." Brae couldn't respond because she actually *did* find that hard to believe.

Rhett just shook his head.

"In three years, you never said anything," Brae said bewildered.

"In case you didn't notice, we never opened up much to each other. And besides, what did it matter? It wouldn't have changed a thing."

Brae dropped her hand from the door. "Yeah...I guess so." She felt bad for never having asked him. "I hope you find her, Rhett," she said. It was all she could muster to offer one leaf of an olive branch to close out their journey.

Reaching to press the close door button, he looked up at her one last time.

"See you around, Thornton."

"I hope not," she shot back with a bit of a smile.

He chuckled, then shook his head.

"Got that right."

The door closed, and a moment later he was gone. Brae could feel the tension in her body falling away as the transport speeder disappeared over the horizon.

"He'll find his way." Brae heard the calm and strong voice behind her as Jeshu approached.

"Are you sure about that?" Brae turned about.

Jeshu looked into the distance after Rhett. "I'm sure. Come, let's catch up with Daeson, shall we?"

Brae found a genuine smile.

"Yes!"

The rest of the day was filled with delicious food and much conversation about what had happened over the last three years. Daeson listened with bated breath as Brae told of the Omega Nebula Event. Her regaling of the strange warrior that held the tear of the hull of the merchant ship at bay so she could escape with Jeshu was of particular interest to Daeson. For Brae, this time with Jeshu, her father, and Rivet seemed so surreal, as if she was in a dream. Watching her father and Jeshu interact evoked the strangest mix of emotions. In one sense it solidified the bizarre reality of who she was and the epic narratives of her parents' lives. In another sense, it made her feel small, insignificant, and afraid. As Jeshu continued to transform into the embodiment of the Son of Sovereign Ell Yon, Commander of all Malakian Immortals, the collision between realms became more and more of an inevitability, and this frightened Brae for she didn't know what it would mean for her and for her people.

The next morning, Daeson and Brae woke to see Rivet waiting for them in the kitchen. Daeson turned solemn.

"What's wrong, Rivet?" he asked.

Brae looked at her dad. How could he possibly tell from Rivet's continually stoic metal expression if there was something wrong? Rivet paused.

"He's gone," the android stated flatly.

Brae's stomach flipped.

"What do you mean?" she demanded. "Where has he gone?"

Rivet slowly turned his head to face her.

"Away."

"For how long?" Daeson asked. "Did he take supplies?"

"He didn't say. He took nothing."

"It begins," Brae heard Daeson whisper.

Rivet's responses were not enough. Brae felt a dark loneliness beginning to swell within her. She went to stand face to face with the bot.

"Why, Rivet? Why did he leave?"

Rivet tilted his head ever so slightly.

"To fight."

Jeshu left Daeson's home early, before the sun crested the morning horizon. Brae would be upset not getting a chance to say goodbye, but he didn't want to have to navigate the questions she would surely have for him. Rivet would be his goodbye, and it would have to do.

Having studied the geography of the entire planet, and especially the area around Jalem, Jeshu set a course southwest. This region was a rocky wilderness with no cities or dwellings for a hundred miles. It was a place he was drawn to for reasons unknown. From the christening of the Protector, Jeshu felt compelled to bear the next few weeks alone as he embarked on a final journey to prepare for the mission his father had given him.

Fully donning the cloak of humanity was revealing. Progressing from infant to adult was a bizarre and intriguing journey to say the least. Like a slow lifting fog, the reality of self-actualization toward that of being not only called by Sovereign Ell Yon but of understanding his exclusively unique relationship as his son was profoundly humbling if not terrifying at first. It happened early, but the full discovery of it took years, and Jeshu knew, would culminate to finality through his voyage into the wilderness right now. As Jeshu had awakened to his royal heritage, there had come a moment midway through his maturing when he also began to understand the beginning, the purpose, and the end of his mission. The very knowing of such a thing was a weighty burden for shoulders so slim. It also incurred a soberness that no other human could understand. The favor of Sovereign Ell Yon helped him carry much of the burden, but what gave him the power to press into such a terrifying end was the silent cry of all humanity yearning for freedom from the bondage of inevitable death...death that had infected humanity by the hand of C'fir Dracus of the Torian Scourge. Ell Yon had looked for a man to bear such sacrifice, but none could reach the mark, for all had been tainted by the evil agent of Deitum Prime. The purification of humanity required the sacrifice of perfection, and thus the tears of Tsiyyon and the Sovereign's broken heart would command his own blood to go forth into the domain of men.

As he grew from child to man, Jeshu had studied, trained, and prepared for his mission, but he knew that all students must be tested to become a master. Although he didn't know what manner of test was before him, nor the length, whether one day or a hundred, the calling to save a galaxy would require the worst of trials to prove out his heart.

Chapter

12

Adrift

Rivet occupied himself with duties in the repair shop while Daeson made breakfast for Brae and himself. Brae didn't help much, which was just fine with Daeson. She found herself in a state of aimlessness, a condition she had never experienced before. The last three years had been so intense with her purpose that she hadn't seriously considered what life after Jeshu would look like.

Daeson placed a steaming hot plate of gilberry waffles on the table between them. Two dishes of fresh fruit, a jar of juice, and a chalice of cream were added to finish the delicious array. Brae smiled, for this was her favorite breakfast.

"Thanks, Dad."

After giving thanks to Ell Yon, Brae built a perfectly portioned waffle, fruit, and cream delight. Her first bite took her right back to her childhood, sitting in this same chair. The galaxy seemed so simple back then. She looked up to see her father smiling at her. His eyes were different now.

"What?" she asked.

Daeson's eyes reddened. "Raviel would be so proud of you."

Brae's eyes immediately threatened to spill tears of her own. She reached across the table for Daeson's hand. "You must miss her so much, Dad. I can't imagine."

Daeson wiped an eye. "Yes…I do."

Brae waited until she could tell Daeson was ready to move on. After a few more minutes of less emotional talk, her dad looked like he had something on his mind.

"Rhett seemed to play a pretty big role in Jeshu's training," Daeson said after downing a bite of breakfast.

"Yeah, he did," Brae replied.

"I also got the impression you two didn't get along so well."

Brae finished taking a drink from her glass of juice. "We didn't get along at all."

She began to wonder where her dad was going with this. She thought of something to change the subject, but Daeson was too quick.

"He left pretty quickly yesterday. Is he coming back?"

Despite their tumultuous relationship, the sheer fact that they had spent three years together essentially trying to accomplish the same goal had forged a bond of sorts, even if she didn't like it. Hearing her dad ask caused a slight twinge of sadness for reasons she didn't understand. It was the first of any such feelings she had ever felt for the man.

"I don't think so. But it's for the best."

"Hmm…you sure about that?" Daeson asked, watching her face closely.

Brae looked up from her food. "Yes," she replied emphatically. "There are people in the galaxy that just aren't compatible. That would be Stryker and me...without a doubt. We didn't see eye to eye on anything!"

"Well, he seemed like a decent guy to me," Daeson said, refocusing on his plate of food.

"You only just met him, Dad. He's the most arrogant, pig-headed man I've ever known. To be honest, I could hardly stand to be around him," Brae countered.

Daeson stopped chewing and just stared at her with eyes that seemed to know things she didn't.

"Hmm," Daeson said. One corner of his mouth turned upward, and Brae immediately responded.

"Oh, please...don't even! I can honestly say that from the moment I met Stryker I haven't had one shred of even the remotest of feelings of affinity for him. And he would say the same about me," Brae huffed. "He couldn't leave fast enough, and I couldn't wait until he was gone."

"You sure about that?"

Brae was getting exasperated, especially with that question. It was his way to get her to rethink her position, but it almost never worked, at least not once she'd become an adult.

"We spent three years together. Yeah...I'm sure."

Daeson nodded. "Okay. Just don't mistake confidence for arrogance. The man is an aerotech fighter pilot. A guy like that has to be confident just to survive."

Brae shook her head, preparing a rebuttal, but Daeson continued.

"What you just went through, with your lives on the line multiple times...I'm pretty sure you wouldn't have wanted some wishy-washy wimp walking beside you," Daeson added.

Brae closed her mouth and thought about that. He had a point.

"Why did he leave?" Daeson asked.

"Probably because of me, but he claims that he just couldn't buy into the Ell Yon, Immortal, Son of the Sovereign concept." Brae shook her head again. "Even after everything he witnessed and then seeing the kind of man Jeshu became. He's denying the obvious and has no faith."

"Really?" Daeson asked.

"Yeah...can you believe it?" Brae said, finally feeling like her dad was understanding how difficult she'd had it with Rhett.

"He sounds like quite an honorable fellow," Daeson said. Brae nearly dropped her fork.

"Did you hear what I just said?" she exclaimed.

"Yes, Brae. I did. Despite him not believing it all, he stuck with you and continued to train Jeshu for three years...I'd say he's fiercely loyal and trustworthy...an honorable man. And from the way you introduced me, he stayed beside you the whole time without having the whole truth." He paused. "Whose fault is that, sweetheart?" he asked gently.

Brae glared across the table at her father, angry for being blamed for Rhett's derogatory attitude and caustic personality...and from her own father at that! He just had no idea what it had been like for her to deal with Rhett on a daily basis. She clenched her teeth. "He would never have believed me, and I was in no mood to bear his incessant condescending comments."

"So, you decided for him whether or not he was going to believe you," Daeson said flatly.

This conversation revived all of her ill-feelings against Rhett, and she didn't like it, especially since her father was actually defending the guy. When he left yesterday, she was certain she would finally have peace back in her life. This was not it!

"You know, I'm not really hungry anymore." Brae stood in a huff, bussed her dishes to the counter, and made for the door.

"Brae," Daeson called.

Brae stopped, her hands clenched into fists at her sides. She waited at the door, her back still to Daeson. She wasn't ready for an apology yet—she needed time to cool down, but an apology is not what she got.

"Just remember, Ell Yon chose Rhett as a mentor for Jeshu just like he chose you...and he makes no mistakes. There must be something pretty stellar about the man."

Brae stepped through the door and exited the house. Just outside, she passed Rivet who was approaching from the repair shop.

"Lady Brae—"

"Not now, Rivet," she said holding up her hand. That whole interchange with her dad had riled her. She needed to be alone, so she took a long walk through her childhood pastures, searching for the peace they had once brought. But alas, no matter how far she went, the words of her father followed.

Before leaving the region and city of Jalem, Rhett felt compelled to discover if there was any hope of reviving his relationship with Quilla. Taking Jeshu's warning to heart, he was careful not to unnecessarily expose himself to any security personnel and, in particular, the Raylean Guard or Terrok's Royal Guard. Being fairly convinced that the massacre at the Omega Nebula was not orchestrated by the Morian Empire, he wasn't as concerned with avoiding Morian commandos, which was impossible anyway since they were everywhere.

The morning after leaving Brae and Jeshu, he caught a transport to a station near the office complex where he knew Quilla had last worked. When it was close to noon, he walked to the courtyard in the front of her building and found a bench by a fountain to wait. He had met her here twice before to catch lunch with her and thought this might be his best bet, feeling that a cold call via a communication device would be too harsh. Before long, his patience paid off. He caught a glimpse of Quilla walking with another woman, and they were coming his way. His feelings for her had never died and seeing her now fully revived them. She was a beautiful woman with a personality that really connected with him. Hope and hurt seemed to occupy his heart the closer she came, and he had no idea what her reaction might be to seeing him now. Fully engaged in conversation with her friend, Quilla was just a few feet away from Rhett when he stood.

"Quilla," he called out.

She stopped midsentence with her friend and turned to look his way. The smile that he had come to love immediately dissolved away, replaced by a look of disbelief, then anger. She stopped walking, as did her friend, then fully turned to face him. Quilla opened her mouth to say something, but instead her eyes narrowed. She then spun on her heel and grabbed her friend's arm, pulling her forward to resume their walk.

"Quilla...please. Can I have just a moment to talk to you?" Rhett pleaded, taking a few steps to catch up to her.

Quilla kept walking, as if trying to ignore him.

"Who is that?" Rhett heard her friend ask.

"He's nobody," Quilla said lifting her chin while quickening their pace.

"Please, Quilla. Let me explain…I didn't leave you on purpose."

At that, Quilla stopped with a stamp of her foot. Rhett saw her clench her fists at her sides then spin about and walk toward him like she was going to run him over. She lifted an accusing finger at him.

"You coward!" she exclaimed. "You didn't even have the nerve to tell me to my face…or at all for that matter! You led me on as if we had something special and then just left me." Quilla glared at Rhett with hard eyes.

"Please just give me a minute to explain," he pleaded as her friend walked toward them to offer support for Quilla.

"Ooo," Quilla exclaimed through clenched teeth. "You even had your squadron cover for your cowardice, refusing to let me even talk to you. I have never been so insulted and humiliated in all my life!"

Rhett held up both hands. "None of that was my choice. I got called out on a mission and things happened so that I couldn't get back home," he tried to explain.

"For three years?!" she shouted. "I don't believe you!"

"It's true, Quilla. Please, can we just sit and talk for a minute?" he asked, glancing toward her friend with as conciliatory a look as he could muster.

Quilla crossed her arms, continuing to glare at him. Her chest rose up and down with deep angry breaths. Rhett looked softly into her eyes.

"Please," he said once more.

Slowly her eyes softened as she seemed to remember the way things with him had once been.

After another 10 seconds of contemplation, she turned to her friend.

"Go ahead, Tamil. I'll catch up."

Her friend eyed Rhett closely. "You sure?"

"Yes...I'm fine. I'll join you in a few minutes."

Tamil gave Rhett a sneer, then turned and left. Rhett motioned to a nearby bench that bordered the broad walkway. Towering trees lined each side, their lofty limbs and branches casting shadows all across the walk. Quilla reluctantly sat down, cold...stiff...arms still crossed.

"Thank you," Rhett said, sitting beside her but not too closely.

"First, I'm very sorry for what happened. I can't give you details because doing so might compromise your safety."

Quilla's countenance shifted to one of skepticism. Rhett was finding this much more difficult than he had anticipated. How do you convince someone of an unbelievable truth and yet still win them over without being able to share everything necessary to do so? He suddenly thought of Brae and the many times she struggled to explain things to him. *Was this the same thing she was experiencing?* he wondered. *What couldn't Brae tell me?*

"I missed you every day I wasn't with you, Quilla," Rhett said.

Quilla turned to look into his eyes, searching for sincerity. She uncrossed her arms.

"What we had was special," he continued. "My feelings for you were...are genuine and strong. Not being able to contact you was one of the hardest things I've ever had to do, but I didn't have a choice...I did it because I care deeply for you."

Quilla's eyes softened, her shoulders dropping slightly as she listened.

"Please believe me...I couldn't even contact my parents or my brothers...in fact I still haven't. You are the first person I've reached out to since this all went down."

The last traces of anger vanished from Quilla's face. Instead, eyes filled with a distant pain looked at him now. She slowly shook her head.

"I don't understand how that's all possible," she said softly. "But I think I believe you."

Tears began to well up in her eyes.

"I really cared for you...you broke my heart, Rhett."

Hearing her speak his name crushed him. For three years he had longed to hear it. He reached for her hand, and she allowed it. She looked down at his hand resting on top of hers.

"I'm sorry, Quilla...I truly am. If there was any way I could have changed what happened, I would have. Can we—"

He stopped short when he felt her slowly pull her hand out from under his. That simple act was enough to shatter his hope.

"I'm with someone now," she said, looking back up at Rhett. She shook her head. "It's been three years, Rhett."

Rhett dropped his head, feeling the end of them.

"We're to be bonded soon," she finished.

Rhett took a deep breath, trying to absorb the pain. He slowly nodded.

"I understand."

A few seconds later, Quilla stood, and Rhett followed. She turned to face him. After taking a moment to wipe her eyes, she smiled at Rhett, then leaned in and kissed his cheek.

"I wish you well, Rhett Stryker."

Rhett tried to smile back. "And I you, Quilla. You deserve a wonderful life."

Quilla looked as if she might shed more tears, so she quickly turned and began walking away.

"Quilla," Rhett called.

She stopped and looked back, eyes brimming.

"It would be best if you didn't tell anyone that you saw me. Okay?"

She nodded quickly then turned and walked out of Rhett's life. He watched her for a time, wondering if she would look back, but she didn't. He wasn't ready to move on. When she disappeared around a distant corner, he sat back down on the bench and put his head between his hands, elbows on his knees.

To torture himself further, he replayed every delightful moment that he'd had with Quilla all the way to the evening before his life changed. The day that Thornton walked into the squadron was the beginning of the end of everything he held dear. *Why oh why did it happen to me?* he wondered. He had sacrificed three years of his life and was forced to spend it with a woman that detested him. Now he had no career, no relationship, and nowhere to go. He was adrift in a sea of humanity with no anchor and no course to set.

"Brae Thornton," he said out loud. "What have you done to me?"

Late in the day, Rhett found his way back to the shuttle and flew to the city of Brohn on the planet's most southern continent. This was home. Being far away from Jalem and the headquarters of the Raylean Guard, he felt relatively safe with little need to hide his identity. Here, he would reconnect with his parents and his two brothers, hoping this reunion would play out much better than the last.

CHAPTER

13

Navi Reborn

Brae wasn't sure what to do with herself. Three years of rigorous purpose was terminated in a day, leaving her in a state of ambiguity. After taking a couple of days to cool down, Brae needed the guidance of her father. Without much said, she took a few tools and began working side by side with him in the shop. She was grateful that Daeson didn't press her for words of reconciliation but let the simple action of her presence be enough.

"When are you going to invest in a decent mapping craft and give up on this old bucket of bolts?" she asked as they teamed up on fixing one of the S-23's control surfaces.

"Really?" Daeson asked. "You want me to trade in the old girl?"

"No...not really." Brae grabbed a fusion wrench. "Let me, Dad," she said, stepping in next to him. "I do get a little worried that this thing is going to flip you over when you're too close to the ground to recover though."

Daeson held the end of the coupler she was trying to loosen. After a minute of hard effort, it broke loose.

Brae wiped her brow then looked over at her father. By the crease in his brow, she could tell something was bothering him.

"You okay, Dad?" she asked. "If you're upset about the other day—"

"Of course not, Brae," he interrupted.

"Okay...then what is it?"

"Have you heard what Prefect Terrok is doing now?" he asked, wiping his hands on a rag then tossing it to the bench.

"I can only imagine. After murdering hundreds of people in an effort to kill Jeshu and then covering it up, there's no telling what that tyrant is capable of," Brae responded, anger boiling up inside her.

Daeson's eyes became fierce, and it set Brae back. She had never seen this look in her father before.

"He's been building a Deitum Prime replication complex right under our noses, and it's nearing completion."

"But what of the Sovereign Sanctums? Surely the Keepers and the Builders of the Protectors have influence and can stop it," Brae offered.

"Ha! The same Keepers and Builders that charge people to be scanned by the Protectors while they themselves have absorbed more Deitum Prime than anyone? They're hypocrites and Terrok is publicly disgracing the precepts of Sovereign Ell Yon!"

Brae became quiet...watching her dad. Though his heart regarding Deitum Prime had always been known, she hadn't seen such a passionate response from him like this before. Perhaps that was part of why it had been hard for her to accept that Elias Thornton was one and the same as the legendary Daeson Starlore. She imagined that she was seeing the real Daeson Starlore once more.

"You're different, Dad," she risked.

Daeson grabbed another tool. With a quick side glance, he moved back under the control surface.

"How so?" he asked.

She grabbed his arm. He stopped and gazed into her eyes. She slid her hand down to his forearm where the Protector was.

"It changes you, doesn't it?" she asked.

Daeson's shoulders dropped slightly. His countenance eased and the corner of his mouth turned up. "Did it change you?"

Brae nodded. Daeson tilted his head toward a bench behind them where they each had a cool drink waiting for them.

"Ell Yon makes us better than we are...fills us with purpose and passion beyond what we can muster on our own. He opens our eyes to what is good and what is evil."

Daeson lowered his head, feeling the Protector with his left hand.

"It's been a long time. He's a patient Sovereign...and forgiving. Ever since Jeshu asked me to christen him, I've been remembering who I was...who I am. I guess I've been playing it safe because..."

Daeson struggled to finish.

"Because why?" Brae asked.

"Because I didn't want anything to happen to you," he said with a sheepish look.

Brae put a gentle hand on his arm. "I love you, Dad, and I understand, but I'm okay."

Daeson covered her hand with his own. "I know."

A troubling thought then landed on Brae's mind. "Just promise me you won't go and do anything too radical."

Daeson smiled. "You either." He took a long drink from his glass. "You mentored and raised Jeshu in preparation for his mission, and soon you will become a student of his, learning the ways of the Navi in a manner humanity has never seen before."

Stories of old began to flash across Brae's mind as she remembered the Commander training Daeson Starlore to be a Navi for the captive Raylean people. Excitement began to well up within her. She stood, a broad smile spreading across her mouth.

"Until then, you train me, Navi Starlore. I will be your sectator, a student of the Navi ways."

Daeson looked up at Brae in a way she had never seen before—eyes like fire and face like flint. What she saw thrilled and alarmed her. This was indeed the Navi of old...the one whom Ell Yon had used to destroy the entire fleet of Jypton.

"You don't know what you're asking, Brae," he said.

Brae lifted her chin while gazing down at her father.

"I'm ready, and if the future holds what you believe is coming, then I'll need every minute of training you can give me."

Daeson set his drink down and slowly stood. "There's nothing romantic about training for battle. This won't feel anything like the stories you love."

Brae didn't flinch. Daeson nodded.

"You don't question me, and you don't complain... ever. Are we clear?"

Brae gave one firm nod of her head.

"Very well, Sectator Starlore. We begin now."

That very day, Daeson began to train Brae in the ways of the Navi. Brae learned just how weak she was in every aspect of her being...physically, emotionally, mentally. For the first two weeks, she had to constantly rebuke herself for wanting to complain or even quit.

Her notion that her father had changed proved out to be as true as ever. She found it nearly impossible to keep up with a man that was over twice her age. She quickly came to understand that, for a time, their relationship was no longer father-daughter. It was master-student...Navi-Sectator. This even translated to when they weren't in training. The emotional distance, she knew, was necessary for Daeson to implement training to its fullest.

The training began with an intense physical regimen, grinding out the weakness of the heart and coming to understand that her limits were not limits at all. Daeson kept demanding more and more from her...pushing her real limits to heights she didn't think possible. Then came serious hand-to-hand combat training with the Talon. On week three, Daeson began to show her the power of the Protector, but she did not don it. Daeson said it wasn't yet her time, and so she accepted that. In truth, she was relieved, for it frightened her.

Each night Brae would collapse in her bed, hardly able to roll over. But slowly, her body strengthened, her mind cleared, and her emotions were bridled, being made obedient to the greater call of a future mission she did not yet know or understand. One evening, after they had finished their last lesson for the day and were sitting down to eat, Daeson slid a glass tablet across the table to Brae.

"It's time to prepare the Raylean people for the Merchant."

"Merchant," Brae said quietly. "That comes from the oracle Micaba. He is the first and one of the few to call him the Merchant. I don't suppose it's a coincidence that we found him on an abandoned merchant ship," Brae mused.

"I think not," Daeson replied. "'Consider the cost of your freedom. Who among us is able to secure it? For he alone is able and shall buy your freedom and your future.'"

"It's one of our oldest," Brae said, reflecting on the first time her dad had read Micaba's words to her.

"When I was a prince on Jypton and your mother first quoted that oracle to me, I had no idea what it meant. Even now, there is a mystery in those words."

Brae picked up the tablet to see a broadcast brief on the coming month-long festival hosted by Prefect Terrok called the "Magnifical." Of course, such events were closely monitored by Subchancellor Pylok and the Morian Empire.

"I don't understand. Prefect Terrok is a monster...why would we participate in this? We've never even attended the Magnifical in past years."

"Because millions of Rayleans from around the planet will be participating, and they have lived far too long without the voice of Ell Yon beckoning them to return to his ways." Daeson glanced down at the Protector on his arm.

"For many years, I determined in my heart that I would remain silent and not make mention of Sovereign Ell Yon nor speak his name to others, but his word burns within me. I am weary with refraining from his call, and I cannot stay silent anymore."

Brae looked up from the glass tablet and into the face of her Navi. Though his words frightened her, she understood, for she felt the burning too.

"How?" she asked.

"I've registered to participate in the aero-skills competition. It's attended by over two million Rayleans and broadcasted globally to a hundred million more.

Rayl needs to prepare their hearts for the coming of the Merchant."

"Dad," Brae began, then saw the gentle but firm look of rebuke from her father. She chose to break their rules this once. She reached across the table and grabbed his hand. Her touch softened his countenance.

"You've never broken a promise you made to me...promise me you'll be okay."

Daeson's eyes warmed, becoming the loving father of his precious daughter again.

"I promise, Brae."

After the tender moment passed, they stood and prepared for bed.

"We have six days to make sure the Starcraft is ready," Daeson announced.

"Starcraft! Really?"

"To win that competition I'm going to need something more than that bucket-of-bolts S-23 now, aren't I?"

"Yes!" Brae exclaimed. "Can't wait for tomorrow!"

As Daeson drew close to Ell Yon through the Protector once again, the fire of his former years as a Navi began to burn within him. He never imagined the turn of events that would allow him to train Brae as a Navi and considered himself fortunate. Her agility and knack for mastering the things of battle were thrilling to watch unfold. He couldn't help but think of Raviel. Brae was so much like her. He also saw himself in Brae, but there was a uniqueness that was all her own. Her ability to perfectly anticipate an outcome was uncanny, perhaps like the oracles of old. It was fascinating for Daeson to watch.

Although Daeson had kept his flying skills somewhat current through the geo-mapping jobs he took flying the S-23, it had been a long time since he had sat atop the power of a craft like the Starcraft. He, Brae, and Rivet opened the workshop's floor revealing the sleek form of what today's aero-tech pilots would call ancient. Memories and emotions rushed in on Daeson as he replayed the countless events where this beautiful machine had saved his life. Though it was ancient to the Rayleans today, for Daeson it was a recent past and the machine was just as powerful and as capable as ever.

The three of them looked down on the Starcraft from above, savoring the moment.

"Well...let's get started," Daeson stated. "Before we even turn on the electrical, we'll do a complete maintenance check on every system. Brae, Rivet has the entire set of tech schematics in his memory banks and can transfer whatever you're working on to one of the glass tablets. Hopefully the last twenty-six years haven't been too hard on her."

"If the festival isn't for three weeks, then why do we only have six days?" Brae asked.

"The entry requirements for a fighter craft are very strict. If necessary, the engine and weapons systems must be de-rated in order to comply with the maximum allowances. Some weapons must be disengaged completely, like those concussion missiles," Daeson explained, pointing to the four canards on each of the dual wings. "And the Starcraft far exceeds their competition allowances. Also, there can't be any other system that will unfairly advantage one pilot over the other...such as a cloaking technology."

Brae whistled. "I have a feeling that's going to be a problem."

"Yes, it is. That's why I need you and Rivet to figure out how to de-rate, hide, or possibly remove tech so we can qualify."

Brae pursed her lips and nodded. "Very well. Let's get to it."

Daeson watched Brae come alive as she poured herself into studying every system in great detail. It was like watching Raviel all over again. Rivet, of course, was an immense help making sure nothing was missed. It wasn't long before Brae had discovered the tech within the Starcraft that didn't fit with the original design. She went to Daeson and Rivet.

"This is one of the Malakian mods, isn't it?" she asked, turning the tablet toward them.

"It is," Rivet said. "And there are several more."

"I can tell," Brae responded. "If I can spot it, surely the festival mechtech inspectors will."

After considering multiple options, they landed on one that they all felt comfortable with that would disguise its intent. De-rating the weapons system and engine thrust was considerably easier than dealing with hiding the cloaking tech, but with long hours and creative design alterations, they succeeded.

By the end of the week, it was time to fire up the Starcraft. Despite Brae's protest, Daeson required the first flight to be solo. On Brae's signal, he fired up the engines, the roar of which brought chills to Daeson and a wide smile to Brae. After a full tech systems check, Daeson carefully pushed the throttles up until he had reached lift-off power. He felt the Starcraft begging to take to the skies, and so he did. Within a few minutes, he was screaming across the countryside, skimming the tops of the 400-foot tall Magalla Lumen trees. The thrill was so invigorating that Daeson had to remind himself to stay focused—after all this was a maiden flight of sorts. After fifteen minutes in the skies, he landed to pick up Brae for her initiation flight. To say that she was giddy was an understatement. As they navigated through some of the terrain they were familiar with, Daeson was reminded of the days when Brae was just a child, begging to join him on his geo-mapping expeditions.

"How are you feeling?" Daeson asked through their com link.

"Amazing!" she returned. "But it kind of feels like you're babying her."

Daeson smiled, knowing full well what Brae was up to. He slammed the throttles to full speed, yanking back on the stick to bring them into a pure vertical climb. The world beneath them shrank away at an exhilarating rate. He heard Brae grunt until the grav dampeners fully engaged.

"Woohoo!" she yelled.

He pulled back short of entering space for fear the Morian security vessels might intercept them and start making demands. Once level, he clicked the com button.

"She's yours, Sectator Starlore...you have the stick."

He felt Brae take control. He had taught her to pilot the S-23, which was a very maneuverable craft, but significantly reduced in power. He had let her fly a couple of different shuttles as well, but the Starcraft was an entirely different machine, sporting raw power, maneuverability, and tech, not to mention its firepower in the form of three major weapons systems. Of all the training as a Navi that Daeson was to give her, he knew that both of them would enjoy this the most.

When they landed, Brae was nothing but smiles that didn't dissipate. Rivet was waiting.

"I see you enjoyed your flight," he said as Brae finished descending the cockpit ladder.

"Oh, Rivet! It was the most exhilarating thing I've ever experienced! This is what I was born for!"

"It is thrilling indeed," Rivet replied.

When Daeson joined them on the ground, Brae enthusiastically wrapped her arms around his neck, giving him a kiss on his cheek.

"Thank you, Dad. That was just amazing. Even though I've logged many hours, I never imagined that flying could be that incredible."

Daeson returned the hug, unable to subdue his own foolish grin, cherishing this moment of Brae's enthusiasm for that which he too loved so dearly. He was already looking forward to the next flight, eager to teach her all he could.

On the day they delivered the Starcraft for inspection to meet the Magnifical Festival Aero-skills competition requirements, Daeson and Brae were both a bit anxious. The only facility on Rayl large enough to handle a competition like the aero-skills contest was the Jalem Interplanetary Spaceport positioned just on the city edge of Jalem. Even though it had been built to be the most advanced and largest spaceport in the Kayn System, the Morian Empire had recently expanded and upgraded it for their own purposes. It was elaborate and well equipped for just such an event as this. As they approached the spaceport, Daeson flew a wide arcing route over the area.

"What are we doing, Dad?" Brae asked.

"Getting a glimpse of Terrok's blasphemous work," he replied.

Just off the left wing was the signature pyramidal form of a Deitum Prime replication complex. "He's a puppet prefect accelerating the demise of our people," he muttered. "His blatant arrogance and rejection of Sovereign Ell Yon is abominable."

Brae was silent. The stirring in his soul was difficult to ignore, even though he was certain Brae wasn't sure what to make of it.

Daeson set the Starcraft down in his designated bay in one of the six massive hangars located on the Jalem spaceport. Their arrival immediately drew significant attention from not only their inspection team and a dozen more mechtechs that had spotted them land, but also from several other pilots that were present for their inspections. After exiting the cockpit, Daeson opened the cargo bay so Rivet could unfold and be available to help answer the inspectors' questions.

As the inspectors gathered, they began murmuring and whispering among themselves while circling the craft.

"She's a relic," one of the mechtechs said as she completed a brief walk-around. Daeson read her name tag— "Largo." Another young mechtech joined her. His tag read, "Foss."

"She's reliable," Daeson said. "An old Jyptonian Aerotech design that I was able to acquire."

"Aah, yes...that makes sense," the first mechtech said. "I love the history of spacecraft and thought I'd seen a variant of one similar to this," she added with a smile.

"It's almost as old as its pilot," Daeson heard one of the other pilots quip to another as they stood gawking at the Starcraft.

The mechtech named Largo smirked, then put her hand on the fuselage as she walked, almost stroking it to soothe the machine. Mechtech Foss walked behind Largo, seeming just as enamored with the Starcraft.

"No fluff...all machine," he said with a smile. "She's a beaut."

They turned to Daeson and Brae.

"Don't worry, we'll be nice to her," Largo said. "It'll take a couple of hours to confirm festival requirements are met. There's a pilot lounge just there. Please stay close in case we have any questions."

Daeson nodded his gratitude then lead Brae and Rivet to the lounge.

"Like I said, arrogant jet jockeys...every one," Brae said as she glared at the sniggering pilots in the adjacent bay. "Reminds me of Stryker all over again," she added.

Two hours later, Daeson, Brae, and Rivet were called back to the Starcraft. It was evident that one mechtech was leading the inspection.

"Who will be piloting during the competition?" he asked.

"I will," Daeson replied.

The man paused, raising an eyebrow. Daeson knew the man was concerned because he looked twenty years older than nearly every other pilot that was planning on competing.

"Have you ever participated in the Magnifical Aero-skills competition?"

"No."

"Any competition?"

"Just one...many years ago." Being judged too old to fly was new for Daeson. He made an extra effort to look pleasant.

The inspector let a smirk flash across his face. "I don't mean to patronize, but the competition can get pretty intense. This is more than just flying around a few anti-grav buoys. Besides this, we also have experienced aero-tech Raylean Guard pilots entered into the competition."

Daeson heard Brae snort next to him. He just smiled and nodded.

The man smirked again. "Well, anyway...we've confirmed your weapons and thrust have been appropriately de-rated, but there are two systems that are rather unique. We don't have the full scope on their functionality, so mechtech Largo would like some clarification."

The man stepped aside and let the lead mechtech forward. She looked at Daeson, offering a genuine smile. She seemed to struggle with how to start.

"Come this way," she said, taking them right to where Daeson knew she would.

Brae gave Daeson a concerning look as they approached the Malakian installed cloaking generator and image projection system.

"Can you tell us about this system? What does it do?" she asked.

"This Starcraft was designed with adaptive cloaking tech. This is just a system I acquired off world to enhance that just a bit," Daeson explained.

"We've completely disabled it regardless," Brae added.

The mechtech exchanged glances with Brae, then looked back to Daeson. He could tell she wasn't really buying it, or at least that he wasn't divulging the full truth. She was smart.

"I see," she said hesitantly.

"Since it appears to be tech that we aren't familiar with, we can't allow the craft to participate without a full set of technical diagrams for this system," the lead inspector declared.

"Seriously?" Brae exclaimed. "It's completely disabled," she protested.

The female mechtech looked apologetic.

"Excuse me, that won't be a problem," Rivet said stepping forward. "May I have your glass tablet?" he asked of the mechtech.

Largo handed it to Rivet. He extended an interface key from his forefinger and inserted it into her tablet's input port. Five seconds later he handed it back to her. The mechtech's eyes lit up as she swiped across multiple pages of diagrams. She showed it briefly to mechtech Foss who was looking on over her shoulder. He nodded, and Largo looked up.

"This will do," she said with a smile and a nod.

The lead inspector looked a bit disappointed. "Very well. You're cleared to compete. Check your schedule for your entry qualifying flight. You must deliver this craft to this bay two days prior to the start of the competition where it will undergo a final inspection and be quarantined. Do not make any adjustments to the operation of your ship's systems between now and then or you will be disqualified. Good luck."

Daeson caught just a hint of condescension in his last two words. Once they were left alone Brae turned to Rivet.

"Did you seriously give them the tech diagrams to Malakian cloaking technology?"

"Of course not, my lady. I rewrote the existing Jyptonian adaptive cloaking tech diagrams to make them look authentic."

Daeson eyed Rivet. "She seems pretty sharp, Rivet. Do you think she'll buy it?"

Rivet tilted his head. "Of course not," he replied. "I could tell by her biological responses that she was for us. She just needed some help to appease the chief inspector."

Daeson laughed. Brae stared at Rivet, shaking her head.

"Is anything the matter, my lady?" Rivet asked.

"I'm still trying to get over the fact that you're not Clunk. Impressive, Rivet...very impressive."

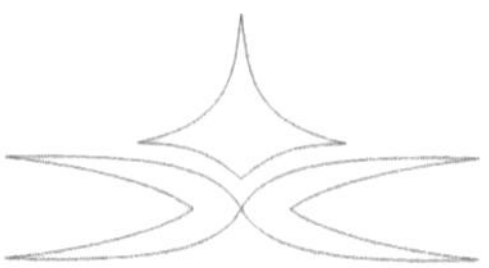

CHAPTER

14

Champion of the Skies

The Magnifical Festival was a celebration that had grown to a global event over the past century. Although the Morians had subjugated the Rayleans, using their productivity and tech prowess to advantage the empire's cause, they did not make slaves of Rayl. There were instances where the needs of the Morian Empire demanded such servitude, but on the whole, the Rayleans were free to conduct business and celebrate in their way as long as it did not disrupt Morian agendas or instigate rebellious acts against Chancellor Krish, First Leader of the Empire. And as such, the Magnifical Festival became an event to help the Rayleans forget their status as a conquered and occupied planet, at least for a few weeks.

Unfortunately, copious amounts of Deitum Prime and lascivious activities were becoming more and more prevalent, promoted and inspired by the heinous behavior of the Raylean puppet prefect, Amidus Terrok. Although Deitum Prime Sanctums had resurfaced from time to time after Navi Raviel's days of purifying the planet, Prime Sanctums were not currently sanctioned by the masses. This was a residual impact of the efforts of the Keepers and the Builders from centuries past. However, the power and lure of Deitum Prime on Rayl had not diminished. As tainted human nature would have it, the distribution and use were relegated to a more subtle but just as destructive nature, finding its way into the byways of Raylean culture. There, its presence was known and winked at, therefore making it impossible to target as an institution. The natural result of such covert use and acceptance was the hypocritical actions of all people, from the lowest commoner clear up to the Preeminent Keeper of the Protectors, Fasa Kylos.

For those whose hearts truly belonged to Sovereign Ell Yon, this was an erosion of the honorable Raylean culture from the inside out. It was intensely discouraging to watch the collapse of something good and right to an inevitable demise without knowing how to stop it. These were the people, studiers of the oracles of the past, that often found themselves asking, "Where have the Navi gone? When will be the coming of the Merchant?"

There were a hundred different facets to the weeks of celebration during the Magnifical Festival, but the favorite of all was the aero-skills competition, a three-week event with over 400 pilots vying to become the Magnifical Champion of the Skies. After having received approval for their Starcraft to be allowed in the competition, Daeson still had two weeks to brush up on his skills as a pilot.

"Dad, do you know what the aero-skills competition entails?" Brae asked the next morning as they were prepping for his first flight of the day.

"Yes, I'm aware. The inspector wasn't wrong…it's a very intense competition with extremely difficult routes and challenges to accomplish."

"I wouldn't say 'difficult'," Brae returned. "More like 'treacherous.'"

"Of the approximate 400 pilots that participate each year, there is an average of 8.4 deaths that occur," Rivet added.

"I didn't need to hear that," Brae said.

"Yes, but Master Daeson did," Rivet replied. "It is important to know exactly what risks you will be facing."

"Give me the criteria for the competition, Rivet," Daeson said.

"There are five routes that will be varied throughout the three-week competition. It is their intention that no pilot will ever fly the same route twice. For each qualifying flight, there will be ten pilots in a heat that will launch at the same time and fly the same route. Five pilots will be eliminated out of each heat. The first round will have 40 heats where 200 pilots will be eliminated. The second round will have 20 heats, then 10, 5 and 2. After five rounds, there will be ten to fifteen pilots left to fly in the championship flight. The championship flight will be a new route that none of the remaining pilots have seen. Points are awarded for each flight based on the speed of completion, finishing position, and weapons deployment accuracy. There are a limited number of target and defense drones in each flight, therefore the crafts leading the flight usually garner the most weapon deployment points."

"And the routes?" Brae asked. "What do we know about them?"

"They only publish general information about the routes, but based on previous years' competitions, an average route is 3,000 to 7,000 miles long and will traverse all three major continents and oceans on the planet. Each route will have five sub-courses, each requiring a particular set of obstacles, targets, and threats that must be navigated and overcome. Each route will take two to four hours to fly. Two imaging sensors are mounted on each competing craft, and there will be hundreds of imaging drones positioned along each route to record and broadcast the results to the world."

"And the prize?" Brae asked.

Daeson glared at Brae. "This isn't about a prize."

Brae smiled. "I figured that out, Dad. I'm just curious what's motivating the other 399 pilots."

"Ah."

"The winning pilot receives the esteemed 'Champion of the Skies' title awarded by Prefect Terrok, a banquet at the prefect's palace in his or her honor, and Morian credits equivalent to five years of wages. There is the additional prestige of being interviewed and lauded throughout the Kayn system via the broadcast network as the best pilot in the galaxy, which I'm sure is the motivation of Navi Starlore."

Brae laughed out loud. "Rivet...you have a sense of humor too?"

"I attempt having one from time to time, my lady."

Daeson didn't laugh. "Actually, that *is* my motivation." He looked at Brae. "The competition is solo of course, but would you like to catch the second seat while I train?"

"Absolutely!" she exclaimed.

"I've created a few simulated routes in remote regions that you can practice on," Rivet said. "Your navigational computer has been programmed with the routes. Be safe, my liege and my lady."

Daeson and Brae launched and flew Rivet's first route in just under three hours. On their return, the three of them debriefed each leg of the flight in detail. It took Daeson a few days to dust off his skills, and he had to admit that his age was a factor in his performance, but before long, he found his rhythm. Brae, of course, enjoyed every second of every flight, learning as much as she could from the master of the sky.

The day before the competition, Brae came to Daeson and asked him to walk with her through the nearby field and grove of trees...her favorite childhood place. The sun was just touching the horizon, casting brilliant orange and yellow flames of light on the undersides of remnant clouds. Not long into the walk, she grabbed Daeson's arm and pulled herself in tight to his side. Daeson smiled, putting a gentle hand on hers as they slowed to enjoy the charming evening sounds, fresh country air, and the spectacular beauty of the sunset.

"These last few weeks have been incredible," Brae said, stealing a glance up at Daeson as they walked. "I just want to thank you for showing me who you really are, Dad."

Daeson patted her hand.

"Ever since you told me that you were the Navi of our history, and of mom being Raviel, a Navi herself, I've struggled to put my life in perspective. From time to time I even struggled with my own doubts. But now, watching you...seeing Ell Yon at work," Brae paused, giving a deep sigh. "There's no going back. I wouldn't *want* to go back."

"You speak like a Navi," Daeson said. "But what I've shown you...taught you...is nothing compared to what's coming, my sweet daughter."

It had been weeks since Jeshu disappeared from their lives.

"How long do you think he'll be away?" she asked.

"I don't know," Daeson answered.

"Will he take on Terrok, or even the Morian Empire?" she asked.

"I don't know," Daeson said again. "Only he knows and will reveal his purpose in his time." Daeson stopped and turned to face Brae. "As hard as it is to fully let you go, it's time. Are you ready?"

Brae looked up at Daeson. She saw both warmth and concern in his eyes.

"I don't know, Dad, especially if I don't know what's coming."

Daeson stroked her cheek then pulled her into his chest.

"You're ready, Brae. The beginning is now," he said calmly.

And so is the end, he said to himself.

Daeson's heat in the first round matched him up with five other first-time entries and five very experienced Magnifical Aero-skills competitors, one of them being last year's champion. Their heat was the third of the day and began with dire news that two craft had collided in the first heat, killing both pilots. Although extra warnings were given, Daeson secretly suspected that Terrok loved the tragedy, for the thrill of potential death would add hype and draw more viewers to the contest.

Rivet and Brae served as Daeson's mechtech crew, but there were also festival mechtechs available to help should extraordinary situations occur. He noticed that the two mechtechs that had served on his inspection team had made it a point to check on them a couple of times during their preparation for launch. All pilots and their support crews were given the route and details of the sub-courses two hours before launch so they could prepare for the obstacles and challenges they would face. Rivet and Brae were instrumental in helping Daeson analyze and prepare for the three-hour flight. Each pilot was also allowed a com link to communicate with their support crew as well as a sensor and telemetry data link during the flight.

"Don't take risks, Dad," Brae warned. "All you have to do is finish in the top five and you move on to the next round."

Daeson put a hand on her shoulder. "Brae, I'll be okay. You don't need to worry."

Brae took a deep breath and nodded.

Daeson and his crew continued receiving ridicule and snide comments from other pilots and crews regarding his age and his Starcraft. They even criticized him for having an android as part of his crew. He had to calm Brae down multiple times to keep her focused.

"The greatest arrogance comes from ignorance," he told her.

"I just want to see their smug faces after they see how badly you've beaten them," she said with fire in her eyes.

"And with wisdom and age comes humility," Daeson added.

Brae huffed. "Yes...I know...I'm sorry."

The signal came for the third heat to begin. Brae and Rivet launched Daeson and soon he was in flight to the lineup. Amidst the cheers of over a quarter of a million people, ten craft were positioned one hundred feet off the ground line-abreast on the west end of the spaceport in what was called "The Boulevard." This was a custom-built arena with seating for 300,000 spectators. The grandstands lined both sides of the Boulevard which was the starting and finishing line for all of the routes orchestrated for the competition. This 500-foot space between the grandstands was dubbed "The Alley." Although this was the first day of the aero-skills competition where only round one heats would be flown, the arena seating was filled nearly to capacity and would be for every heat of every round. This is because the earlier round seating costs were much less expensive and attainable for the commoners compared to the later rounds and especially the championship, for which the cost of a Boulevard seat quadrupled. Therefore, the composition of the crowd shifted from commoners to the wealthy and prominent citizens as the competition progressed. If a competition was ramping up to be especially exciting, "Standing Admission" was offered to those who couldn't afford a grandstand seat. During inclement weather, two massive energy shields would activate, one for each of the grandstands bracketing the Boulevard. The actual spaceport terminal was located on the opposite side of the spaceport complex to allow a reduced operation while the competition was underway. The spaceport tower served as the contest observation and judging platform and began each race with both an audio and brilliant visual launch display sequence.

Daeson waited for the launch signal, his hand patiently resting on the throttles. The route for this round was 7300 miles in length with five sub-courses positioned on two continents. The first five hundred miles was a sprint before they would encounter their first sub-course. The entire spaceport tower column illuminated with three red flashes followed by a steady green, and the race was on. Ten spacecraft instantly accelerated out of their launch positions in the Alley to leave the Boulevard in a wash of engine plume.

Daeson slammed the throttles to full power. The acceleration was everything the Malakians had designed it to be, but once he reached competition max thrust, the engines throttled back to maintain within the specified limit. At nearly 3000 miles per hour and a few hundred feet off the ground, the terrain was a blur. Rivet had pre-tuned the Starcraft's radar for all avian life that might result in catastrophic results if he hit one. Daeson knew that he had to stay at the front of the pack to avoid the backwash of any leading craft, keeping an eye particularly on the previous champion.

In less than ten minutes, the pack of ten craft was approaching the first sub-course, a zigzagging passage through a huge forest of Magalla Lumen trees with a max course altitude of 300 feet. Since the tops of the trees were over 300 feet tall, there was no flying over the forest. Thirty-five target and defense drones were placed throughout the forest sub-course as well as five phase cannons which had reduced power that would momentarily disrupt a pilot's concentration and decrease his or her route score if hit by one.

Daeson and three other craft reached the forest first where one phase cannon unleashed a barrage of shots at each of them. There was an instant jockeying for position to avoid being hit and for a good entry vector to the forest. Daeson juked right, then barrel rolled over the top of another craft while pulling his throttles back to the entry velocity they had calculated he could safely navigate the forest. Even still, it would

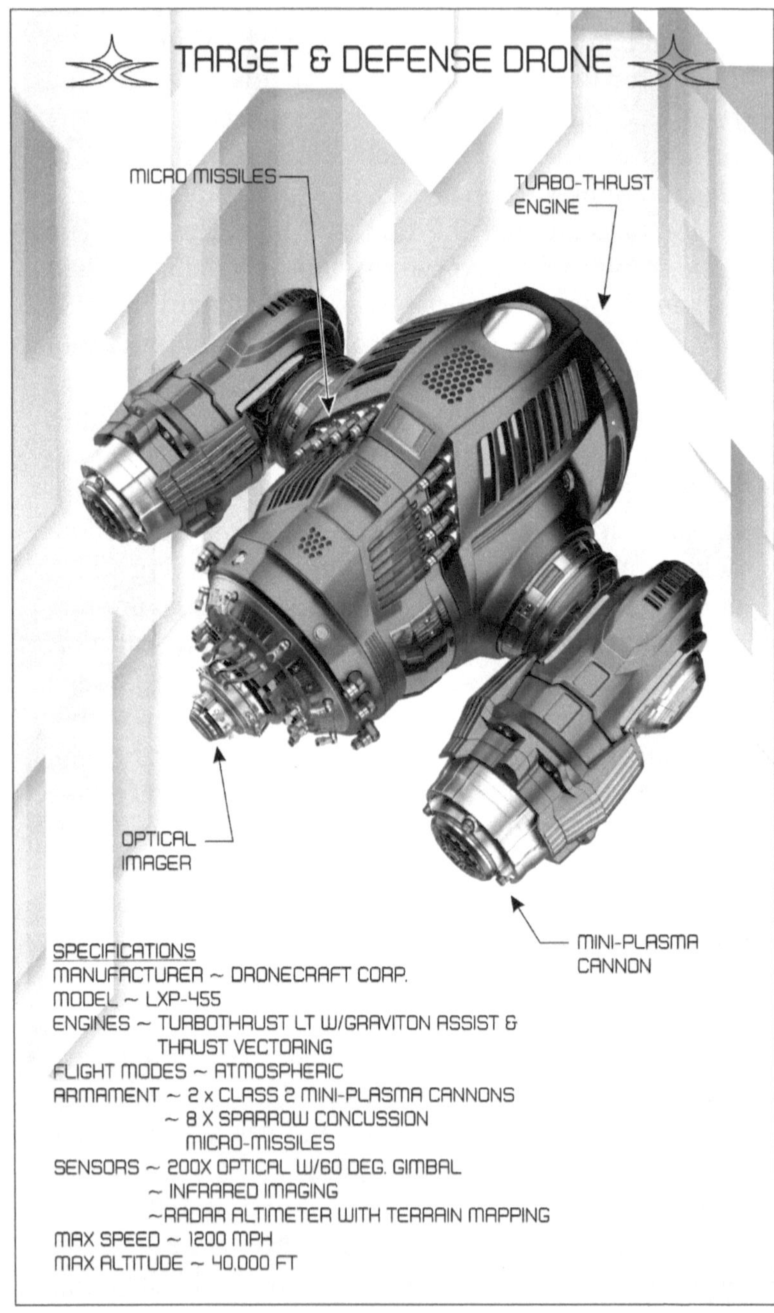

SPECIFICATIONS
MANUFACTURER ~ DRONECRAFT CORP.
MODEL ~ LXP-455
ENGINES ~ TURBOTHRUST LT W/GRAVITON ASSIST &
          THRUST VECTORING
FLIGHT MODES ~ ATMOSPHERIC
ARMAMENT ~ 2 x CLASS 2 MINI-PLASMA CANNONS
           ~ 8 X SPARROW CONCUSSION
            MICRO-MISSILES
SENSORS ~ 200X OPTICAL W/60 DEG. GIMBAL
          ~ INFRARED IMAGING
          ~RADAR ALTIMETER WITH TERRAIN MAPPING
MAX SPEED ~ 1200 MPH
MAX ALTITUDE ~ 40,000 FT

be a daunting challenge, having to make over thirty hard-G turns for this first sub-course. At over 500 miles per hour, Daeson entered the forest in third place. Besides the course obstacles and targets, there were other unplanned challenges. Daeson knew this particular forest was home to the Terridon, a massive flying reptile that was very territorial. Long ago, this was the same forest where he and Raviel had fought several and barely survived. Though their numbers had reduced over the centuries, they were still very much present here.

"We're scanning for Terridons," Brae radioed, keeping calls short and to the point so that Daeson could focus on flying and targeting with minimal distraction.

"Copy."

Daeson banked left, pulling hard on the stick to navigate the first 90-degree turn. Rolling out he targeted the first target drone and fired. His shot went wide as he prepped for the next turn. It took three more turns before he could relax and find his rhythm. For the next twelve minutes, Daeson scored 21 drone hits and avoided every phase cannon but one. He became frustrated with the craft he was following, having to go slower than anticipated to avoid colliding with him. And yet it wasn't reasonable to attempt passing within the narrow course walls lined with massive trees and with all the other distractions in play.

The next sub-course came seconds after exiting the forest—an inverted steep dive down into an adjacent canyon that ran for 200 miles to the Medda Ocean. Once again, a route altitude cap forced the pilots to fly subsurface and navigate the treacherous jagged canyon walls. Daeson's last twenty years as a geo-mapper gave him a significant advantage for this sub-course, but he had to adjust for the considerable increase in speed he was flying with the Starcraft compared to the S-23. Once in the canyon, Daeson waited for the right opportunity to attempt passing the two leading craft. One of them, last year's champion, attempted to squeeze him between a towering spire and his own craft to negate his attempt, but Daeson deftly performed an inverted negative-G barrel role underneath the threatening craft. Dropping beneath his competition and being inverted, Daeson nearly skimmed his canopy along the surface of the river at the bottom of the canyon. Unknown to Daeson, that risky move was captured perfectly by a broadcasting drone, causing the watching world to erupt in cheers and exultations for Daeson. It was the beginning of his rise to popularity with the masses. Within minutes, the number of viewers for the third-heat flight doubled as the global spectators shared the thrilling clip with friends and families everywhere.

Daeson was able to easily keep his lead through the canyon. With two sub-courses complete, three more remained—a low-level flight on the ocean along a volcano-active reef with sporadic lava and geyser eruptions, a subterranean flight through a massive crystal cave, and an intense aerobatic flight through antigravity fields with floating islands. Throughout the remainder of the route, Daeson exchanged leads with the former champion multiple times. And although neither of them would be eliminated in this round, Daeson knew that this would set the tone for the rest of the competition. The back-and-forth battle for the lead also roused the world to a near frenzy watching an unknown pilot with a craft that was a relic from the past threaten their former champion.

In the antigravity field, Daeson was king, and his dominance as a premier fighter pilot became obvious to the planet. With a short 75-mile sprint home, Daeson crossed the finish line to the riotous roars of every man, woman, and child attending as well as millions more across the planet.

Every heat winner was given the honor of landing on a special platform in the Boulevard before the attending crowd of 300,000 people. This gave the broadcast specialists the opportunity to ask a few questions about the flight in support of the Magnifical Festival spirit.

With the guidance of the festival mechtechs, Brae and Rivet helped Daeson land his Starcraft on the winner's platform. He was oblivious to the thunderous applause and cheers until his engines shut down and his canopy came up. The cacophony of sound was deafening. As he stepped off the ladder, Brae greeted him with a quick hug.

"You were amazing, Dad…and they love you!"

Daeson looked up and down the Boulevard, his spirit falling with each passing second. He had been here before, for he knew how fickle his people could be. He knew the state of their hearts. Memories of him, Raviel, Tig, Kyrah, and hundreds of other valiant servants making gallant efforts, often paying the ultimate sacrifice to turn the hearts of the people back to Sovereign Ell Yon, filled his mind. Where they had failed, could Jeshu succeed? It was hard not to be pessimistic.

Daeson and Brae walked to the edge of the platform while Rivet remained with the Starcraft. The platform was positioned midway down the premier side of the arena grandstand seating. Just off the landing platform was an elevated honors stage with seating placed in a semi-circular fashion round about it for 500 additional people. These were reserved for the Raylean elite and esteemed political and military figures. Since this was just one of the heats for round one, there were only a handful of elite present with a few more seats occupied by tournament officials.

As Daeson approached the honors stage, the voice of the Boulevard announcer filled the space, but his words were nearly drowned out by the cheering crowds.

"Elias Thornton, victor of heat three in round one!" an announcer exclaimed, building on the already energetic crowd. "Now our broadcast specialist, Zee Palla, will ask Elias, pilot of the Starcraft, a few questions."

Daeson handed Brae his helmet as he stepped up to the waiting broadcast specialist. The crowd hushed to silence, as did the millions across the planet. Zee Palla smiled, eager to capture this moment with an unknown underdog for a world of onlookers. This was as much her moment as it was Daeson's. Silent video drones were positioned around the stage so that anything Zee Palla or Daeson said or did was captured and broadcast.

"Elias, it is fair to say that you are virtually an unknown here at the Magnifical Festival, having never competed before. Despite your age," she said with a gleam in her eye, "that is, compared to the other pilots, you won the flight today, even defeating last year's champion...simply remarkable!"

Cheers rose up, and she waited for them to subside. "Unlike every other pilot in the competition, you have no listed sponsor. For whom do you fly?"

The crowd hushed to absolute silence. Daeson took a few seconds to glance from one end of the Boulevard to the other, capturing the eye of every single person present. Then his gaze fell to the black pyramidal structure in the background towering above all other structures in the area…Terrok's Deitum Prime replication complex. His heart became heavy with grief at the sight of it. When the moment was right, he spoke.

"I fly for one and only one…the Immortal Sovereign Ell Yon."

His response left Zee Palla speechless and the crowd dazed. He turned and began walking back to the Starcraft.

"Wait," Zee Palla called, "I have more questions."

But Daeson didn't turn back. Instead, slowly the crowd began cheering once more until over the course of the next 60 seconds, they were at a full roar. At the Starcraft, Brae was smiling ear to ear.

Once Daeson had launched to return the Starcraft back to their designated hangar bay, Brae and Rivet recovered their equipment and jumped on the mechtech hover ferry that had brought them over. It was piloted by mechtech Foss with lead mechtech Largo in the front seat beside him. She turned about to speak to Brae.

"Your pilot…your Starcraft," her eyes glanced to Rivet, "your android—there's something…unique about all of this."

Brae noticed that Foss had leaned his head back to listen as well.

"I've never seen anyone fly like that," she continued. "What's happening? Who is he really?"

"Elias is my father," Brae explained. "He has served Ell Yon before and has a message for our people. Be patient, I'm sure there's more to come."

Largo stared at Brae for a moment, then turned back to face the front.

"At last, Rivet," Brae said quietly. "He will once again speak truth to the Raylean people."

Rivet was silent for a moment.

"Yes, my lady. But I'm afraid your enthusiasm may be misplaced."

Brae's stomach turned, knowing that Rivet was as Daeson had said, much more than he seemed.

"What do you mean, Rivet?"

He then turned his head to look at Brae.

"There is power that does not want to hear this truth, and I fear this will not end well."

Brae's former state of glee was crushed in a moment. *How could this be? How could such applauded victory be so quickly turned to demise?* she wondered. She tried to be encouraged by reminding herself that Rivet was still just an android, not an oracle, but it did little to dissipate the gathering cloud of darkness over her soul.

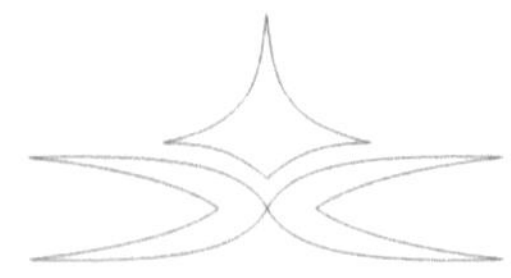

CHAPTER

15

The Eyes of Power

Because there were so many heats to complete in the first round of the competition, Daeson didn't fly again until the fourth day of the tournament. During those days, investigation and speculation by the broadcast specialists turned into a global phenomenon. Remarkably, they were able to discover almost nothing about Daeson's former life or his family history. The mystique around him built massive amounts of anticipation for round two of the competition. No longer did the other pilots jeer or belittle him because of his age. They had all watched the recorded footage of his flight and stood amazed, offering instant respect for the man and his Starcraft.

After Rivet's warning, Brae considered talking with her father about her concerns but anticipated his response and decided against it. She tried to envision a hundred different scenarios, but each one ended with the entire planet returning to serve Ell Yon and welcoming Jeshu as their world leader. Such an outcome wasn't unprecedented in their history. Raviel had done it. Daeson had done it. Surely Jeshu could and would do it. Wasn't that the whole point of his mission...to revive their people's faith in Ell Yon?

For the second round of the competition, Daeson was placed in the fifth heat, usually the most watched flight because of the timing in the day. But with the anticipation of watching him fly already at a climax, Brae was pretty sure he could have flown in the middle of the night and garnered the same turnout.

Once the route was issued, Daeson, Brae, and Rivet studied, analyzed, and briefed, coming up with a plan for each sub-course. Daeson climbed the ladder to his Starcraft and began strapping in. Brae climbed up after him, standing on the ladder to make sure he was set.

"You know...I thought we agreed you wouldn't take any risks," she said, handing him his helmet.

"Actually, sweetheart, that's what you suggested, but I never agreed to it," he said with a smile. "I'll be careful, Brae, but you know what's at stake. You don't gain anything without taking risks."

Brae leaned into the cockpit and gave him a kiss on his cheek.

"Do be careful."

Twenty minutes later, the signal to launch was given, and ten round-two crafts blasted forward out of the Boulevard in a sprint to their first sub-course. This route was 500 miles longer than Daeson's first flight and had sub-courses that were just as challenging. Treacherous narrow-channel runs through Waterfall Canyon, heart-pounding ridge crossings over Glacier Mountain, tight turns and high-G maneuvers through Rock Tower Gardens, and a vertical climb to a short slipstream jump arriving at the moon, Barra, for a low gravity flight through multiple deep craters and trenches were just four of the five sub-courses.

Brae watched with bated breath as her father took the lead after the second sub-course, tallying record-setting scores by his speed and by hitting nearly every target drone while finishing far ahead of the other nine pilots. Particularly unusual for round two of the aero-skills competition, the arena was filled to capacity, and the planet watched to see for themselves if the grand stories of this obscure geo-mapping pilot were exaggerated or indeed accurate. They were not disappointed.

When Brae escorted Daeson to the Boulevard honors stage, the thunderous applause and cheering did not abate. The announcer tried several times to gain the crowd's attention but to no avail. Unlike round one, the elite seating around the honors stage was over half full. Brae gazed across the mass of people, this time with a tempered response, seeing as she imagined Daeson was seeing. She glanced at him, trying to discern his countenance. Unaffected by the overwhelming adoration, she could see concern behind his stoic eyes. Only when Daeson stepped onto the honors stage and came to Zee Palla did the crowd relent of its cheers, for they were eager to hear more from this mysterious pilot.

Zee Palla's smile was broader than ever as she addressed the largest audience of her career.

"Elias Thornton, you have once again amazed us with your superior piloting in round two of the tournament. The planet is eager to know who you are and why you have waited so long to share your incredible skills with us. Please tell us, where did you learn your piloting skills?"

As before, Daeson waited until the silence in the air was almost eerie.

"People of Rayl, turn your hearts back to Sovereign Ell Yon. You have made a mockery of his precepts, basking in the immersion of Deitum Prime. Sorrow your hearts and return to Ell Yon for he has not turned a blind eye to your debauchery, nor does he wink at your façade of obedience to his oracles' teachings and commands. Sovereign Ell Yon is not far away as you have come to believe...he is here...among us even now."

Zee Palla and every soul in the Boulevard and everyone watching the broadcast looked on in utter silence. In just a few words, Daeson had crushed the jubilant spirit of the festival, bringing the harsh message of truth from the heart of Ell Yon to their ears.

Ten seconds after Daeson finished, the first jeers came. Zee Palla attempted a follow-up question to the one that Daeson had ignored, but she was so flustered by the moment that her words were nearly incoherent. Pockets of rebuttals rippled through the crowd as the fervor of anger intensified. Brae's heart quickened. *Why this message and why now?* she wondered. Surely there was a better way to turn the hearts of the people. This clearly wasn't working.

Daeson stood immovable, absorbing the rebuke as many in the crowd stood to shout and curse at him. The ruckus escalated until festival security became nervous at the commotion. Then in one quick deliberate motion, Daeson thrust his open hand into the air, and the Protector blasted forth a brilliant vertical column of blue Immortal energy reaching far above the heights of the Boulevard stadium seating. Every soul hushed to frightened silence as they beheld the power of Ell Yon through the Protector for the first time in their lives. Daeson held the burning tower of Ell

Yon's judgment for ten long seconds, letting fear and astonishment grip the hearts of Rayl. Then in an instant, Daeson squeezed his hand into a fist, and the column of purging energy exploded outward in a wave of resonant power that pierced through the bodies of every single attendee and beyond. It was terrifying to watch as it continued in all directions outward at blinding-fast speed across the planet, stopping nowhere and opening the eyes and ears of those it pierced.

At that moment, every person fell back into their seats, mouths open, and eyes full of fear. Zee Palla stumbled backward, falling onto her backside as she tried to scoot away from Daeson.

"A Navi has come!" one woman shouted.

Shouts of alarm and exclamation echoed throughout and across the Boulevard. Daeson went to stand over Zee Palla, stark fear on her face. He reached down, offering a hand to her. Timidly she took it, and he lifted her to her feet.

"Are you okay?" he asked.

She nodded nervously, looking down at the hand that held hers and the Protector on his arm.

"Who are you?" she asked with trembling voice.

Daeson said nothing. He turned and joined Brae back on the platform with Rivet and the Starcraft. A few minutes later, they were back at their hangar bay preparing to leave. Brae was silent until they were in the speeder and nearly home.

"I don't suppose you could prepare me a little the next time?" she asked.

"I've asked Ell Yon the same thing many times before," he said quietly. "What I say isn't planned, Brae. Ell Yon gives it to me as I speak." He looked over at her. "It will be the same for you one day."

"I see," she said. "I heard some of the people claiming you are the ancient Navi Starlore reborn."

Daeson laughed. "Imagine that."

The Sovereign Sanctum of Jalem was the premier sanctum on the planet. For devoted followers of Ell Yon, visiting this Sanctum at least once a year was an important part of their commitment as a Raylean. This Sanctum of Jalem was where the Master Builder of the Protectors, Krisha Monae, conducted the operation of replicating Protectors by acquiring omegeon from the collector array and infusing the particles into the micro chambers to make the Immortal technology functional. This was also the chief operating office for the Preeminent Keeper, Fasa Kylos, and his associate Keepers, managing the tight security and distribution of each of the six Protectors to other key Sovereign Sanctums around the Planet. Much to the chagrin of both the Builders and the Keepers, unexplained damage to many of the omegeon collectors in the array at the Omega Nebula had occurred just when they were about to collect and attempt to create a seventh Protector.

"Have you heard, Preeminent?" a Keeper Associate asked when he found Fasa Kylos about to don the Jalem Sanctum's most treasured possession, the first Protector, or so they believed.

"Heard what?" Kylos snapped.

"Forgive me for the intrusion, Preeminent, but a Navi has appeared at the aero-skills competition wearing—"

"A Navi?" Kylos exclaimed turning to face the man. "Impossible! A Navi must wear a Protector and we have them all accounted for and secure."

"But Preeminent...he *was* wearing a Protector!"

Kylos's face turned stone cold.

"It must be a forgery...no omegeon in the microchamber," Kylos contemplated.

"No, Preeminent. By this man, the Protector has awakened...like the times of old."

Kylos's brow furrowed. "Who else saw this?"

"The whole world, Preeminent...the whole world!"

Kylos glared at the Associate. "Gather the council!"

Prefect Terrok was renowned for his wild mood swings which invariably led to a constant elimination and promotion of advisers and administrators. This fostered a significant level of fear and anxiety in all who served him. Since the Omega Event, he'd had no less than five first advisors. The most recent, a man by the name of Aunder, was the most successful of them all with a tenure of over one year. The man had the ability to navigate Terrok's rash emotionality, feeding him only information that tended to subdue and appease him.

Years earlier, when Terrok in his paranoia had initiated a dark plan to eliminate the potential rise to power of a prefect foretold by multiple oracles, he had then followed the execution of the mission by purging all who were privy to the plot. As a result, there was no one left to identify anyone associated with that horrific event. It was well understood that the topic of such a morbid plan and the subsequent purging of his staff was never discussed in the presence of Prefect Terrok nor with each other for that matter. When the occasion arose for Terrok to be informed of unwelcome news impossible to hide, Aunder's quasi bold, matter-of-fact approach seemed to work best, but it was frightening to watch, not knowing if Terrok would unleash his rage on the man at any moment.

Inside the luxurious walls of the prefect's palace, there was tumultuous activity as the current advisers and administrators met with Prefect Terrok to discuss the recent phenomenon that had happened after the round-two flight of the aero-skills competition. Terrok was standing in front of a large wall that was displaying exquisite graphics from edge to edge.

"Who is this man?" Terrok asked, a smile on his face as he watched highlights from the flight. "He's a flying genius! And look at how many people are attending and watching my festival!" he exclaimed pointing to an inset on the display showing a variety of statistics.

"We're not sure, Prefect," an advisor offered. "He seems to be a nobody...an old geo-mapper with a home on the outskirts of Jalem."

Terrok shook his head. "Oh...he's much more than that, I promise you. I must meet him! Finally, we have a real hero of the competition we can applaud. Bring him to the palace to enjoy our evening entertainment."

The advisors and administrators looked at each other, each waiting for the other to speak up. When there was no reply, the prefect turned around, eyes filling with anger at their dismissal of his command. Terrok's Deitum Prime-assimilated body was a strange and frightful wonder. Born a small, slender man, he found the accentuated enhancements of Deitum Prime a delightful alternative to his natural state. Nearly grotesque bulging muscles rippled across his body, especially when anger threatened to unleash the full effect of Dracus's curse. His mind teetered on the edge of maniacal responses if not kept in check by his entourage.

"You may not want to do that, Prefect," Aunder finally spoke up. He walked to the display and motioned for the video to advance to the end. There, in larger-than-life form stood Elias Thornton.

"—you have made a mockery of his precepts, basking in the immersion of Deitum Prime. Sorrow your hearts and return to Ell Yon for he has not turned a blind eye to your debauchery, nor does he wink at your façade of obedience to his oracles' teachings and commands."

Terrok swiped, and the wall went black. He stood still as did his advisors and administrators.

"There's more, Prefect."

"I don't want to see it," Terrok said through clenched teeth, his bulging neck and facial muscles quivering.

"You...really need to, sir," Aunder dared say.

The advisor carefully went to the display. Reactivating it, he positioned the video, then let it run. Terrok stood in awe as he saw the Protector explode in blue flames of power up and then onto the people. The advisor then shut down the display, turning to face the fury of the prefect.

"The Keepers and the Builders have no idea who he is," another advisor voiced.

At that, Terrok's face lightened, then a smile began to spread across his face until the man was near ecstatic.

"Those crooked cronies don't know who this man is?" he exclaimed.

Aunder slowly shook his head, unsure how to react to his prefect's growing elation. Terrok laughed out loud, clapped his hands, then laughed some more until he could hardly contain himself, nearly dancing about in delight. Although his advisors had grown accustomed to Terrok's manic mood swings, this was certainly unexpected.

"This is wonderful," he wheezed. "We'll use this!" he shouted. "This will be the best festival in decades! He's a broadcasting dream, drawing millions of viewers and filling the Boulevard to capacity already in round two."

Terrok's advisors and administrators tried to rally with the prefect with fake smiles and half-hearted laughter, but when Terrok left the room to enjoy his mirth, his entourage immediately fell silent and somber.

"Navi and wayward prefects are historically disastrous," one of the advisors whispered.

Aunder stared at the door Terrok had departed through.

"Yes."

Rhett's family was overjoyed to see him. He did his best to explain the circumstances by which he had found himself unable to contact or communicate for so long. Although they didn't fully understand, they honored his silence on much of his story, knowing his character and trusting in him. Rhett gave himself a few days to relax and try to make the adjustment from his absurd previous three years to whatever this was going to be. The truth was, he felt utterly lost for the first time in his life. Ever since he was just a boy, he'd wanted to fly fighter craft—it was in his blood. He came from a long line of Raylean Guard pilots dating back hundreds of years. Now, with the world thinking he was dead, what could he do? One week into his return, he began looking for something productive to apply himself toward, but nothing held his interest. He even applied for a pilot geo-mapping position, but his introductory flight felt so pointless. In a way, he felt as if these last three years had ruined him. Eventually he reached out to Major Kamp, searching for a thread of hope that he might rejoin his squadron.

"What happened three years ago is never discussed in the squadron," Kamp had told him. "Everyone thinks you're dead, so if you show up now, there's no telling what kind of storm would be unleashed. No one's looking for you, so you'd better stay away for your own sake."

Even though the conversation ended with Kamp promising to keep in touch and even hinting at some information he'd discovered, the exchange brought Rhett to a whole new low, discouragement saturating him. He often found himself taking long evening walks through the city of Brohn, aimlessly wandering through different sections of the city. It was as if he was looking for something. Whatever it was, he knew not.

After a few weeks of living an ambiguous life, he was becoming frustrated and more confused by his inability to respond to anything with some semblance of motivation. One evening, Rhett ventured into the heart of Brohn, wandering through the City Central Gardens Park, a twenty-acre wooded and flowered atrium offering a stark contrast to the glass, metal, and stone edges of the cityscape. Just when he was ready to turn back home, he passed a stone bench that called for him. He sat, running his hand along the smooth worn edges of the quiet companion to any who would tarry with it. Feeling despondent, he began to contemplate his sorry state, wondering where his life would now take him since his life-long dream to fly as a fighter pilot in the Raylean Guard was over forever. With head in hands, Rhett wasn't sure just how long he had wallowed in his self-pity. He only just realized that someone had sat down on the bench when he heard a deep voice next to him.

"Why are you here? Your life isn't over…it's just beginning."

Rhett laughed within himself, suspecting that some elderly gentleman who spent his empty life walking his poonta canine in the park was about to share some philosophical insight.

"And how would you know—" Rhett began, lifting his head to look the man's way, but he stopped midsentence. The eyes that were looking back at him were made of galactic fire, his gaze as firm as steel. The man didn't move…didn't smile.

"Who are you?" he asked.

The man stared at him a moment longer then stood.

"Open your eyes, Stryker. There are people that need you…and you need him."

Without another word, the man left. Rhett didn't even consider following—one doesn't follow a man like that. The encounter deeply troubled Rhett for many reasons, perhaps the greatest of all was having to face the likelihood that whoever the man was, he didn't seem to be from this world…or reality. Facing such a possibility would force Rhett to reconsider his carefully crafted beliefs regarding reality and superstition. And worst of all…that Brae Thornton might be right.

In the three days that followed, the hype over Daeson's competition performance and even more so, his message, had traveled to every hall and home on the planet. People began showing up at Daeson's country home, some to rebuke him, some to interview him, most to hear more of his message from Ell Yon and to follow him. Brae was disquieted, for in just a few days, the serenity of their country lives had been shattered, and she realized that it was probably gone forever. It dawned on her that she was quickly becoming an integral part of one of the stories of Navi Starlore much like she had listened to and dreamed of many times as a child and a youth. She also concluded that living such a saga wasn't as romantic as hearing about it. In fact, it was everything but.

By the time Daeson's heat for round three was to begin, there was a near frenzy. Festival security had to post extra guards at their hangar bay just so they could arrive and prepare for the flight.

"Dad...what's happening?" Brae asked.

Daeson put a hand on Brae's shoulder. "Don't be troubled. Rayl is being prepared for the Merchant. They are hungry for the truth."

Brae put a hand on his arm, feeling the Protector beneath his sleeve. It eased her mind knowing her father had the protection of Ell Yon with him. She nodded.

Daeson launched and twenty minutes later they were given the green light. Although these pilots were clearly more experienced than those of his previous heat, by the beginning of the fourth sub-course, Daeson was clearly leading the pack, flying maneuvers and hitting target and defense drones like no one had ever seen before. After landing in the Boulevard, Brae and

Rivet met him at the platform amidst riotous cheers and fanfare. Brae was nervous.

"Dad, the honors stage seating is full of Builders and Keepers," she said, looking that direction. "And Prefect Terrok and his advisors are there too!"

The news didn't seem to alarm Daeson a bit. She grabbed his arm.

"Just tell me this is going to be okay," she said. "That *you* are going to be okay."

She looked up into his eyes and could already see the spark of Ell Yon. He offered the faintest of smiles, then walked to the honors stage. The announcer didn't even try to proclaim him as winner, for the crowd wouldn't allow it. The sonic assault of 300,000 cheering voices was almost painful. Zee Palla was waiting, attempting to smile but failing. She held tight to her own hands, trying to keep them from shaking. Brae saw Terrok lean over and whisper something into the ear of his first advisor. Once Daeson was center stage, the roar of the crowd hushed to silence. He scanned the Boulevard from one end to the other.

"Do not cheer for me, fellow Rayleans. I am but a messenger of things to come. There is darkness in the halls of Rayl...in the chambers of our Sovereign Sanctums."

Brae bit her lip as she watched the Preeminent Kylos and his Keepers grow red with anger. Daeson pointed a finger at the elite...at Kylos.

"The hypocrisy of the Keepers and the Builders will come to an end, and you will see the coming of one to whom I cannot compare to even a single hair on his head. Turn from your love of Deitum Prime before it's too late. Ell Yon is here...he is now...and he will expose the lies and deception of all who falsely claim to obey the oracles and his precepts. You have been warned!"

There was no eruption of applause nor cheers that filled the air as Daeson stared back at the people and their leaders. Kylos slowly stood, fury on his face. Brae could see he was eager to rebuke Daeson, but the whisper of another Keeper in his ear stayed his tongue. He glanced about the watching masses, then stormed off the platform seating. The rest of the Keepers and Builders quickly followed. Brae noticed that Prefect Terrok wore a pompous smile.

"Rivet, we need to get out of here as fast as possible."

"Yes, my lady," Rivet replied. "I agree."

As Daeson left the honors stage, the crowd awakened from their stupor, at first with reserved applause, but with each passing moment the roar of the crowd intensified. By the time Daeson was climbing into the Starcraft to return to the hangar bay, the crowd was standing in an ovation that didn't diminish. Festival security had to contain a throng of people from trying to come to him.

"I'll meet you at the hangar bay," Brae shouted as she signaled Daeson to spool up the Starcraft engines and launch. When it was time to make their way to the hover ferry, the frenzy of the crowd was so intense that she and Rivet were cut off. Rivet stepped forward.

"Thornton," Brae heard a familiar voice call out.

She turned to see mechtechs Largo and Foss motioning for them to come their way. They had sequestered a security detail to help forge a way out.

"This way!" Largo shouted.

"Come on, Rivet," Brae said, quickly making her way to them.

With the help of the security detail, they were able to load into the hover ferry and make their way out of the Boulevard.

Largo left her seat to sit on a chair across from Brae. "Your father...who is he really?"

Brae hesitated, but Largo's eyes pleaded with her.

"Are the rumors true? Is he a Navi? We must know," Largo added, glancing toward Foss who was flying the ferry.

"Yes," Brae said. "He is a Navi."

Largo's eyes lifted with hope. She reached for Foss's shoulder, and the man briefly turned his head to acknowledge a mutual satisfaction at hearing her words.

"What's to happen?" she asked.

"I'm not sure," Brae said. "I just know that he would say there is one much greater than he who is coming soon."

Largo's brow furrowed with confusion, then her countenance began to dawn with illumination.

"We should move quickly, my lady," Rivet said as Foss brought the hover ferry to a stop at the hangar bay where Daeson was just now exiting the Starcraft.

Brae stood to disembark, but Largo caught her hand.

"Thank you. There are many who've waited so long for this good news."

Brae smiled, squeezing her hand.

The activity at the hangar bay was better than at the Boulevard but still uncomfortable as pilots, mechtechs, and security personnel began closing in on them. Daeson, Rivet, Largo, and Foss made quick work in recovering the Starcraft as Brae focused on packing up essential equipment. She reached for the handle of a case containing her flight processor interface module but as she did, a strong hand grabbed it ahead of hers. She looked up to see the face of the man who had startled her.

"Hello, Thornton," Rhett said with a smile as he lifted the case. "I got this for you."

Rhett Stryker was the last person on the planet that she expected to see. A flurry of thoughts and feelings rushed through her, none of them very positive. She hadn't yet sorted out the rebuke Daeson had given her on Rhett's behalf which tended to further frustrate her. She grabbed the case from Rhett.

"Don't bother yourself, Stryker—I got it."

She walked quickly to their speeder to load the case into the storage compartment.

"Suit yourself. I just wanted to help," he said following behind her. He turned his head left and right.

"Where's Jeshu?" he asked.

Brae pressed the panel to open the speeder's compartment.

"Not sure...haven't seen him in weeks," she replied.

"Hmm." Rhett looked unusually unsure of himself. "You have quite a show going on here."

Brae finished loading the case into the speeder, then turned to face him.

"Show?" Brae crossed her arms while turning to face him. She immediately could feel her previous snippy self vying for control. She despised this version of herself, but Rhett just had a knack for evoking this response from her. The last few weeks had been such a wonderful return to her normally peaceful and self-controlled Brae.

"What are you doing here, Stryker?" she asked.

"Hey...I just thought I'd check to see if you and your father are doing okay."

"I'm fine...he's fine." Brae flashed a fake smile. She didn't have time for this. She just wanted to go home.

Rhett stared back at her, but not with the resentful look she was used to seeing in him. He glanced toward

Daeson who was just finishing a final inspection of the Starcraft.

"Geo-mapper, huh?"

Brae followed his gaze to look at her father. "He is," Brae replied, "and a bit more."

"A bit more? Why didn't you tell me he was a Navi?"

She looked back at him. "I thought that would have been obvious," she said tersely.

Rhett opened his mouth to respond, then stopped and forced a smile instead.

"Well...I don't know where this is going, but he's caused quite a stir."

Brae glanced at the gathering crowd, many of them shouting out for Daeson to come and speak to them. She then felt a hand on her shoulder. It was Rhett's.

"Thornton...if you need help, just let me know."

Brae looked at his hand, then back to Rhett's eyes. *Was he serious?* she thought. *What was he up to?*

"Thanks, but we'll manage," she replied, desperately wishing he would move his hand.

Seemingly sensing her discomfort, he immediately dropped his hand, pretending to punch her in the arm to assuage the increasingly awkward moment they were having, but that only made it worse.

"Okay then...good luck with the next round," he said, turning away.

Brae tilted her head, feeling really weird. Rhett didn't look back as he disappeared into the gathering crowd.

"Are you ready, Brae?" Daeson asked.

She jolted.

"Yes! I can't wait to get out of here."

Rhett walked away from that extremely awkward encounter with Brae feeling two feet tall. He wished he had never even talked to her now. These past weeks had been a time of serious self-reflection. Without a squadron to be part of, and still trying to stay under the radar, he had been forced to consider all that had happened and his response to it. Leaving Jeshu and Brae, even though life with her was pure misery, had been much harder than he ever imagined. He attributed it to the fact that as captain of the Event mission, those two were the only other survivors, and he had felt a sense of obligation to them. He figured that the longer he was away from them, the less he would feel that pull on himself. But that was not the case, and he began to wrestle within himself. Some nights were long and frustrating as he tossed upon his bed dealing with what he considered misplaced loyalty and obligation. It came to a head when he watched the first round of the Magnifical Aero-skills broadcast. Rhett just about fell out of his chair as he watched Elias Thornton fly that archaic Starcraft to a stunning victory. Then after watching round two, the moment Brae's father opened his mouth to speak to the people, Rhett had been compelled to offer help despite Brae's dislike of him and probable refusal should he offer. That, and the eerie encounter with the park visitor.

I'll give this one honest try, he had thought. *Then at least I'll be free of her forever.*

And so he did, and it went as awfully as he had imagined.

"That's it...I'm done. Now I can get on with my life," Rhett muttered as he walked away.

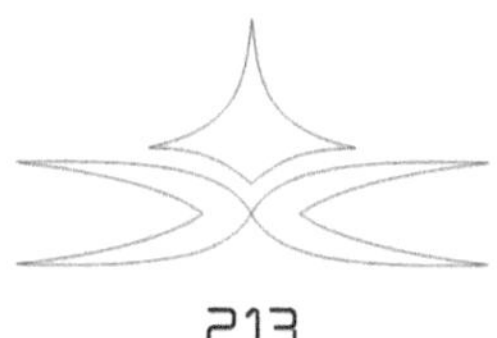

CHAPTER

15

The Consequence of Truth

Round four was Daeson's most challenging flight thus far with higher skilled pilots to defeat and sub-courses that were slightly out of his element, but by the end of the fifth sub-course, he had garnered enough of a lead to soundly defeat all ten pilots in his heat. The message he delivered afterward was much different than anything Ell Yon had given him to speak thus far. Once again, Brae was as stunned as the audience he spoke to.

There wasn't a single empty seat in the Boulevard, nor in the platform elite seating area around the stage. In fact, there were people standing in every square foot of space that had visual access to the stage that Daeson was now approaching. Zee Palla had learned her role and seemed much more comfortable. She smiled as

Daeson approached, then stepped back and to the side, allowing him to be front and center. The Keepers, Builders, and royal staff, as well as Prefect Terrok, were all there, displaying everything from fury and disdain to anticipation. Daeson scanned the crowd once more, waiting and listening for the Protector.

"When will you believe...when will you submit... when will you follow...when will you acknowledge your own captivity to the effects of Deitum Prime? Dracus has offered you pleasure and power and in exchange you sell him your souls. Do you not know that this existence is only the beginning? Deitum Prime has penetrated every hall of power on Rayl, including that of your esteemed prefect!"

Daeson's gaze fell on Terrok. "You have despised the precepts of Sovereign Ell Yon, and even now are building a Deitum Prime replication complex in our midst! Your mockery of our bonded ways is despicable." Daeson lifted his right hand to point a finger at Terrok whose face was now red with fury. "You are an offense to Ell Yon, and your judgment is sure!"

Three hundred and fifty thousand people seemed to shrink back in fear and hold their breath. Daeson waited for the Protector to unleash its condemning judgement on Terrok, but it did not. Slowly he lowered his hand. The apprehension was palpable, emphasized by ominous silence as the eyes of the planet turned to Terrok, the Morian Empire's Raylean puppet prefect. The prefect slowly rose, his Royal Guards readying their weapons.

Daeson walked to the edge of the stage, turned and left, leaving the prefect and all of Rayl in a state of stupor. This time, no one dared come to Daeson or Brae. Their progression back to the hangar bay was unhindered. The only ones that dared come close were Largo and Foss, but even they were silent.

When they arrived back at their country home, no one was there. The words Daeson had spoken had effectively isolated them from every other soul. Brae was both relieved and very afraid.

"Dad, you attacked the prefect...even the Morian Empire won't stand for that," Brae said as she, Daeson, and Rivet sat talking on the front porch, something they hadn't been able to do since this had started.

"Terrok isn't just a puppet of the Morian Empire, Brae. He's a puppet for Dracus, and one of the worst our people have seen in a long while."

Brae shook her head. "There's no recovering from this."

"A Navi doesn't ever recover," he said solemnly, "because words of truth have consequences. We often bear those consequences, especially when those that need to hear it are in power. Prefect Terrok is a conduit of evil for Dracus and even though the people know it, they need to hear it spoken and to see him confronted. That will always be the role of a Navi."

Brae and Rivet exchanged looks.

"How do you see this ending, my liege?" Rivet asked.

Brae watched as Daeson's eyes warmed toward the android.

"I don't see the future, Rivet...you know that. My whole life has been singular in purpose, and that is to hear the voice of Ell Yon and obey. Now it's to prepare the way for Jeshu. Speaking the truth, even if it's hard to hear, is the manner in which I am supposed to fulfill this duty. Where this ends is in Ell Yon's hands."

Rivet looked as if he were processing Daeson's answer.

"I think you would have made an excellent politician, my liege," the android finally said.

Brae stifled a laugh. "I agree, Rivet."

Rivet turned his head to look out toward the surrounding landscape. Brae looked that direction, but the dark of night made it impossible to see.

"My liege, there are eight armed people approaching from that direction." Rivet stood and pointed to the southwest.

"This isn't the end…it's the beginning," came a loud voice out of the darkness.

Daeson and Brae stood, joining Rivet.

"Who's there?" Daeson called.

"Don't be alarmed. We're friends."

A lone figure stepped out of the trees from the southwest. He continued with his hands held out until he was ten paces away.

"What do you want?" Daeson asked.

"We've been watching you…hearing you at the competition. You're the Navi we've been waiting for. Today you made that clear, having exposed Terrok for being a puppet of the Morian Empire, the true enemy of Rayl."

Brae rested her hand on the Talon at her hip, having become accustomed to wearing it for the past three years. Another man and a woman stepped up beside the first.

"We would like to speak with you about joining causes. You're not alone in your mission to free Rayl. There are many able and willing to support you in this cause."

"Partisans," Daeson said.

The three stepped closer.

"Yes. And we are many. We believe that with your leadership, the time is right to rise up and reclaim our planet. Clearly you're not afraid of Terrok or even the Morian Subchancellor Pylok. We're not afraid either and are ready to join you."

Brae looked to her father. Could this be the beginning of a new future for Rayl...to rid their people of an evil prefect and eventually the shackles of the Morian Empire? Was an army of trained Rayleans just waiting for a leader? This sounded much like what Daeson Starlore had done for their people numerous times in the past. She imagined Jeshu stepping in with Daeson Starlore at his side to lead this force on behalf of their people. Brae was hopeful.

"Though the enemies of Rayl are many, the empire is not who we must fight. I'll have no part of your plan."

Brae's heart sank. "Dad?" she said softly.

Daeson shook his head once. The silence from the three partisans was telling.

"All enemies of Rayl are worth fighting," came their leader's reply.

Five long seconds of silence filled the air between them, and then turning about, they left.

"Why, Dad? I don't understand," Brae said, turning to face Daeson.

Daeson continued to look into the dark of night.

"I don't fully understand either, Brae. Just that things are about to change in a significant way. Our true enemies will be revealed, and former enemies will become friends. This is the mission of Jeshu."

That night, Brae was more concerned and more confused than she had ever been. The future seemed so hopeful and so uncertain all at the same time. *When will he return?* she wondered.

"That backstabbing, ungrateful, backwoods, hick of a pilot has disgraced me in front of the whole world…in front of the Morian Empire!"

Terrok was pacing back and forth in a fit of rage before his advisors and administrators. They retreated from the man, fearful of the potential frightful transformation that was threatening to take over his body.

"And to accuse me of not honoring the Raylean tradition of bonding!" Terrok turned on his first advisor. "What does that mean…why does he lay such unsubstantiated accusations against me?" he shouted with droplets of spittle flying from his mouth, neck muscles bulging.

The first advisor retreated in fear, unsure if he should answer.

"Why?" Terrok shouted louder.

"Because the women you are with, you are not bonded to?" he timidly suggested.

"Bah! I support any Raylean that wants to be bonded. This is outrageous. And besides this, many of our people want the Deitum Prime replication complex!"

Terrok turned away, pacing once more. "Something must be done with this fanatic!"

"Honorable Prefect," an approaching advisor called. "The Preeminent Keeper Fasa Kylos is requesting to speak with you."

Terrok stopped. "What does that two-faced pompous Keeper want with me?"

"He claims he wants to talk to you about a mutual problem…Elias Thornton," the advisor replied.

Terrok's dour face began to illumine with delight.

"Send him up," Terrok ordered.

"He insists on you meeting him in the courtyard...something about not wanting to risk exposing himself to a place so saturated with Deitum Prime."

Terrok scowled. His advisors cringed, waiting for Terrok to explode in another fitful rage. Terrok walked to the end of his pacing pattern, then threw up his hands.

"Aahg!" he shouted then walked to the door. "Aunder...come!"

Terrok's first advisor hurried to catch up with him. Within a few minutes, Prefect Terrok and his first advisor, Aunder, were face to face with Preeminent Keeper Fasa Kylos and two of his associate Keepers as well as Master Builder Krisha Monae. The walk to the courtyard had settled Terrok enough to feign civility.

"What brings such honorable officials to my humble abode?" Terrok asked with outstretched arms and a smug smile.

"Stop with the façade of respect, Terrok," Kylos rebuked. "You and your ridiculous festival have created a hero that is an enemy to us all!"

Terrok scowled.

"And now there are rumors that he has banded with the Partisans and is building an army to fight against the Morian Empire," Aunder added.

"He wears one of *your* Protectors," Terrok countered. "You do something about that, and I'll take care of Thornton. A Navi isn't a Navi without a Protector."

"It's not one of ours," Kylos replied. "And he's not a Navi."

Terrok's expression became rigid. He leaned into Kylos.

"And how is that possible, eh Kylos? Perhaps you're not the high and mighty Keeper you thought you were." Terrok glared at Kylos until he flinched.

"I have an idea," Master Builder Krisha Monae said, stepping forward to save her counterpart. All eyes turned to the intelligent and contemplative Builder. "We aren't the only ones that want to see him destroyed. If we move quickly, we should be able to have everything in place by the championship round."

Monae now had the attention of all as she began to lay out a plan to bring about the demise of the obscure man heralded as the long-awaited Navi.

Two days later, Daeson flew the semi-final round flight, defeating the other nine pilots soundly. His message to all of Rayl continued to be a call to return to Ell Yon and to chastise the Keepers, the Builders, and Prefect Terrok.

During the three days that they waited for the championship round of the aero-skills competition to begin, the Raylean people slowly rediscovered their courage to support Daeson, seeing as though he wasn't arrested or punished for his public chastisement of Prefect Terrok after the previous two rounds. The championship aero-skills round was the crowning event for the Magnifical Festival, and therefore every industry and business had closed its doors so the planet could watch. By now even most of the Morian Empire occupation force was eagerly anticipating the final round, hoping this dark horse competitor would once again give them a spectacular show.

By the time the ten final pilots were lined up in the Alley of the Boulevard, the crowd was proclaiming riotous support for Navi Thornton, the Starlore Navi reborn. Brae and Rivet were at their support station, synced up with com and telemetry to Daeson's Starcraft. The Boulevard and every square foot of the spaceport were now occupied by hundreds of thousands that had come to see the spectacular skills of Elias Thornton and also to hear his words. Security had been doubled everywhere, and much to the annoyance of Prefect Terrok, Morian commandoes were now watching and policing the fringes of their grounds. It was a sign of nervous oversight by the mightiest force in the galaxy. It was also a sign that they were beginning to question Terrok's ability to keep his Raylean people under control.

Daeson had experienced the fury of planet leaders many times before, and so he was quite certain that Terrok would attempt some form of retribution due to his public accusations. The form of that retribution was yet to be discovered.

After much fanfare and lengthy introductions by the announcer, the launch signal was given—the ten finalist pilots and their fighter craft were off. Just ten minutes into the sprint to sub-course one, it became evident what Terrok's retribution plan was, or at least what part of his plan was. Two of the competitors positioned themselves on Daeson's right and left, then abruptly jinked into him in an attempt to crush his wings in a midair collision. At the last second, understanding their intention, Daeson pulled up, narrowly missing the squeeze maneuver. Both craft collided into each other causing a midair collision destroying the engine of one and causing significant damage to the fuselage of the other. One pilot was forced to eject while the other was able to recover and remain in the competition. Suddenly Daeson became aware that every other craft he was flying against was now a major threat.

"Dad, we just learned from our mechtech friends that Terrok has offered a huge bounty for any pilot responsible for taking you out!" Brae radioed.

"Yes...I've figured that out," Daeson radioed back. "I'll just have to get ahead and stay ahead. I'm increasing my entry velocity into the first sub-course."

"That isn't advisable, my liege," Rivet said. "Your entry velocity into the glacial trench is already pushing the limits of the Starcraft."

"That's a risk I must take. I can't watch the trench walls and my competitors at the same time."

The first sub-course entry was upon them. The other eight craft slowed from sprint velocity to an acceptable entry speed, but Daeson delayed his deceleration which sling-shot him into the lead. Five seconds later, he slammed his reverse thrusters into position causing a ferocious deceleration just as the jagged white edges of the massive glacier formation flew by his canopy. It was a treacherous move since he had to immediately execute a thirteen-G turn to avoid colliding with the crystal blue walls of the trench. Back at the Boulevard, Brae and millions of spectators held their breath as a plume of snow and ice obscured the view screen, the wash of his Starcraft blasting into the ice and snow. Two seconds later, Daeson and his Starcraft rocketed clear of the death-defying maneuver. The planet erupted in shouts and cheers, for the nefarious plot of the other competitors was now well understood. Daeson pushed his skills to their very limit, narrowly missing the spires of opaque death. Once again, the planet was stunned by the display of superior airmanship of this no-name pilot that had shaken the powers of Rayl.

On the next sprint, Daeson discovered a new threat. Although he was leading the remaining six pilots, for two had collided with the glacier walls in an attempt to keep up with him and his Starcraft, this position made him vulnerable in a way he didn't expect. The second and third-place craft behind him began targeting his Starcraft and firing their plasma cannons—full force cannons that were not de-rated. Rivet was faster, however, remotely activating Daeson's rear energy shield before the plasma rounds could hit and significantly damage the Starcraft.

"Thanks, Rivet," Daeson radioed.

"My pleasure, my liege."

Daeson had to tap into every last ounce of concentration and skillset he had to survive the remaining sub-courses and the sprints in between. But despite Terrok's plots, Daeson not only survived but was leading the six pilots remaining now. By the time Daeson was approaching the fifth sub-course, the entire Boulevard was booing every time a competitor would try to take Daeson out. But Terrok was not yet done. During the fifth and final sub-course, both the course plasma cannons and the target and defense drones started firing back with destructive power, at times firing multiple salvos only at Daeson's Starcraft. After taking two hits, one to his right engine, he began to lose ground. The crowd and the watching planet became furious. By the time the final four craft exited the fifth sub-course and had begun their sprint back to the Boulevard, Daeson was under an all-out attack from competitors and targeting drones alike. Like wild dogs chasing a wounded Kalazoo beast, the spectacle of Terrok's reprehensible scheme against Daeson had the crowd in an angry frenzy. Brae was out of her mind with rage as she watched Daeson perform aerial combat maneuvers that most onlooking pilots and certainly spectators had never seen before.

"My liege, if you are to survive the day, the time is now," Rivet radioed.

"Did you make the adaptations I asked for?"

Brae turned, looking at Rivet. If the android could have smiled, he would have. "Yes, my liege. At your command."

"Engage."

Rivet tapped in a sequence through the telemetry interface, and Daeson felt his Starcraft surge to life. The power indicator for the engines and his weapons instantly rose to 100 percent. The dormant concussion missiles on his wing canards pulsed to life showing "ACTIVE." Daeson turned on the targeting drones first, taking them out one by one until none remained. The three other craft seemed to have completely forgotten that they were in the aero-skills competition as they continued to hound Daeson with burst after burst of their plasma cannons. Now with a nearly fully functioning Starcraft, Daeson deftly positioned and targeted each one. Rayl looked on in stunned adoration as they witnessed the fighter pilot of the ages out-maneuver and outgun the very best pilots the competition could muster against him. In a final one-v-one maneuver with the remaining craft, Daeson took the fight pure vertical in a spiraling barrel roll dance until he was able to make the final shot, disabling the last of Terrok's pilot pawns. As he recovered from his nearly stalled-out fall, he pushed his throttles to full speed and rocketed through the Boulevard in a ground-shattering victory pass that sent the crowd over the top in jubilant shouts and cheers.

Terrok, Kylos, and every man and woman holding Raylean power sat in humiliating shame for the spectacle that Daeson had made of them, revealing their twisted hearts in such a public forum. Terrok pulled Aunder close to him and issued one final order.

Over the past three hours, Brae had watched in agony and with thrill as her father and childhood hero overcame insurmountable odds. Seeing Daeson face and conquer the worst Terrok could throw at him in front of the entire planet and come out victorious was euphoric. Surely it was over for Terrok and his cronies...surely the Keepers and their false claim of power would now collapse and make way for the true and honest leadership of the Merchant. Daeson Starlore had prepared the way, just as he said he would. To the public shame of Terrok, Daeson had exposed the prefect's wicked heart.

Brae cheered with the masses as Daeson circled the Boulevard, preparing to land. But as he slowed and descended, making his final pass down the Boulevard, the unthinkable happened, for Terrok would not... could not allow such flagrant insolence to stand. Two class three plasma cannons rose up from beneath the Boulevard platform, unleashing a barrage of fire at Daeson and his Starcraft. Being slow and low to the ground, there was nothing he could do.

"No!" Brae screamed, as did nearly 400,000 Rayleans.

In seconds, the power of the cannons overwhelmed the Starcraft, and it careened out of control. Brae watched in horror as Daeson and his Starcraft crashed at a perilous upright angle into the ground in the Alley between the Boulevard grandstands. Immediately, dozens of Terrok's Royal Guard continued the attack, advancing on Daeson and his Starcraft as it came crashing to a halt. The entire Boulevard erupted in mayhem as cannon fire, explosions, and a raging crowd all collided in a cacophony of revenge and revolt. Brae began running to the Starcraft, Rivet beside her scanning for threats that could harm her. She drew her Talon, but before she could target soldiers that were firing on Daeson, a faction of the Partisans began taking them out. Smoke and fire obscured much of what was happening and people were screaming and running in all directions, most to safety, some to battle.

All at once, three of the four concussion missiles on the Starcraft rocketed off their rails flying upward and over the Boulevard grandstands. Brae watched in utter confusion. Had Daeson fired them? And at what? Seconds later it became clear as they penetrated and exploded the pyramidal Deitum Prime replication complex just one mile off the spaceport property. This added an entirely new level of mayhem to the chaotic world of the Boulevard.

Brae resumed her sprint to Daeson as the canopy of the Starcraft began to rise. Immediately, multiple plasma bursts blasted into the canopy and all around Daeson. Surely, he would unleash the Protector, just as he had done countless times before, but alas, he did not. Instead, Daeson stood on his seat to exit the cockpit, but that's when the first plasma round hit him.

"No! Dad!" Brae screamed. She was still nearly 100 yards away. She saw him crumple over the edge of the cockpit, not dead but severely hurt. Brae would not reach him in time. The moment seemed to freeze, and she knew...almost saw the end of this tragedy, and it terrorized her.

"Rivet, save Dad!" she yelled.

Rivet hesitated, clearly trying to process odds and loyalties.

"Please, Rivet...save him!"

Rivet looked one last time at Brae, then sprinted ahead twice as fast as Brae could run. In seconds, Rivet was to the Starcraft amidst smoke and fire. Brae watched with hope in her heart as she saw Rivet leap up to the cockpit and lift her father up. She was still 50 yards away when her world shattered. Two perfectly aimed shots from one of the class three cannons tore into the Starcraft's fuselage fuel tanks. The explosion disintegrated the major structure of the Starcraft, and the resulting concussion threw Brae backward twenty feet.

The world nearly went black as Brae fought to remain conscious. All sounds were muffled, as if she was submerged in water. Thoughts were difficult to form, but there was one dark thought that came crashing in on her...Dad! She blinked, trying to regain her senses, but they refused to come. She rolled and then felt it. Extreme burning pain in her right thigh. The pain accelerated her return to consciousness, but it would soon overwhelm her. She looked down, seeing a jagged six-inch shard of metal protruding clear through her leg. She cried out, pleading for the end to come. She glanced to where she had seen Daeson and Rivet, but the only thing that remained were charred and burning pieces of the Starcraft. In that moment, she died with them. How could it be that Daeson Starlore had come 1500 years through Raylean history to die this pointless death at the hands of the evil Prefect Terrok?

Brae fell back to the ground, tears and screams involuntarily rising out of her. She closed her eyes to the agony of it all, waiting for Terrok's Royal Guards to finish her.

"Get up, Thornton!" a voice called. She felt a tugging on her arms and shoulders. "Get up!"

She opened her eyes to see Rhett bent over the top of her. Above him smoke, fire, and chaos continued to reign. She clutched at his shirt.

"I can't, Stryker...I can't. Just leave me."

Plasma fire mixed with shouts and screaming were happening all around them.

"No! Come on—get up!" he shouted as he began lifting her to her feet. The pain was nearly putting her back into unconsciousness. She screamed with every movement, but Rhett wouldn't stop. "If they get to you, they'll kill you."

Rhett was able to get her up on her one good leg, then wrapped her arm over his shoulder, forcing her to walk with him. After just twenty steps she collapsed to her good knee, crying out again for the movement in her pierced leg. The blood had now fully soaked her lower leg.

"Leave me, Stryker," she pleaded.

"Hang on to my neck," he ordered, as he lifted her up, cradling her back and her knees in his arms.

Brae hung tightly onto his neck as Rhett trotted her out of the Boulevard Alley amidst rioting people and plumes of smoke. She was barely aware of being placed on a hard surface as pain and loss of blood began to push her into unconsciousness.

"My father..." she mumbled, then the world went black.

CHAPTER

17

Wounds of the Heart

With the fortuitous help of two mechtechs, Rhett was able to get Brae clear of the Boulevard and onto his shuttle. Time was of the essence, so he dared travel just far enough to be outside of Terrok's immediate reach but not so far as to jeopardize Brae's chance of surviving her life-threatening wound. He took her back to Zareth, a place he was very familiar with, remembering a medtech there that he could trust. Within a couple of hours, he had Brae secure and being treated in a safe location. After three days of surgery and treatment, Rhett was relieved to hear from the medtech that Brae would live and be able to keep her leg. On the fourth day, Brae awoke to the reality of her injured leg and a broken heart unable to cope with the reality of the now. Silence was her response to such deep grief. The next day, Rhett waited outside Brae's room as the medtech replaced bandages and checked Brae's vitals. When the medtech exited the room, Rhett pulled her aside.

"What's the prognosis?" he asked.

The medtech frowned. "Her wound is healing, but her spirit is completely broken. Unless she recovers psychologically and emotionally, this will cripple her in more ways than one. She needs to get out of that bed and start walking."

Rhett slowly nodded. "Okay...thanks for this. I don't know what I would have done without your help."

"I think the hardest part is yet to come," she said, then left.

Over the next four days, Rhett did his best to care for Brae, not only delivering food and water, but making multiple attempts to break her free from the silence of her utter despair.

On the eighth day of her recovery, Rhett went to the door and waited, trying to gather the intestinal fortitude to try one more time. He knocked gently on the door, but there was no answer. He opened the door just far enough to peek in. Brae was in a sitting position on her bed, still and quiet.

"May I come in?"

Brae looked his way, then back straight ahead without answering. Rhett pushed the door open further, slipping through carrying a cup of hot liquid.

"Hey, Thornton...how you feelin' today?" he asked, feigning a chipper attitude.

Brae didn't move. Rhett's shoulders dropped. Images of seeing Brae watch her father being killed by Terrok's Royal Guards flashed across his mind. He couldn't imagine what that would be like or how he would react, but he knew that somehow she had to break free from it or it would ruin her forever.

He came to her bedside. Setting the cup down on the nightstand beside her, he fumbled for something encouraging to say. Even when things between them were at their best, he'd found it impossible to speak encouragement to her. Each day his efforts became more and more difficult.

"I brought you a cup of your favorite tea."

Brae turned her head to look at the cup, then for the first time since she had revived, she lifted her gaze up to him. She looked so incredibly sad. Despite all of the friction that had existed between them for years, he couldn't help but feel extreme sympathy for her. He took a risk. He sat down on the bed beside her, gently resting a hand on her forearm. He pushed into her personal space, looking her right in the eyes, close enough to see the dual blue-green colors of her irises.

"Look, Thornton, I can't imagine what you're going through, but I just want you to know that you're not alone. I'm here, and I'm not going to leave you."

Rhett watched as Brae's eyes became wet, her lower lip quivering ever so slightly. He knew that she hated appearing vulnerable, especially with him around, so he offered a quick smile then lifted his hand from off her arm, intending to stand and leave. Before he could rise, Brae grabbed his arm. He turned back to look at her. Two tears trickled down her cheeks, and she made no attempt to wipe them or turn away.

"Please don't leave," she whispered, her voice trembling.

Rhett turned back.

"Oh...okay."

Ever so slowly, Brae leaned into him, turning her head until she was resting on his chest. Her shoulders shook as she began to weep.

"Hey there, Thornton…it's going to be okay," Rhett said, gently wrapping an arm around her shoulders. This single act of tenderness seemed to open her heart, and her weeping became deep sobs of sorrow. Rhett wasn't sure what to do. This was a side of this tough, stoic woman he had never seen—didn't think existed. He put his other hand on her head, letting her melt into his embrace. Then he understood that he was all she had. Her closest friend had died. Her father had died. Even her strange android had been destroyed, and Jeshu was nowhere to be found. If even just for a few minutes, he decided to put away all of the ill-feelings between them and do this for her. He fully expected that when she was ready to pull back, the old Thornton would revive and be ready with some insults, but he was okay with that. He could be strong for her now.

As Brae exposed the deepest parts of her grief, she wrapped her arms around him and hung on as if to a lifeline. Minutes passed as Rhett held and soothed her, his shirt becoming wet with her tears. Finally, the sobs subsided, being replaced with deep cleansing breaths.

"I'm so sorry," she said between staggered breaths. "I'm so very sorry."

"It's okay," Rhett said. "No need to be sorry."

She shook her head, then released her grip on him. She pulled back and reached for a tissue to wipe her face.

"There's every need to be sorry. My father tried to tell me you were a good man, and I was too stubborn to see it. I've treated you terribly." Brae bit her lip. She lowered her head briefly, then looked back into his eyes in a way that moved him. "You stayed with me through everything. Even when I pushed you away you...*you* came to rescue me. And here you are again. Please forgive me, Rhett...please."

Rhett found himself wildly unprepared for anything like this from her. Surely this was just a momentary lapse in her rigid personality that was only being manifested by the intense grief she was experiencing. At least that was what he told himself as he straightened.

"I...ah...of course, Thornton. We're good. Don't sweat it."

Brae's brow furrowed. She nodded her acceptance of his forgiveness then looked as if she might break down again. More tears came. He reached for a couple more tissues and handed them to her. He smiled, trying to encourage her.

"You hungry?" he asked.

Brae nodded.

"Okay," he said. "I'll fetch some food for you."

Rhett readied to stand up again, but something inside him didn't want to go. He was afraid that by leaving he would break this moment and never see the soft side of Brae Thornton again. He turned back to her, softening his heart. He looked into her eyes where something different was now looking back.

"You were right about me."

Brae tilted her head, questioning. Rhett briefly dropped his gaze to his hands then back up to her.

"I *was* afraid," he said nodding. "You were absolutely right. Seeing what we saw with Jeshu and knowing in my heart who he was and what it would mean scared me. It scared me because I didn't feel like I was worthy or capable of being the man I was supposed to be for him or for you."

Brae reached out and touched his arm.

"I'm sorry I left. I should have been there for you, your father, and for Jeshu through all of this."

Brae's eyes reddened once more, and she leaned into him. This time their embrace was for each other—an embrace that healed the words and wounds of their past. Though it lasted but a few seconds, Rhett felt something fresh wash over his soul. When they broke, they broke as friends and not as forced accomplices.

"I'll get you that food now," Rhett said, standing and walking to the door. He felt as though both of them had ventured a bit far to be comfortable anymore. At the door she called to him.

"Rhett?"

He turned, looking back at her.

"Thank you."

Rhett nodded. "When you're done eating, we're going to get you out of that bed and start walking, okay?"

"Will you help me?" she asked.

"Will you fight me?" he returned.

"Probably."

Rhett sighed. "I'd expect nothing less, but yes...I'll help you anyway."

"Good," Brae said, her eyes still kind toward him.

Rhett left the room with a whole new world of feelings rumbling inside him.

"Don't expect anything to change once you get her better," he said to himself as he walked down the hall, but deep inside, he couldn't help but hope something had.

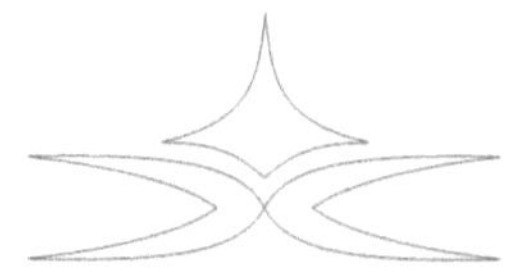

Chapter

18

The Lure of Darkness

Without provisions or clothes beyond what was on his back, Jeshu subjected himself to the brutal ways of the wilderness. Hunger and thirst became his companions as he began to empty himself of any measure of comfort. The realm of the Ruah was just out of touch, beyond the temporal boundary where mortal eyes could not see. Pushing away the comforts of humanity drew him to the brink of peering beyond and into his former domain where his father dwelled. With parched lips and an empty belly, it was hard not to yearn for his former glory as the Prince of the Malakians. Jeshu wandered for many weeks, sipping tepid water to keep just this side of death. And although he had no Protector to whisper assurance and speak strength into his soul, the presence of his father was with him...he could feel him, solidifying the truth of who he was...heir to the throne of power, Commander of all Malakians, Ruler of Peace,

Son of Ell Yon! In the crucible of suffering, Jeshu spent every waking moment in a journey to join his life to the mind and the will of his father.

Jeshu knelt to scoop a handful of murky water, hoping to wet his cracked lips and swollen tongue. The sun was nearly set, the air quickly cooling to temperatures that would soon bring shakes and shivers. The first indication that he wasn't alone was the slightest waft of a most delightful aroma. He lifted his head to see the dancing light of a campfire off the craggy walls of a rock outcropping just ahead. He had lost count of how many days it had been since he left Brae and Daeson. Was his testing over? He knew that he had reached the limit of his physical endurance. The anticipation of the end of his suffering was significant. He rose up and walked toward the light, the enticing aroma growing with each step. *Surely there would be cool water there as well*, he thought. In the distance he saw the flickering flame and its attendant. Jeshu nearly called out, but there was not enough moisture in his throat to enable him to form the words. He trudged onward, willing each foot to step forward. The closer he came to the fire, however, the heavier his heart became with understanding. A man sat on a stump poking and adjusting the wood fuel to a perfect position for spit roasting. He never looked up, even as Jeshu approached. Just beyond the fire, Jeshu stopped, watching the man attend to his meal as if he was all alone. Minutes passed.

"I know who you are," Jeshu said, eyeing the hooded man.

"Do you? Do you really?" the man asked, looking up for the first time from his roasted meat. A sardonic smile spread across his face. He tore a small slab of meat from the spit and took a bite.

"And you know who I am," Jeshu finished.

The man swallowed then ran his tongue across his teeth as if attempting to dislodge a stuck morsel. He took another bite, not waiting to clear his mouth before talking.

"Sit," he said, motioning to the opposite side of the fire where a stone was conveniently positioned, a perfect sitting height to position Jeshu slightly lower than the man. "Sit, sit, sit."

Jeshu considered the offer, then obliged. His feet were sore and his body weary. Easing the weight off his legs was welcome.

The man smiled. "You must be hungry," he said, reaching across the fire to offer Jeshu a seasoned smoldering wing and thigh from the roasted avian carcass. The sweet smell of roasted meat teased his nostrils with delight. His stomach, swayed by the aroma, churned with hunger pains.

Jeshu waited...silent. After a few seconds, the man's face filled with disdain.

"Have it your way," he said, letting the succulent meat fall into the fire.

He then grabbed a fist-sized stone and threw it to Jeshu. Jeshu instinctively reached up and snatched the stone with his left hand.

"If you won't eat my food, then eat your own. Surely the son of Ell Yon has the power to call to the Ruah and secure a morsel of food so he won't die. If you're not delusional...if you truly are Ell Yon's son, then make food for yourself. There's no harm in this. No one would begrudge you a little food to sustain you." The man cocked his head to one side, feigning a sympathetic posture.

Jeshu felt the weight of the rock in his hand. His stomach once again reminded him of his duty to supply it with sustenance. He took a deep breath, then let the rock fall to his feet.

"My food is the voice of Sovereign Ell Yon. By his words, I live."

The flickering light of the fire on the man's face seemed to ignite a dark passion inside him.

"Well then, let's get to it." C'fir Dracus paused, pointing a half-eaten leg at Jeshu. "Ell Yon's love affair with these degenerate humans is remarkable if not comical. It will be his...and your undoing." Dracus continued to chew and talk, pausing only long enough to swallow and slug a gulp of drink, allowing the enticing liquid to dribble out of the corners of his mouth. "I mean, look at you," Dracus exclaimed motioning with his free hand toward Jeshu. "Exposing yourself to death, disease, mortality...and for what? So you can save a handful of these miserable creatures?" Dracus shook his head in disbelief. Throwing the remaining half-eaten leg bone into the fire, he sighed as if unimpressed with everything about Jeshu. After taking a long drink from a chalice, he stood.

"Come—I want to show you something," Dracus said, turning to walk away from the fire.

Jeshu stood but hesitated. This dark Immortal could not be trusted, that was for sure. How far dare he allow this interaction to go? Dracus turned, looking back over his shoulder.

"What frightens you most, me or the weakness within you?"

Jeshu's eyes narrowed. An ancient memory awakened concerning Dracus. A memory promising justice for the crimes of which this Torian was guilty. He followed, ever wary of Dracus's nefarious schemes. Just beyond a small grove of trees, Dracus tapped a sequence on his wrist control and a sleek command transport ship shimmied into view, decloaking before their eyes. A walkway extended from the side of the ship as they approached. Dracus continued a steady gait right up the ramp, disappearing into the belly of the craft as if expecting Jeshu to follow. At the base of the walkway, Jeshu hesitated again. Mooring his identity as the true Son of Ell Yon had been an intense process over the past few years, but there was one final tether that needed to be secured to finish his journey. He understood that somehow, exposing his humanity and all of its vulnerabilities to the archenemy of the Sovereign was part of this final leg. He stepped up and into Dracus's ship. Moments later, the craft lifted up and away, leaving the dwindling orb of Rayl behind. Jeshu watched through a massive observation deck window as Dracus initiated a slipstream jump without the aid of a slipstream conduit. Twenty minutes later, the ship emerged from the jump at a perch normal to the spiral plane of the Aurora Galaxy. The splendor of trillions of stars was breathtaking.

Dracus came to stand beside Jeshu. He looked over at the young man, a subtle smile on his lips.

"Watch," Dracus said as he activated a holographic overlay on the glass window before them. Sequential pinpoints of light illumined then expanded to show either a solar system or a cluster of systems, each identified by their names, cultures, and governments. Nations and peoples of the galaxy began filling the display before Jeshu.

"Behold, Jeshu. Everything you see is mine. This is true power. Ell Yon didn't give these worlds to me...I took them! And that which I take, I can give away." Dracus paused, seeming to carefully consider his next words. "My lieutenants contest with one another to rule just one of them. Acknowledge me as Sovereign of the Aurora Galaxy, and it's all yours. Billions upon billions of humans will worship at your feet while you lead them in peace and prosperity."

Jeshu was stunned by the sheer enormity of it all. He couldn't deny Dracus his claim…this *was* power. His thoughts teetered on that notion for a few seconds, daring to imagine what leadership of the galaxy under a good ruler could bring, then he turned to look at Dracus.

"Ell Yon is the one and only true Sovereign. To him and him alone must all knees bend and acknowledge as Sovereign of the Aurora Galaxy."

Jeshu watched Dracus's eyes darken with frustration that hadn't been evident before. With a quick swipe of his hand, all of the worlds and his offer disappeared in an instant.

"Your loss." He crossed his arms, continuing to stare at the vivid starry display, his genius mind formulating a final plot. Slowly his head turned toward Jeshu.

"I have one last thing to show you," Dracus said, then turned and left.

Jeshu took a deep breath, trying to imagine what the enemy of his father was planning but failing to do. He went to a cushioned seat and sat down. He yearned for the voice of his father. Would a Protector give him that? In the far reaches of space, subject to the cruel plots of Dracus, Jeshu felt utterly alone. Sorrow threatened to fill his soul at the absence of Ell Yon's presence. Surely, he had not been abandoned at such a time as this. He closed his eyes, searching with his mind…waiting…calling. But all he found was the frail fabric of his humanity threatening to undo his great mission before it began. Fatigue was crushing the final reserves of energy that remained, and his body began to feel as if it weighed five hundred pounds.

Nearly an hour passed without Jeshu realizing it, his thoughts teetering between meditation and sleep. The jostling of the ship and the faint noise of extending landing struts revived him to full consciousness. Jeshu opened his eyes to an alien world crafted for agents of darkness. Behind him, a door opened, and the extension ramp reached out and down to touch the ground beneath the ship. A blast of hot dry air assaulted him. Dracus motioned for Jeshu to follow him as he walked down and out of view. Once Jeshu had disembarked, Dracus was nowhere to be seen. The ramp behind him receded, and the ship powered up its engines. Before he could find shelter, it rocketed up and away, leaving him in a painful skin-searing wash of dry dust and glass. The aura of the desolate world upon which he had stepped permeated Jeshu.

The planet Haleo, without its original protective atmosphere, was too close to its red dwarf star for temperatures amicable for human existence. This world was a labyrinth of blood-red amethyst crystals ranging in size from microscopic to towering monoliths. Large concentrations of anti-gravitons were evident in the great fields across the landscape and in the floating crystal structures that meandered across the dusky orange skies. The atmosphere was host to an ever-flashing electrical storm without cumulonimbus formations to carry the discharges. Instead, the frightening electrical borealis display was caused by continual bombardment of charged particles from its red star which interacted with the floating amethyst crystal monoliths. Ribbons of electricity often arced from sky to crystal, ground to crystal, and even crystal to crystal. At times, a discharge would shatter a larger floating crystal and all sections devoid of anti-graviton particles would rain down from above in fatal shards of glass-like spears.

Where crystals had not formed, the soil that remained was too dry and desolate to support any fruit-bearing life. The grasses and fungi that did grow were food for the sparse organisms that helped comprise this grim ecosystem. Reaching five to six feet in length, large foraging poisonous centipedes and spur-nosed moles with sharp teeth and long claws for digging competed for the scarce food supply, often preying upon each other, the victor usually determined by size. But the king of Haleo predators was a creature that had adapted most gruesomely to its crystalline habitat, the Pike Scorpion. Its proclivity to readily absorb Deitum Prime was attested by its unusual size, growing to as large as five feet from head to curled tail. The creature's biology allowed for absorption of microscopic amethyst crystals into its protective exoskeleton shell, replacing as much as 80 percent of its normal chitin constituent. This made for a nearly impenetrable crystal-chitin armor. Hosting an effective poison delivery system, the pike scorpion's tail could shoot toxic spears of chitin-crystal shards infused with a deadly toxin. On such a hostile planet, there was little in the world of Haleo to inspire hope of any kind.

Somewhere in the recesses of his mind, Jeshu had heard of this place. It too was a product of Dracus's doing...or rather undoing. In eon's past, this world had once been the jewel of the galaxy. Malakians would travel from afar to gaze upon the wondrous beauty of the glimmering purple amethyst landscape. Shimmering displays of distant sunsets, aqua seas

HALEO CREATURES
PIKE SCORPION
POISONOUS CENTIPEDE

abundant with marine life, and a landscape rich with forests and wildlife were now only distant memories for the Immortals that had visited Haleo. Of all the planets in the galaxy, this place seemed to shout loudest of the curse of Dracus, for Deitum Prime works its vilest work on that which is most beautiful. Not only had Deitum Prime destroyed and altered the nature of life on the planet, but its devastating impact on the intricate balance of the environment and geological structure had utterly destroyed its beauty forever.

Jeshu took in the terrifying display, hearing from within his soul the raging screams of a Deitum Prime-laden world. And yet beneath it all, he could also hear the weeping of a paradise lost. It reminded him of the silent screams of humanity pleading to be free of the prison Dracus had used to capture them—the prison of Deitum Prime.

Never was nor ever would there be fought a greater battle than the one that was about to happen on this remote planet between Dracus of the Torians and the Commander of all Malakians. The silent arena of creation held its breath, as did every warrior in the Ruah, both Scourge and Malakian. Although all of humanity was ignorant of this mighty duel, their very fate hung in the balance. The future reclamation of the galaxy would be won or lost here, and Jeshu felt the weight of every soul and every living cell of creation on his shoulders.

The air was hot and dry, subduing the ancient stench of a dying planet. His heart broke for what Haleo symbolized. He closed his eyes, searching the gaps in his mind for final understanding and purpose. Still, something eluded him. Where his mind had not yet been awakened or he could not yet see, trust in his father filled the void and held him firm. His rapid growth from child to boy to man had been unique and challenging in every way. His first human memory was of the kind face of a young woman. Brae Thornton was his tether during many days of both exciting and frightening enlightenment. He was just a child when he began to understand his great purpose, and she had mentored him through it. Like awakening from a deep sleep, Jeshu had to daily strive for wisdom and understanding, at times desperate to find it all out at once but unable to do so. Even now, as he was on the verge of facing his nemesis, Jeshu searched the empty corners of his mind. Deep down, he knew there was one more thing to understand…one more thing to fight for.

"How do you like what I've done with the place?" Dracus's dark and sordid voice called out to Jeshu from the edge of a large amethyst monolith to his right.

Jeshu looked his direction. The Torian Immortal was holding out his arms, a glib but evil smile on his lips.

"Come and see," Dracus implored.

Jeshu walked his way, trying to ignore the dozens of micro-cuts in his face, neck, and arms. As he approached Dracus, a wide canyon opened up before him, exposing the gruesome splendor of this morbid world. He joined Dracus on the precipice of a great crystalline structure overlooking the canyon. Far below, movement caught his eye. Two pike scorpions were fighting over the carcass of a large spur-nosed mole. Jeshu watched the gruesome duel from the ledge upon which they stood, wondering what about this place could possibly supplement any scheme Dracus was planning. He broke his gaze from the valley to look at Dracus just a few feet away. The image of the

Immortal Torian shimmied for a moment, as if threatening to disappear like a vanishing hologram. He then realized that Dracus had momentarily deactivated his interphasal translator.

"Ell Yon is powerful," Dracus began, casting a leery gaze toward Jeshu, "as is his son, commanding countless Malakian warriors." He paused, allowing Jeshu time to acknowledge his confession. "You can't see them, can you?" Dracus asked. "Jump, Jeshu. It is foretold that they'll protect you."

Jeshu's eyes widened. Jump? He looked out over the amethyst speckled canyon, large floating spires of jeweled glass lumbering through its rocky channels. A hundred feet below him, jagged spears of amethyst gleamed in the noon-day rays of the sun. For one brief moment, he imagined the realm of the Ruah, the domain from which he had come. Being fully human, there was no interphasal translator to deactivate so that he could glimpse across the fringe of the two realms. Were his warriors there? Were they watching? If they were under his command, why couldn't he remember any of their names?

Dracus stepped close to Jeshu.

"If you are indeed the son of Ell Yon...jump," Dracus whispered.

Shivers flitted up and down Jeshu's spine at the sound of evil so close. Without looking away from the glassy abyss of the canyon, Jeshu answered.

"My father and I are one. I know him, and he knows me. I need not prove my identity to you, but if I am not the son of Ell Yon," Jeshu paused, closing his eyes to hear the quiet voice of Ell Yon, but his voice was not there, "then why are you here?"

Jeshu slowly shook his head, stepping back from the canyon's ledge.

"No," he began to say, but his tongue and his body resisted. Suddenly he felt his feet sliding across the ground as some dark force pushed him the last couple of feet toward the edge of the canyon. He turned to see Dracus's hand outstretched, a glowing stream of red energy emanating from it.

"You think yourself so wise, Son of Ell Yon," Dracus spewed his hatred onto Jeshu with each word he spoke. "Ell Yon gave your weak Navis the Protector, but I have created the Destroyer, tapping into a technological force infinitely more powerful!" Dracus shouted, his eyes glowing red with Immortal rage.

Jeshu strained against the paralysis that encased him. With all his strength, he lifted up his right arm while opening his hand, resisting the push of Dracus. Now perilously close to the edge of the canyon, Jeshu pleaded for Ell Yon's help. The heel of his foot was now hanging off the last vestige of solid ground. Pebbles and shards of amethyst were sliding beneath his foot, careening down the cliff face as they broke from beneath the last two inches of his foothold. At that moment of utter peril, when the noose of defeat was tightening around his neck, Jeshu felt the power of Sovereign Ell Yon fill his soul as a Protector...his Protector translated from the Ruah and onto his outstretched arm. The synaptic connection was instantaneous, ending the quest of his journey, but was it too late?

"No!" Jeshu declared as the Protector awakened.

Powerful blue streams of energy erupted from his Protector. The collision of Immortal power was brief, temporarily blinding both Dracus and Jeshu. In the confusion, Jeshu moved forward and away from the precipice of death before Dracus could recover and consider what had happened. The enemy of Ell Yon stood straight. Sneering, he brushed the Destroyer with his left hand as if dusting it off.

"You ignorant fool—you have no idea what's coming!" Dracus exclaimed. His face contorted with rage as he unleashed the full power of the Destroyer on Jeshu.

Dehydrated and weak, Jeshu was slow to react. A wave of bone-crushing force hit him full on, throwing him dozens of feet through the air. He landed on his back, jagged edges of smaller crystals tearing his flesh as he slid to a stop. Pain enveloped him, further hindering his ability to fight. He forced himself to a kneeling position, trying desperately to focus on a counterattack. He lifted his hand, but before his mind could even form the thought, a second blast of dark energy smashed into his frail body, blasting him into a horrifying tumble across rock and crystal. He fought to remain conscious as waves of pain threatened to fully seize his mind. On his back once more, he blinked, trying to wipe away blood from a gash on his brow that was seeping into his eyes. He rolled onto his hands and knees, desperate to fight as he knew he must, but finding no strength left in him to do so. He slowly lifted his head to see Dracus walking toward him, a loathsome smile on his face.

"You're going to discover just how painful it is to be human, Son of Ell Yon."

Dracus tapped a sequence on his control band and the space around Jeshu filled with a dreadful sound. He turned to see a pike scorpion rise up from a crevice just to his right, its tail poised. Jeshu noticed a small technological module implanted on the front side of the creature's head. The high pitch clicking sound of the scorpion was sonically debilitating. Jeshu winced against the assault on his ears. He turned the Protector toward the scorpion's direction but from his left came another. Nearly faster than his eye could see, this nightmarish creature shot a three-inch needle-sharp crystalline shard toward Jeshu, which found its mark, penetrating deep into his left shoulder. Jeshu screamed against the toxic invasion. He blindly shot the Protector, but the blast of energy fell wide of its mark. Another air-splitting shard from the first scorpion pierced his back, sending Jeshu to the ground. The pain was unbearable. He was vaguely aware of the dark figure standing over him. Another few taps on Dracus's arm band and Jeshu felt powerful pincers from the two scorpions collapse on the lower portions of his forearms. They pulled in opposite directions, stretching Jeshu's arms outward until he was flat on his back, the one shard pushing deeper into his body. Dracus leered over Jeshu with delight.

"My agreement with Ell Yon was that I could test you in any way I saw fit, as long as it didn't kill you." A deep staccato laugh punctuated his words. "But then again, I never was very good at keeping my word."

Jeshu tried to muster the energy to free his right arm from the bone-crushing grip of the pike scorpion so he could engage the Protector, but it was simply impossible. Dracus knelt down beside Jeshu, wrapping the fingers of his right hand around his throat.

"You shall die before you even begin your miserable mission," he exclaimed through clenched teeth.

Jeshu felt and heard the powerful energy of the Destroyer on Dracus's arm building to a crescendo. A discharge this close to his head and with no protection would surely kill him. He closed his eyes, straining against the avalanche of pain that was crushing him.

Please, Father—Sovereign Ell Yon, deliver me from this evil, Jeshu pleaded.

In that moment of desperation, the spark of the Immortal Sovereign ignited within Jeshu, and he fully discovered his last tether. The Protector flickered wisps of blue energy and Dracus froze, a fractional moment of fear filling his eyes. He commanded the scorpions once more and Jeshu felt the pressure intensify, the bones of his arms nearly collapsing beneath the force. But it did not matter for Jeshu could see past this moment of despair and into the brilliant future of a galaxy subject to the white throne of the Sovereign. Unstoppable power began to flow through the Protector, but it did not flow outward to destroy his enemies, at least not yet. It flowed inward, into the body, mind, and soul of the Son of the Sovereign, forever binding the son to the father in a fashion unknown in both realms.

Jeshu opened his eyes, glaring into the evil abyss of Dracus's soul. The archenemy of Ell Yon understood in that moment his great folly, for before him was the source of power by which all matter in the universe consisted. The terror on the face of Dracus was acutely apparent.

"No!" Jeshu commanded, and as the word formed on his lips, the inexhaustible power of the Protector exploded from his mouth and into the body of Dracus. The ancient evil warrior flew backward thirty feet, colliding into a massive crystal monolith. Simultaneously, shockwaves of Immortal power flowed out from Jeshu's chest down both arms and into the bodies of the pike scorpions. In an instant, every molecule in the creatures' bodies erupted, disintegrating the horrid forms to microscopic dust. In that moment of completeness, the body of Jeshu, Son of

Ell Yon, became the Protector. However, the expulsion of such energy consumed the last of Jeshu's temporal being. He could hardly lift his head to determine the state of his enemy, but a moment later, it was obvious this was not over. The horrific sound of dozens of pike scorpions closed in on him. Before Jeshu could even roll from off his back, four massive Malakian warriors appeared on each side of their Commander, weapons drawn and ready. Ten feet away, another thirty appeared, forming an impenetrable circular wall of Immortal protection for their Sovereign. Their Talon-style weapons of judgement began destroying each grisly creature as they dared approach their fallen Commander.

One of the nearest warriors knelt down to Jeshu, reaching for him. They locked hands.

"Kalem," Jeshu whispered.

"Be still, my lord," Admiral Kalem said gently, his voice trembling with pain and anger. "We are here."

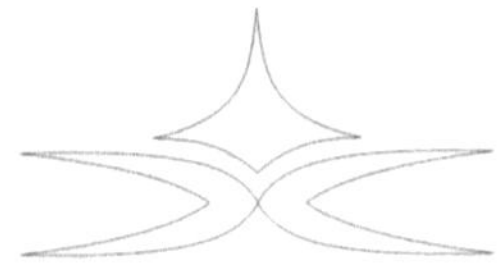